RAPPERS D-Lite

SA'ID SALAAM

STREET CHRONICLES

Published by:

G Street Chronicles
P.O. Box 490082
College Park, GA 30349
www.gstreetchronicles.com
fans@gstreetchronicles.com

Cover Design: Hot Book Covers
                 www.hotbookcovers.com

ISBN: 978-0-9834311-9-0
LCCN: 2012937133

Join us on our social networks
Facebook
G Street Chronicles Fan Page
G Street Chronicles "A New Urban Dynasty" Readers' Group
Twitter
@gstrtchroni

Dedication

This book is dedicated to

Sean Craven, aka Sharra-Abdul - the best MC you never heard,
My angel *Zakiyyah Salaam,*
Darius 'Uncle D' Jennings,
Cameron Forest
and
Dondi Gant
try to rest in peace.

Acknowledgments

All praise goes to Allah, Lord of everything in existence. He created the pen and allowed me to push it.

To Ma Dukes, Diedra…you were right about everything.

Grandma Rainey, you are my hero.

G Street…let's get it!

To hip-hop and all those who've died trying.
To the Top Ten who've ever done it:
Rakim
Jay-Z
NAS
Biggie
Pac
Eminem
Melly Mel
Ice Cube
KRS 1
Chuck D

G STREET CHRONICLES
~A NEW URBAN DYNASTY~

WWW.GSTREETCHRONICLES.COM

CHAPTER 1

Grammy night! My limo glided to a stop at the coveted red carpet. I took a deep breath as the door was pulled open by a tuxedo-clad attendant.

I emerged from the vehicle and was immediately engulfed by the bright lights. My name was being called from every direction by the drove of fans vying for attention. I did my best to accommodate everyone, waving and smiling as cameras snapped and flashed.

"D-Lite, how does it feel to be nominated for both an Oscar and a Grammy in the same year?" asked the lovely Amira Muhammad from Black Tree TV.

My publicist had prepped me well, so I gave her the same scripted answer I used in all interviews. "It feels great! It's been a fantastic year, and I have some fantastic fans," I said graciously before resuming my grand entrance.

As I made my way inside the venue, I greeted all the other stars, exchanging compliments. "Loved the album," I said to Fifty. "Hot video. We gotta do something together," I mentioned to Rihanna.

Queen Latifah and I exchanged Hollywood kisses on both cheeks. NAS gave me a pound and invited me to an after-party.

"Oh, shit! There goes Jay!" I said, ducking before I could be spotted. Jay-Z had been bugging me to be on a song with him for months. Don't get me wrong: I mean, Jay is cool, but he was starting to act like a groupie.

I turned my head and walked quickly toward the door. I almost made it, but *Beyoncé* spotted me just short of the entrance. "There he is!" she screamed, alerting Jay-Z to my presence.

"Oh, man! D-Lite! D-Lite!" he squealed. "Man, I love you! You're my favorite rapper."

I tried to ignore him and get inside, but his voice grew louder as he drew closer.

"D-Lite! D-Lite!" I heard right behind me, until I felt a hand on my shoulder.

* * *

"David Light! Earth to David!" Mrs. Hunter, my fifth grade teacher said, shaking my arm. "Boy, are you daydreaming again?" she asked, shaking her head and causing my classmates to crack up. "You're supposed to be taking a test, young man," she admonished. She picked up my test booklet only to see that it had been completed already, and I still had thirty minutes to spare. "Humph!" she grumbled, putting the test back down on my desk.

When Mrs. Hunter went back to her desk, I went back inside my head. I spend a lot of time in there. Most of the time, the happenings in my head trump the ones happening in reality.

The bell rang, signaling the end of the school day, causing everyone to scramble out of their seats.

"Put your tests on my desk on your way out!" the teacher said loudly so as to be heard over the din of the exodus. "Mr. Light, I need a word with you before you leave," she announced as I neared.

I put my test on the growing stack and waited.

"In trouble again?" Desean snickered as he passed. "We'll be out front."

Desean is my best friend in the world. We have known each other since we were babies because our moms are good friends. We'd only recently found out that we weren't really related. We had been calling each other's mom "Auntie" for so long we thought we were actually cousins.

"What'd I do now?" I asked, exasperated, once the last student left.

"Boy, what am I going to do with you?" she asked sincerely.

I shrugged my shoulders for a reply since I didn't quite understand the question and *"Stop sweating me"* seemed inappropriate.

"You are, beyond a doubt, one of the best students I have," she said, smiling proudly. "The best and the worst. You have the brains to achieve anything in life. You are full of potential. Please don't waste it," she pleaded. In her thirty-plus years of teaching in the Bronx, she'd witnessed the streets eating plenty of souls who, like me, had potential.

"I won't, I promise," I replied solemnly, affected by her genuine concern. I knew that was what she wanted to hear. I even threw in an "I'll do better from now on" for good measure.

"Yeah, right." Mrs. Hunter chuckled at my canned response. "What do you want to be when you grow up?" she asked.

"A rapper!" I exclaimed, almost before she could get the question out.

"Ugh! That rap…stuff is fine, I guess, but even with that, you will need an education," she lectured. She would have had the same response had I said I wanted to be a street sweeper or a truck driver, of course. "Here," my teacher ordered, handing a piece of paper to me.

"What's this?" I enquired looking at the list of foreign words.

"Vocabulary words. Rappers need to be articulate," she said smugly. "Now, I want you to look each of these words up and use it correctly in a complete sentence—a sentence other than the one used in the dictionary as an example," she added, remembering how I'd tried her the last time.

"Aw, man!" I whined. "Who gets homework on the last day of school?"

"Only the rappers. Now you have something to rap about," she chuckled as she gathered her belongings to leave for the day. "Don't let me down, Mr. Light."

When I got outside, Desean was waiting with Shelby, our third musketeer. She was part of our crew. Even though she was a pretty girl with her long hair and hazel eyes, Shelby was a straight-up tomboy. She could run, jump, play ball, and even fight with the best of them. We lived on the same floor, on opposite sides of the elevator. "Dag, boy. What choo did now?" Shelby complained.

"I ain't do nothin'," I shot back.

"A-yo, how much homework she gave you?" Desean laughed.

"This much!" I said, throwing a wild hook that he barely ducked.

Desean grabbed me, and down we went, wrestling on the sidewalk. We were rolling around on the concrete, laughing as we both tried to pin one another. Shelby couldn't decide who's side to be on, so she started kicking us both.

It was incidents such as those that made our half-block journey home take upwards of a half-hour. Our school, PS 129, was actually part of the building we called home.

Home was a massive structure that extended the entire length of Ogden Avenue from 166th Street to 167th. PS 129 flanked it on 166th, while a huge parking structure took the 167th Street side. The top of the parking garage was used as an all-purpose park.

Our neighborhood was the Highbridge section of the Bronx, an area known for stick-ups and shoot-outs. It ran from Yankee Stadium on 161st Street all the way to the 181st bridge.

We had our share of drama, but our block was relatively peaceful. The basketball tournaments in Nelson Park were second only to the world-renown Rucker.

What we were famous for were the block parties that took place every weekend during the summers. The park over the garage was used for bike-riding and softball during the day, but at night, it transformed into an open-air disco. With such a draw, it became the spot for established rappers to shine, as well as a proving ground for newcomers.

That was where I first met and fell in love with rap. I was hooked instantly, and I heard my calling. The shit was a religious experience for me. Rappers were treated like royalty. The adulation and awe they inspired was amazing. In rap, I saw my future. I saw my destiny.

* * *

"Boy, how many times I gotta tell you to bring your behind straight home," my mother demanded as soon as I stepped foot inside the house, some thirty minutes after school let out.

"Um, I had to stay and talk to Mrs. Hunter," I said, thankful to have a valid excuse. "You can call her if you don't believe me."

"Boy, I just seen you and Desean rolling in the street. No wonder y'all be messing up all your school clothes. Now sit down and do your assignments," she ordered.

I was about to ask how she knew about the vocabulary list, but she beat me to it.

"Yeah, I already spoke to her, so get busy. I swear, you the only child I ever heard of to get homework on the last day," she chuckled, amused by my dilemma.

My mom stayed on me, but I knew it was for my own good. She worked hard to take care of me by herself. That was why I worked hard in return, to please her. I was a straight-A student, and besides an occasional fight or my constant daydreaming, I stayed out of trouble.

I never met my father, and my mom refused to even talk about him. She used to get so upset when I asked about him that I finally stopped asking. It didn't really matter, though, 'cause no one I knew had a father—not a live-in one anyway.

I quickly found the definitions to all the words on the list and wrote them down. I intended to write out my sentences, but the sounds of kids playing destroyed my concentration. Having heard enough fun being had without me, I decided to pack it up and finish later.

"Your homework is done already?" my mother asked as I gathered my papers.

"Um, *I'm* done," I replied, amused by my clever play on words.

I met up with Desean and Shelby, who were sitting on the steps of our building. I knew exactly where they would be since they wouldn't ever go far without me. Even though I was the shortest and the youngest, I was the leader of our little crew. "Y'all waitin' on me?" I asked, taking the first set of stairs in a single bound.

"No!" Shelby spat curtly, finally beginning to show some semblance of actually being a girl.

"Nigga, ain't nobody sweating you," Desean added.

Nevertheless, they both fell in line behind me.

I decided to hit Nelson Park to see if anything was popping. We walked over to the next block, horse-playing the whole time. Nelson Park wasn't much of a park, as parks go. There were no trees, no grass, and the one remaining swing was on its last leg. The concrete "tree house" offered the best view of the park. From it, we could see all that the small oasis had to offer.

Seating was first-come, first-served, so we were lucky to find the place empty. We kicked the empty crack vials and forty-ounce bottles out and posted up.

When the older guys began picking teams to run a full-court game, Desean was an early pick. At age ten, he was already one of the best players in Highbridge.

"Y'all going to camp this year?" Shelby asked.

"Man, I hope not," I whined, dreading being shipped upstate for summer. Every year, Desean's mother and mine sent us to summer camp so they had time to get their groove on.

"Least y'all will be together and having fun. I gotta go to my dad's in North Carolina." She groaned miserably. Every year, Shelby's mom sent her down South for the same reasons as ours did. "Gotta see my sister," she griped, frowning as if the word "sister" left a foul taste in her mouth.

"What's wrong with that? I wish I had a brother," I said, watching Desean manhandle the young men on the court and reasoning that I did sort of have a brother after all.

"My sister makes me sick! All she talks about is clothes, hair, makeup, and boys," Shell spat.

"Well, if you were a real girl, you would like that stuff too." I laughed while bracing for impact.

As expected, Shelby came after me, and we began to tussle. She almost had me in a headlock when I spotted King-Stan entering the park. "Hold up!" I announced seriously, glad to have a way out of the chokehold. "They about to spit," I said, jumping down from the structure.

The cipher had just formed as I reached the grove. King-Stan was our local rap legend, royalty in that part of town. "Set it off!" Stan ordered, and his sidekick quickly complied and began beat-boxing with his mouth.

One by one, every one kicked a few verses, and I was no exception. When my time came, I went for broke. Everyone was rocking right along with me until the dude next to me cut in, cutting me off.

He was O-Phryme, another legend from the Bronx River projects uptown. As if it wasn't bad enough that he had cut me short, he went after the King. He called King-Stan out, hurling insult after insult. O-Phryme was on a mission to expand his rep'. He wanted to be the man, and that meant a battle. To be the man, a rapper had to go 'hood to 'hood, eating M.C.s as he went. He had already beaten the Milk-Man up in Soundview and K.O. over on Boston Road. Now, he was in Highbridge talking real reckless about our hero, but Stan wouldn't take the bait.

"Son, you wanna battle? Be in the big park on Saturday," said the King as he turned to leave.

"A'ight, that's what's up!" O-Phryme agreed. "Just don't chicken out."

After leaving the park, the three of us ripped and ran for a few more hours until the streetlights came on. It was before that, actually, 'cause as soon as they began to flicker, kids scrambled in every direction.

I was so tired from the day's adventures that I fell asleep as soon as I finished my dinner. The next thing I knew, my mother was in my doorway, yelling for me to get ready for school.

"Come on, Ma! It's the last day. I may as well stay home. We ain't gonna do nothing," I pleaded.

"First," my mother said, placing a hand on her hip, "ain't ain't a word! And second, if you ain't play around during your test and get homework, I would let you."

Oh shit! My homework! I thought about showing my mother the word "ain't" in the dictionary, but I ain't crazy. I jumped up and rushed around in an effort to get to class early and finish my assignment. After eating an English muffin topped with enough butter to clog an artery, I left my apartment.

Shelby was in the hallway already when I cam out, and she hit the button to summon the elevator. Her mother made her dress like a girl that day in a dress with ribbons in her hair. "One word, and I'ma kick your ass," she warned as I neared.

"I ain't say nothing." I chuckled. "I'm sayin' though…" I tried my best not to laugh, but the sight was too much for me. As far as I was concerned, Shelby was a boy. "I'm sayin', though, you look like one of them poodles they dress up with the—"

WHAM! Shelby slugged me just as the elevator door opened with a *ding*. The passengers, an elderly couple, gasped as we tumbled inside. Since she didn't have her sneakers on, I got her down pretty quickly. I would have had her pinned if the couple hadn't intervened.

"Boy, you don't fight with no girls!" the man said, pulling me off her.

"You should be ashamed of yourself, young man," his wife said, helping Shelby up.

"That's not a girl! It's a poodle dressed up like a girl," I said, laughing.

Shelby pulled away from the old woman and came after me again. I was laughing too hard to defend myself, so she quickly pinned me. I would have been in trouble if the elevator hadn't reached the lobby by then.

Desean was waiting there in the lobby when the doors open. "Man, y'all at it again?" He sighed and began to try and separate us. "What you got on?" He chuckled at Shelby's girly get-up. "You look like one of them pood—"

WHAM! Shelby swung on Desean, and now I had to be the peacemaker. When I finally got them separated, she had lost all her ribbons and looked disheveled. "It ain't over," she announced before storming off. "I got y'all."

* * *

"Okay. I have Monopoly, Clue, Scrabble, and checkers," Mrs. Hunter said as the class settled in. "And…how about some music?" she said, producing a small boom box.

"Yeah!! Wild 101!" someone yelled, causing the class to cosign on the idea. "Wild 101! Wild 101!" we all chanted in support of our local hip-hop station.

"Uh…no." Our teacher laughed and hit the play button on the radio. When she did, the room filled with jazz. The soothing music immediately calmed the room, and we all became engrossed in play.

Before I knew it, the half-day school day was almost over, and I still hadn't written my sentences. I scrambled to pull out my work and get it done as the clock began to speed up.

Mrs. Hunter saw me and raised an eyebrow. "Don't you have something for me, Mr. Light?" she asked knowingly.

"Yes, ma'am. Just checking it over," I lied. My mind was coming up empty on how to use the new words in sentences—that was, until a funky jazz instrumental came on, and the words began to form in my head. I was tapping my foot to the beat as the words began lining up, then poured out of the pen, spilling onto the paper. I wrote…

THIS *INNOCUOUS* ATTEMPT IS TO MAKE YOU *VACILLATE* IN YOUR OPINION OF RAP…

IT'S A *FALLACY* TO SAY IT'S *BANAL* OR *FATUOUS* CRAP…

THIS *AMORPHOUS* ART FORM WILL BE *UBIQUITOUS* IN A MINUTE…

IT'S *URBANE* AND *CAPRICIOUS*, SO DON'T BE TOO *FLIPPANT* TO GET WITH IT…

I HATE TO *IMPORTUNE* YOU WITH AN *INSIDIOUS* ADJURATION…

BUT I HOPE YOU *ACQUIESCE* BY THE END OF YOUR VACATION. D-LITE.

I wrapped up my rap just as the bell rang to end the school day and year.

Mrs. Hunter was yelling her end-of-school speech in vain. "Read every day! Stay out of trouble! Blah…blah…blah…"

I fell in line with the crowd of escaping students and tried to get past my teacher.

"Yeah, right, boy." She chuckled, extending her hand to collect my assignment.

"Oh, my bad." I laughed and turned in the work. I got outside and paused to watch her reaction.

Her lips were twisted into a *"Yeah, right,"* expression as she read. The expression changed into a smile, then morphed into laughter.

Mission accomplished, I thought, and with that, I turned to leave, heading for another summer in the Bronx.

CHAPTER 2

The Bronx was buzzing with anticipation of the upcoming battle between King-Stan and O-Phryme. Since the DJ for Wild 101 lived in our building, the whole city had heard about it. DJ Wayne and King-Stan were good friends, so the promotions were slanted in the King's favor. He constantly played songs from his mix tape that Stan was featured in.

Highbridge was a rough area, but it was well established that block parties were off limits. There were no stick-ups and no gunplay allowed, simple as that. Someone would probably get their ass whipped, but it was the Bronx; a party in the Bronx ain't a party unless someone gets their ass whipped.

That Saturday, like every Saturday, I was tasked with giving the house a thorough cleaning while my mom was at work. She left me a detailed list explaining what to do and how to do it. Every Saturday I also got called back upstairs to redo some or all of my chores, and that Saturday was no exception. I was busy cleaning the streaks on the windows, left behind by my rushed job.

"Don't make no sense!" my mother griped as she inspected my work. "Look at this shit. Boy, I should make your ass stay in the house all day," she grumbled.

The more she complained, the deeper inside of my head I went. I got to the point where I could no longer hear her voice over the music in my mind. Since I had a beat, I began to rap.

IF I HAD A GENIE TO GRANT THREE WISHES...
I'D USE THE FIRST ONE TO WASH DEM DISHES...
THE SECOND ONE TO STOP MOM'S BITCHING...

AND THE LAST TO SWEEP AND MOP THE KITCHEN...

MA DUKES IS HOLLERING, BUT I AIN'T LISTENING...

A diamond mine in my mind, so my rhymes be glistening…I gotta—"

"Boy, are you listening to me?" My mother yelled, inches from my ear, snatching me back into the real world.

"Yeah! Dang, Ma!" I shouted back, pissed about the interruption.

It took another hour to finish, and I was back on my way.

* * *

Shelby and Day (my nickname for Desean) were in the usual spot on the stairs when I went back out.

"Dag! You stay in trouble," Shelby said with a sneer.

"Moms had you cleaning up again?" Desean added.

"She be buggin', yo. Got me doing all that woman's work," I spat.

"How is cleaning up woman's work?" Shelby demanded indignantly, placing a hand where her hips would one day be.

"You wouldn't understand 'cause you ain't no real girl," I teased, knowing I would get a reaction.

"That's it!" she yelled, rising to her feet. "I'ma kick your ass just like I did before," she said, referring to the one time we did get into a real fight.

"Girl, that was a tie," I said, feeling wounded by the memory.

Desean moved in to break it up before it got too serious. "Damn! Look at all these heads," he said as he moved between us.

We looked around and marveled at all the people milling about. The big park was slowly filling up, even though Wayne had yet to set up his equipment.

Black Joe, the building weed man, was posted up on his step, making a killing. The bodega across the street had a line just to get inside. Once customers got in, they stocked up on Philly blunts, forties, and Newports.

We decided to go play hand ball until the festivities began once night fell.

It was just before dusk when Wayne and crew began setting up their gear. Huge speakers were strategically placed so sound waves would bounce back off the building, into the park. The turntables inside their coffin were hooked up and illuminated. Next, mikes were connected and checked with the requisite "Mike check…one…two…" The entire area was then roped off to prevent common people from getting too close. It was a makeshift stage as well as a ghetto VIP section. Only those who were somebody or were with somebody special could get beyond the ropes.

Wayne was still getting set up when he looked up and caught my eye. "A-yo, Dave, come here," he ordered.

"Me?" I questioned, pointing to myself to be sure. Although we lived in the same building and saw each other quite often, I was surprised he knew my name—surprised and honored.

"Yeah, you, son. Your name is Dave, right?" he said as I ducked under the ropes to get to him.

Hey! I'm behind the ropes! I must be somebody! I shot a quick glance around just to see who saw me moving behind the ropes.

"A-yo, B, grab me a Nick from Joe and a blunt from across the street—oh, and a forty," Wayne said, handing me a $10 bill.

Desean and Shelby looked puzzled as I shot off on my mission. It only took a few minutes to grab everything. Where else besides the ghetto can a ten-year-old buy weed, alcohol, and tobacco, no questions asked?

"Stick around. I'ma need you to make a few more runs," Wayne advised.

He allowed me to keep the two bucks that were left, so I decided to share with my crew. "A-yo, run and grab us a big bag of Cheese Doodles and three quarter waters," I commanded in the same authoritative tone that Wayne had used to speak to me.

Shelby frowned but said nothing as Desean snatched the money and ran off. When Day came back, we stood separated by the ropes and devoured the snack.

"A-yo, B, your peeps can chill with you," Wayne said, granting Shell and Desean access.

"They cool," I replied quickly, not willing to share my limelight.

When the preliminary battles began, the crowd got hyped. They loudly cheered or jeered the M.C. on the mike. More would-be combatants got turned away than actually took the stage.

As for me, I took in every word uttered by everyone who touched the mike. My mind analyzed each bar for accuracy, articulation, grammar, and diction. At the same time, I watched the crowd to see what moved them.

Once the mikes were warmed up, King-Stan came up and ran through songs from his and Wayne's latest mix tape. Since Stan was Highbridge's own, we all knew all the words and rapped along with him.

It was a powerful sight: thousands of people reciting his words. The next sight was equally impressive, as the massive crowd began to part like the Red Sea.

The commotion stopped King-Stan mid-verse, and he, too, curiously watched the spectacle.

A hush fell over the park as O-Phryme and his entourage came into view. The mood was so serious that it scared me. I looked to where my friends had been standing, but they were gone.

"Y'all ready for the battle of the year?" Wayne asked with all the enthusiasm of a *Friday Night Fights* announcer.

The crowd went ballistic as their reply. The two contestants faced off like gladiators as Wayne laid out the rules. "A'ight. You know the drill. Same beat, one-minute rounds," he said, looking back and forth from man to man.

O-Phryme and King-Stan shot odds and evens to determine who would go first. Stan chose odds and threw one finger to O-Phryme's two, securing the right to flow last.

Wayne selected the Pete Rock classic, "They Reminisce over You," for Round 1. O-Phryme jumped right into the smooth track with equally smooth lyrics. His verse was generic on the surface, speaking about his car, jewels, and skills, but his delivery was extra. Son could have spit his ABCs and made it sound dope.

Stan played his own hype man, whipping the crowd into a frenzy before he began. His verse was so-so, but the crowd was already amped up.

Round 1 went to the visitor on my mental score card.

Wayne threw on the instrumental to M.O.P.'s smash "Ante-up," causing the crowd to take it up another notch.

This time, O-Phryme came out like a savage. His voice became gruff, and he was almost growling. I was scared for Stan after that brutal verse.

The King came out pretty much like he had in the first round. That was when I realized he only had one style. I vowed then and there to be as versatile as water and go with the flow.

Round 2 went to O-Phryme as well, as far as I was concerned. He was eating Stan's food off his own plate.

"A'ight, we tied up," Wayne announced, to my surprise. "Last joint for all the marbles. Let's get it!"

KRS One's 'hood classic "South Bronx" came on, and the park erupted. The crowd lost their minds, and so did O-Phryme!

He straight murdered Stan with the hardest, most aggressive, violent lyrics I'd ever heard. He was actually out of breath when he came to the end of his verse. O-Phryme had been eating good off that verse, smashing M.C.s all over town, but now he was in Highbridge.

"Drop it," Stan said to Wayne, who responded by dropping the needle back on the wax. He then name-dropped half the people in the park, drawing a loud response from the partygoers. Stan named all the streets, bodegas, and weed spots, instilling pride that translated into whoops and hollers.

When it was all said and done, King-Stan was declared the winner. In all fairness, had the battle taken place up in Bronx River, or anywhere else on the planet besides Highbridge, O-Phryme would have easily won.

O-Phryme gracefully accepted the loss and gave the champ a pound. They vowed to have a rematch in the near future.

Wayne kept on spinning records until the police shut him down a little while after 2 a.m.

I stayed around and helped break down the equipment.

"Here you go, B," Wayne said, extending another $10 bill. "Good looking, son. Fuck with me next week."

"Bet!" I exclaimed, accepting the money and position at the same time. I had a job with DJ Wayne!

I then headed upstairs to face the real music, coming from DJ Ma Dukes.

G STREET CHRONICLES
~A NEW URBAN DYNASTY~

WWW.GSTREETCHRONICLES.COM

CHAPTER 3

Summer was only two weeks old when Desean and I left under protest to go to summer camp. For all the bitching we did, you would have thought our mothers were sending us to Camp Crystal Lake to hang out with a guy in a hockey mask.

Shelby had been shipped south the previous week, but she didn't go out without a fight either. She only relented when her dad promised her karate lessons. She vowed to kick my ass with her new skills as soon as she got back.

Once me and Day settled in at camp, we had a blast. As usual, we were the only black kids at camp. All the other campers were rich white kids. The culture exchange was good for all. We learned a lot from them, and they from us.

Being up there in the fresh air and clean water made me realize just how bleak our existence in the ghetto really was. Hearing the other kids talk about summer homes, vacations, and backyards with swimming pools made me yearn for the better things in life.

We still had a month and a half left of summer when we got back to the Bronx. Me and Day would walk and explore all over the city. We walked down to Harlem hospital to visit Desean's mother at work or over to Lincoln hospital to see mine at her job. One of our favorite places to go were the polo grounds, where the world-famous Rucker Park was located.

There, it was street ball at its finest. It was the place to be for ballers of all kinds. There were the ballers who handled the rock on the court and other ballers who handled rocks on the block.

Rap royalty was usually in attendance, with their entourages in tow. I was captivated by the respect they commanded. They were ghetto celebrities, working the crowd like politicians—shaking hands, giving hugs, signing autographs, kissing babies, and the whole nine.

While Desean watched the court, I watched the people. I saw my future—or at least the future I wanted for myself. Not only did I want to be rich like my white friends, but I also wanted to be famous. I wanted people to scream my name. I wanted them to love me.

We also began hitting all the block parties within walking distance. For us, that meant anything short of Connecticut. We were up on Boston Road or down on Trinity, Soundview, Leman, Bronxdale. Wherever a mike was being checked, I was there.

I began to study different rappers, taking note of their every word, their every movement. I took note of how an M.C. could captivate an audience more with his swagger than with his lyrics. Some of the wackest rappers would have the crowd totally enthralled, even though they weren't saying anything.

Every night when I got in, I hit the books. I scoured the dictionary and the thesaurus to improve my vocabulary. I studied analogies as a science. My mom was proud of my semantics and improved communication.

I also worked on my swagger. I tried out different personalities daily. One day, I walked with a limp and talked with a lisp. The next, I'd switch it up and speak with a raspy voice and a ditty-bop. My mother was getting concerned that I had become bipolar, but I was just trying to find myself.

I also experimented with different names to go by. "D-Lite" was too generic. I needed something with flair. I went from "M.C. Fan" cuz I was so cool to "M.C. Flame" cuz I was so hot. "Bionic Boy Wonder" on Monday; "Rapper D" on Tuesday; and "Sugar Foot" by Friday. The shit was ridiculous!

Luckily, my best friend Desean came through and saved the day. "A-yo, son," he began sincerely, "you the coolest nigga I know. Just be yourself."

I guess he got tired of hanging around with all them different people every day.

That was our life, day in and day out, with nothing really changing. Then, when I was thirteen, everything did change.

I came downstairs to find Desean posted up in our usual spot. He was talking to some new girl who had her back to me. I was checking her out as I approached, admiring her long, pretty legs and equally long and pretty hair.

"What up, Day?" I said, dropping my voice a few octaves, hoping to impress the new girl.

He just laughed without responding.

When the girl turned around, my eyes went straight to her chest. Little ma had a nice set of tits and...*What? Shelby's face!* "Shelby?" I asked in disbelief. She'd gone down South looking like me a couple of months earlier and came back a woman.

"Yeah, it's me." She giggled. She giggled like an actual girl. "How was your summer?" she asked.

"Not as good as yours," I replied, my eyes glued to her brand new breasts.

"Boy, quit!" she said, giving me a shot on the arm.

"Yeah,, that's you." I chuckled, rubbing my sore arm.

Not only had Shelby changed physically, but mentally and emotionally as well. Things between us changed so fast that neither of us knew what was happening or how to handle it. Puberty had hit us pretty hard. Sometimes we caught ourselves just staring at each other. Other times, we would get caught up in an awkward silence, unable to decide what to say. I had gotten into the habit of doing and saying things to impress Shelby. She, in turn, would giggle and act girly.

Desean was the only one who realized what was going on. He was the lover of the crew, with a different girl every other day. "Y'all niggas need to stop frontin' and go with each other," he said matter-of-factly.

"You buggin'!" I exclaimed, feeling embarrassed.

"Buggin'!" Shelby cosigned.

"Whatever. I'm out." Day chuckled, leaving us to deal with the situation alone now that the cat was out the bag.

"He be buggin'," Shelby said, breaking the silence.

"Yeah, Day crazy," I agreed. "He play too much."

"So, how's the rap thing coming? I heard you been blowing up," Shelby said, stroking my ego.

"I'ma be that dude soon," I said confidently. I was in my element when music was the topic of discussion. It was the only thing I was sure about.

"Yeah, right." Shell giggled, twisting her lips.

"No joke! I got over 200 songs written already," I replied emphatically.

"A'ight. So spit something," she dared.

"Bet. This one called 'Highbridge,'" I said triumphantly.

"Naw…hit me with a freestyle." She laughed.

"A'ight. Gimme a subject," I said.

"Me. Spit something about me," she replied.

> SHELBY, SHELBY, DON'T TRY AND FRONT, BOO…
> YOU KNOW GOOD AND DAMN WELL THAT I WANT YOU…
> YOU CAN SEE IT IN EVERYTHING THAT WE DO…
> THAT'S HOW I KNOW THAT YOU WANT ME TOO…
> SO, SHELBY, TELL ME, IF YOU THINK I'M CRAZY…
> IF NOT, THEN IT'S TIME FOR YOU TO BE MY LADY."

Shelby grinned broadly before rushing in and hugging me tightly. She let up her vise-like hold enough or us to share our first kiss.

We slammed our faces into each other's, bumping our teeth as we did. Shelby took the lead and slid her tongue into my mouth. When she did, my dick got hard instantly.

Her eyes grew large when she felt the wood on her leg. "I-I gotta go," she uttered before taking off up the stairs. Shelby stopped at the door, turned around, and blew me a kiss before disappearing inside the building.

CHAPTER 4

High school was the first time the three of us would not be going to the same school. It would be a major adjustment not being together, but for different reasons, we all went to different schools.

Day was heavily recruited by schools all over the city but settled on Dewit Clinton. They were a powerhouse already, and Day would slide right into the vacant point guard position. He was now six-one and had ridiculous ball-handling skills. He had been showing out all summer in the Rucker, and his name was ringing.

Shelby was so goddamn fine now that her moms put her in St. Ann's Catholic Academy up on 180th and Grand concourse. It was a futile attempt to keep the wolves at bay, because the little plaid skirts were straight-up sexy. I always wondered why Catholic schools had all the girls wearing short skirts, but seeing all those thighs every day kept me from complaining.

As for me, I chose Walton High on 183rd and River. I chose it for one reason: It was the party school, and it was where all the fly kids went. Since I was so fly, the choice was easy.

It took some doing, but we managed to ride to and from school together every day. We could catch the Number 13 bus down the hill to Yankee Stadium, then jump on the D train to head uptown. We walked Shelby to school, and Day would bag a different girl every day. Then, we walked over to my school on River. There, Desean would hop on the 4 train a few stops to his school. The process reversed itself again in the afternoon.

My school, being the party school, was full of wannabe rappers, would-be singers, could-be models, and a host of other dreamers. The lunchroom was a mini club, complete with music and alcohol smuggled in the backdoor. There was always a cipher going on, and anytime a group of M.C.s got together, there would be a battle. The shit was inevitable; rap is a competitive sport.

In a month's time, I had smashed every rapper in school. By then, I had so many words and phrases at my disposal that my freestyle was incredible. My mind could instantly process my sight into words. A mortal rapper didn't stand a chance.

It got to the point where niggas would bring niggas from other schools to battle me. The security guards were rap fans, so they let the ringer in—or led them to the slaughter is more like it.

DJ Wayne finally put me on a mix tape, and I went HAM! After that, he took me all over the city and let me spit. The word got out quick: D-Lite got next!

If there's a downside to being on top, it would have to be the fact that someone is always shooting for your spot. Many-a-day, I would have to eat a rapper on the train ride home.

If there's an upside, it would have to be the girls. I was a celebrity, and honeys were throwing themselves at me left and right. I loved the attention, but Shell had my heart. She was still running every time my dick got hard, though, and I was losing patience. To make matters worse, I had to hear tales of Desean's frequent sexual conquests.

The last day of school arrived, and I was surprised to find Desean already at my school when the doors opened. "What's good, fam'? What you doin' here so early?" I asked before giving him a pound and a hug.

"Gotta meet with that girl April at Shell's school. Ma got that super head," Desean said, wincing at the memory.

"Damn, son! You hit her too?" I asked, feeling surprised and probably a little jealous.

"Naw, I ain't fuck her yet. She just gave me some skull that day I met her," he replied nonchalantly. "What's wrong with you, yo?" Day asked after I began sulking.

"Shelby still fronting on the na-na," I admitted sheepishly.

"Son, Shelby ain't got the only pussy in New York! You got bitches throwing panties at your ass. You better fuck something," he exclaimed.

I was in a foul mood when we got to Shelby's school.

"Hey, baby!" she sang as she rushed over to kiss me.

April and Day greeted each other with their tongues.

"What up?" I replied dryly, not partaking in the kiss.

Shelby frowned like she wanted to say something, but she let it pass. "Hey, Day. Y'all ready?" she said, snatching my hand.

The four of us took off toward the train station.

Shelby squeezed my hand tightly to prevent me from pulling it away. "What's wrong, baby?" Shell whispered as we huddled on the crowded train.

"Nothing," I shot back, displaying attitude.

She was about to say something slick until some commotion caught our attention.

"There he go! There he go right there," a dude said, pointing me out. It was some dejected rapper I had battled earlier in the year.

"Beef?" Desean asked, making his way over.

"Naw. This little nigga tasted like chicken." I laughed.

"Bet you can't fuck with my nigga Ace. He's from Brooklyn!" he said, as if Brooklyn was something special. "I got whatever that my man will eat your food."

A muscular dude stepped from behind him, looking me up and down menacingly. He was tall, dark, and handsome in a thugged-out way. His hair was neatly braided, flowing flawlessly into his thin sideburns and beard. He sported a row of gold teeth along the bottom of his mouth. His well-developed muscles looked like they'd been built on Riker's Island or upstate and were accented by a crispy white wife-beater. He was at least twenty-four or twenty-five, but he had no problem stepping to a kid. "You s'pose to be the king?" he said, frowning. "Nigga, you wack!"

"Un-uh. This my time," Shelby said through clenched teeth, squeezing my hand for emphasis.

"Yeah, B, I'm with my girl. Maybe I'll get you tomorrow. Why don't you make an appointment?" I said arrogantly.

"Son scared!" he announced loudly, hoping to impress the spectators to instigate.

It worked, and the crowd began to murmur. They smelled blood and wanted to see a battle.

"Tell you what, lil' man," I said to the kid I battled before. "Come through to the rec' center tonight. You can bring your gorilla, and it's whatever." I then turned my back on them and turned my attention to Shelby.

"A-yo, give him a taste," Ace's sidekick urged.

"Gimme a beat," Ace demanded. On cue, his flunky hit played on the boom box. An old "Gangstar" beat came on, and Ace rapped to my back,

> "THIS LITTLE THING HERE S'POSE TO BE THE KING?...
> YOU MUST KNOW THE TYPE SHIT THAT I BRING...
> YOU CAN'T STAND THE RAIN, AND I BETCHA...
> FUCK WITH ACE, YOU GONNA LEAVE ON A STRETCHER...
> YOU AIN'T HARD. I SEE IT IN YOUR LADY'S EYES...
> EH, Y'ALL, THIS NIGGA IS SOFTER THAN BABY THIGHS."

The crowd began to whoop and holler, hoping to incite me to battle.

I wanted to get at him, but Shell was holding me back. "Rec' center, 11 p.m." I said over my shoulder. I grudgingly resisted Ace's taunts and the instigation of the onlookers.

The train pulled into the station at Yankee Stadium, and we moved toward the door.

"Eleven o'clock! Little hand on 11, big hand on 12." I chuckled as I walked off onto the platform.

"A-yo, that nigga called you baby thighs!" Desean laughed.

I tried my best not to laugh, but that shit was funny. "Baby thighs? Damn." I chuckled. "I gotta get that nigga.

On the bus ride up the hill, Desean and April were making out real hot and heavy. She had her tongue down his throat while he firmly palmed an ass cheek.

To be honest, the shit pissed me off. I snatched my hand out of Shelby's grip and changed seats.

When we got to the building, I walked quickly inside, leaving my friends behind. We were all supposed to hang out at Shell's house since her mother wouldn't be in till after 12. I wasn't feeling particularly sociable, so I played the crib.

I studied my rhyme books, looking for something to spit at Ace if he had the heart to show up. In the end, I figured dude wouldn't show. *Why would a grown-ass man travel all the way from Brooklyn to battle a kid?*

I made it downstairs to the rec' center just before 11. Since it was part of our building, I didn't have to travel far.

Wayne's parties usually drew a good crowd, but I couldn't recall ever seeing one that packed. A couple of kids got turned away by security just as I arrived at the door.

"They waiting on you," the guard said urgently when he saw me.

They are?

They had to be, because all eyes were on me as I entered. Desean had both April and Shelby on the dance floor.

When Shell saw me, she rolled her eyes and turned away. She still tapped Day and alerted him to my presence.

When Desean saw me, he made a beeline to me, leaving the girls on the floor. "Fuck you been, son?" he asked excitedly. "E'rrybody waiting on you."

"On me? For what?" I asked curtly as I surveyed the crowd. "A-yo, who the fuck is all these people?"

"Brooklyn niggas," he answered ominously. "They with Ace."

"Ace is here?" I blurted out, hating the fact that I heard fear in my own voice.

"Yeah, he here with a bunch of niggas. They poppin', too, son—chanting all that Brooklyn shit," he said animatedly.

I had known Day my whole life, so I knew he was trying to gas me up. "Brooklyn, huh?" I chuckled. "Do they know where they at?"

"I can't tell. They already got into a little squabble with Buckhead and them niggas from the projects," he added.

That surprised me, because Buckhead was a straight goon. He wasn't the type to get into 'little squabbles'. He shot niggas! "Word?" I said, showing my disbelief.

"Yeah, but them niggas left—went back to the 'jects, I guess," Desean answered with a shrug.

Wayne spotted me and cut the music, causing a groan from the dance floor. "D-Lite to the DJ booth! You got work to do," Wayne said, sounding irate. "Y'all came for a battle. Now y'all 'bout to get one!" Wayne announced as I made my way over.

Ace arrived at the DJ booth at the same time as me. We stood there mean-mugging each other as Wayne laid out the rules.

"We gonna do shit a lil' different tonight. One beat, one verse. One shot, one kill," he said, changing the game.

We agreed on a NAS track to keep the music borough neutral. After shooting odds and evens, Ace went first. He whipped his supporters into a frenzy with their little chant, then spit pretty much the same verse from the train. They put on a good show and were still screaming Brooklyn after Ace finished.

When I lifted the mic to my mouth, the room fell silent. *Damn!* I still hadn't figured out what to say, but Wayne dropped the beat and forced my hand. Having no other choice, I jumped into Ace's ass with both feet.

"BROOKLYN, HUH?...

YO, YOU IN THE BX. WE SEE SEX AND MURDER EVERY DAY...

WHERE EVERYONE HAS A GUN, SO BE CAREFUL WHAT YOU SAY...

WHERE EVEN RATS AND ROACHES SMOKE BLUNTS...

LEAVE NOW BEFORE SOMEONE JACKS YOU FOR YOUR FRONTS...

COME TO THE BRONX, SON, YOU BETTER COME RIGHT...

THIS SILLY NIGGA BROUGHT FISTS TO A GUNFIGHT...

BOBBING AND WEAVING AND THROWING JABS AND BODY SHOTS...

WILL GET YOU IN THE MORGUE ON A SLAB WITH YOUR BODY SHOT...

I'M AS THOROUGH AS MY BOROUGH, BX TILL THE DEATH...

WHO YOU CALLING SOFT, WHEN YOU BABY POWDER IN THE FLESH?...

SO FUCK YOU, YOUR MOMS, AND WHATEVER SHE'S COOKING...

FUCK YOUR FAGGOT DADDY AND MOTHER FUCK BROOKLYN!"

With that, I dropped the mic and walked off as the crowd went wild. Everyone parted and made a hole for me to pass.

"D-Lite has left the building," Wayne shouted over the hysteria.

Shelby caught up to me just as I reached the elevators. "Oh, baby, you killed it!" she exclaimed, embracing me tightly.

I accepted the hug stiffly and remained silent.

Shelby pulled back to make eye contact before speaking. "Baby, you still mad at me?" she purred sweetly. "I didn't even do nothing."

"That's the problem. You won't do nothing," I pouted.

The elevator door opened, and I walked in with Shelby at my heels.

"Is that what this is about?" she asked, pushing my hand away from the button. "If I don't put out, then you ain't fucking with me?"

"A-yo, we cool, ma," I said indifferently, pressing the button for our floor.

"Okay then," she said, hitting the button again for emphasis.

"Okay what?" I inquired as we rose.

"Okay. I'ma give you some pussy," she said in such a hostile tone that I changed my mind.

"I'm cool," I responded, watching the lights rise with each passing floor of the elevator.

"Cool? Nigga, you been chumping me off all day in front of my girl 'cause you want some ass. Now you talking 'bout you cool?" She chuckled. "You gon' get it whether you like it or not."

"Okay," I said meekly, as if I was being forced into it.

We kissed for the rest of our ascent. When the door opened on our floor, we held our lip-lock—all the way down the hall, even as I fumbled to unlock the door. We fell inside the apartment and scrambled to the sofa, still kissing the whole while. We stripped down to our underwear and lay on the sofa.

I slid my hand down her panties and marveled at how wet she was. "Come on. Let's get you out of these wet things before you catch a cold," I teased, pulling at her panties.

She gave tacit approval by lifting her hips enough for me to remove them. Next came her bra, followed by my boxers.

I took position between her legs and prepared to enter her. That was easier said than done since we were both virgins, and I didn't have a clue what I was doing. It took some work, but I finally got inside of her with a gasp from the both of us. I took two good pumps, and it was over.

"What's wrong?" she asked, confused at why I suddenly slumped over, out of breath.

"I came," I said, still struggling for air.

"Already? Inside me?" Shelby exclaimed.

I was saved from answering by someone pounding on the front door. "Lite, open up!" I heard Desean shout from the other side.

I found my boxers and slid them on while Shelby gathered her clothes and scrambled to the bathroom. "Fuck you banging on the door like police?" I snapped, pulling the door open.

"They shooting!" he said, rushing inside with April close behind. The way he ducked inside, you would have thought "they" were right behind him.

I peeked down the hall just to make sure "they" weren't. *Who the fuck is "they" anyway? And why "they" stay in so much shit? "They" fighting,*

"They" shooting, "they" said…"they, they, they…"

"Them Brooklyn niggas got into it again with them niggas from the PJs. Then, e'rrybody started bussin'," Desean explained dramatically. He looked down at my boxers, then around the room. "A-you, where Shell at?" he asked suspiciously.

"Yeah, where my girl?" April echoed.

"In here!" Shelby said, cracking the bathroom door.

April rushed over and went in. "Ooh!" she exclaimed when she noticed Shell wasn't dressed either.

"My nigga." Desean chuckled, extending his hand.

"Man, who got shot?" I replied, pushing his hand away.

"I ain't stick around to see. As soon as they started shooting, we bounced."

Shelby got dressed and came shyly out of the bathroom with April in tow, grinning from ear to ear and almost looked proud.

"I gotta go before my mother gets in," Shell announced. She came over and gave me a peck on the lips that caused April to giggle.

"A'ight, ma," I said, giving her ass a tap as she turned to leave; that drew another giggle out of April.

When the girls left, Desean and I settled on the sofa and recounted the night's events.

"Oh, Joe said to give you this," Desean said, producing a neatly rolled blunt. He set it on the coffee table, and we just stared at it for a few minutes.

"Fuck it, let's blaze that shit," I announced, grabbing the cigar. I went in the kitchen and lit it off the stove.

"Where your moms?" Day asked when I returned, blowing smoke.

"Don't get home till eight," I replied before choking on the weed.

We choked, gagged, and coughed our way through our first blunt. I was super-high, and I loved it. There was always music playing in my head, but never so loud and so funky. I longed to have a mic in my hand as rhyme patterns swirled around my brain.

"A-yo, I'm mad hungry!" Day announced, signaling the onset of the munchies.

"Say word!" I cosigned, leading the way to the kitchen.

Desean and I started with all the leftovers. Then we polished off the ice cream. Next, we decided a little breakfast was in order and made bacon, eggs, and hash browns. Not quite done, we ended up baking a cake at three in the morning. We'd finally subdued the munchies, but we'd destroyed my mother's kitchen in the process. Too tired to clean up, we decided to crash out and get it in the morning.

I heard my mother come in the next morning after working all night. I prayed she would just turn left and go to her room. "Here it comes," I said ominously when she took a right.

"Oh, hell no!" she screeched when she entered the trashed room. "A-yo, what's up with my kitchen, B?" she said, now standing over me. For all her college and sophistication, my moms is mad ghetto when she gets mad.

"I got it, Ma. Be easy," I said, trying to calm her down.

"Don't got it. Get it!" she yelled, giving me a kick for emphasis.

Desean was amused and began laughing.

"Oh, shit ain't funny, nigga. You was down with the move. Get your ass in here and help," she said, giving him a kick too. "I know my shit better be spotless before I get up," she ordered as she stormed off to her bedroom.

"I'm out," Desean announced as soon as my mother cleared the room.

"A-yo, B, you gotta help me clean this shit up, son!" I protested.

"No can do, my man." Day chuckled, putting his sneakers back on. "I gotta ride uptown with April, then shoot up to co-op and pick up Yolander."

"Just gonna walk out on me, huh?" I asked, turning the faucet on.

All I heard in reply was the door closing behind him as he walked out.

A few seconds later, I heard Day's familiar pounding on the door. I pulled it open without even bothering to see who it was and headed back to the kitchen.

"A-yo, son, I killed that nigga last night," I bragged over my shoulder.

"That's exactly what we're here to talk about!" a strange voice replied behind me.

I quietly spun around to see two rather large detectives. They held up their badges more for intimidation than identification.

"Are you David Light?" the smaller of the two asked, reading my name from a pad.

"Uh…yeah, but what you want with me?" I stammered.

The larger cop moved on me and had me cuffed and out in the hallway before I could react—before I could scream for my mother.

"Just need a few words," the small cop said soothingly as we rode the elevator down to the lobby.

They led me to their car for the short ride over to the 44th Precinct. Once inside, I was led upstairs and into a bleak interview room.

"Have a seat," the big cop said, removing the cuffs. He shoved me into the chair just in case I didn't understand what he meant by it.

"We'll be with you in a sec'," the small cop said as they left.

I was left alone for at least an hour, so I entertained myself by performing in front of the two-way mirror. I relived the battle of the previous night, trying to recall all the lyrics.

"Hey, Dave! You a'ight? Need anything?" the small cop asked when they finally returned.

"A ride home," I said wistfully.

"You ain't going nowhere!" the big cop boomed with a snarl.

"Look, Dave, we wanna help. Tell us your side of the story," the small cop said sincerely. "Let us help you."

"I honestly don't know. I left right after I battled dude," I said meekly.

"A gun battle? You guys had a gun battle?" big cop interjected.

"Gun battle?" I laughed. "What is this guy talking about?"

"You think this is funny? We got a dead guy in the morgue, and you're laughing?" big cop yelled, slamming a huge fist on the table. He rose from his seat as if he was about to come around the table.

Luckily for me, the small cop grabbed him before he could get to me. "Easy, Mitch. He's gonna cooperate. The last thing you need is another brutality charge—not with the last one still in a coma," small cop said, calming his partner. "Okay, Dave. Why don't you tell me about this battle of yours?" he coaxed.

"Ain't shit to tell. I killed that nigga," I said arrogantly.

"It's okay, Dave. Everybody kills sometimes," the small cop said, patting my hand to comfort me. "Most natural thing in the world, killing. I remember my first. You remember your first, Mitch?"

"Yeah, I remember," big cop said dryly.

"Well, he wasn't my first," I bragged.

"No?" both cops asked in unison.

"Shit no! I been murdering cats since I was, like, eleven. Anybody step to me, I'ma let 'em have it," I blasted, ignorant to the hole I was digging.

"Okay, David. It's okay," small cop pleaded. "What did you do with the gun?"

"Gun? What gun?" I asked, looking back and forth between the police.

"Yeah, the gun. Did you toss it after the battle?" big cop asked, leaning in intently.

"Whoa! Y'all talking about the shooting?" I asked, dumbfounded. "Man, I was long gone before they started shooting," I added.

"Who is 'they'?" small cop asked.

I was about to go into my "they" spiel when another cop opened the door and stuck his head in.

"Let me have a word with you guys," he said to his comrades.

"Stick around," big cop said sarcastically as he cuffed my wrists to a ring welded to the steel table.

In the hour or so it took before the cops came back, I entertained myself again by freestyling in the mirror.

"Good news," small cop said, smiling when he returned alone. "We got it all worked out," he said as he uncuffed me.

"So I can go?" I asked, rubbing the cuff marks from my wrists.

"Of course you can," the police replied, as if it was the craziest question he'd ever heard. "Hey, thanks for helping us out," he added, along with a pat on the back.

"Oh…well, okay. You're welcome," I said, not sure what assistance I had provided.

Luckily for me, there were so many cameras on hand to capture the battle, and a couple caught the shootout afterward. It seemed them cats from the projects had laid on Ace and company to come out. When they did, all hell broke loose, and Ace's younger brother got hit. He died on the way to the hospital.

I declined the offer of a ride back home and sprinted the block and a half back to my building.

My mother was sitting on the sofa fuming when I walked in. "Boy!" she said, pausing to breathe fire. "You better have a damn good excuse for leaving that kitchen like that."

I did, but when I told her, she didn't believe me.

She jumped up and marched me right back to the precinct. Mom read both police the Riot Act, then marched me back to the apartment. "Now get my kitchen clean," she barked before retreating back to her room.

CHAPTER 5

The local news and radio covered the shooting incident for over a week: "Rap Contest Turns Deadly" was the common headline.

Since Wayne hosted his own show at Wild 101, my verse was broadcasted all over the city. Every time it played, I basked in the attention.

"I don't know why you keep listening to that, baby. That's bad publicity," my mother said naïvely.

"No such thing as bad publicity, especially for a rapper," I corrected.

My mother frowned at the condescending tone, then sucked her teeth. "Boy, don't let this go to your head. Don't forget who you are," she warned.

"I know who I am. I'm D-Lite, the rapper, south Bronx's finest," I shot back.

"No…you are David Light Jr., pain in the ass," she replied.

"Junior?" I said, hitting below the belt. I knew my mother's aversion to my pops would quickly end any conversation, and that time was no exception.

My mother frowned up and walked out of the room.

I know who I am! D-mother-fucking-Lite!

* * *

Our summer camp days were over, but Desean spent most of the vacation at one basketball camp or another. Shelby went south for a few days after the rec' center battle, leaving me all alone. For the first time in my life, I was without both of my best friends at the same time.

Turned out I wasn't alone for long. Since Wayne had me performing at every gig he played, there was no shortage of people who wanted to hang out.

In the end, I linked up with Big Hank from the projects. He was my age but already 6'4", weighing in at a solid 250. As an added bonus, he was weed man Joey's little brother. He had a never-ending supply of weed, and I began smoking every day.

For me, marijuana was an amplifier. It made everything more intense and took my freestyle to another level. After I smoked a blunt, the music began playing in my head, and line after line of rhymes just appeared.

I was becoming quite the local celebrity and loving all the attention. The majority of attention was coming from my female fans. All these girls were throwing themselves at me, and that was a recipe for disaster. Fact was, I was getting a good deal of booty, which Wayne referred to as "the spoils of war." It was pretty much stick-and-move since I didn't want to get caught up. I had a girl and told every groupie so beforehand. None of them cared. I couldn't blame them; I mean, after all, I am D-Lite!

This one Spanish chick did manage to get me open. Ma looked like a teenage J-Lo. I started going out of my way to get up to Riverpark Towers to see Maria.

Maria hated condoms and said she couldn't feel it. I resisted for a sec', but all that nasty sex talk of hers wore me down. Talking about, "Yeah, Papi, get this pussy. Feel this hot pussy. Listen to it, Papi. It was talking too!"

Mami had me fucked up, and I was running up in her raw all summer. That, too, was a recipe for disaster.

When Desean finished camp, he took his rightful spot by my side. He was amazed at how much I'd changed over the summer. Not only was I smoking weed daily, but I was now getting as much ass as he was. He joined me and Hank as I continued my panty raid on New York City.

* * *

"Shelby's home," my mom sang one night when I returned from a show.

"That's what's up," I replied nonchalantly and plopped down beside her on the sofa.

"Yeah, right, boy." My mother chuckled, passing me the phone.

"Hey, Dave. Shell isn't feeling well. Give her a call in the morning," Shelby's mom advised.

Instead of calling, I walked down the hall as soon as I heard her mom leave for work. I rang the doorbell a couple times, then headed back when I didn't get an answer.

I made it as far as the elevator before I heard Shelby's door open. "Hey, baby," she called out weakly.

As usual, she looked great when she came home from down south. The bronze tan brought out the flecks of gold in her hazel eyes. The sun had also bleached her hair to a sandy color.

Damn! She got thicker too! "What's good, ma?" I said, giving her a peck on her lips as I entered her apartment.

She sucked her teeth and sat in the chair across from me instead of beside me on the sofa. "You know I hate that 'ma' shit," she spat bitterly.

"That's why you way over there?" I asked.

"No. It's 'cause you stink. You smell like stale cigars." Shelby frowned.

"You stink! And I know you better get your ass over here!" I demanded playfully.

She sucked her teeth again before getting up and joining me on the sofa. I tried to give her a hug, but as soon as I did, she gagged. Shelby jumped from the sofa and shot into the bathroom. Even from all the way in the living room, I could hear her throwing up. She returned a few minutes later, looking seasick. Shell bypassed me and fell back into the chair across the room.

"Fuck wrong with you?" I asked, feeling far more sympathetic than I sounded.

"Morning sickness," she replied curtly.

"I don't get it," I said, dumbfounded.

"Duh! Morning sickness! Pregnant!" she snapped.

"I'm not sure what you mean," I replied, still unable to process the information.

"Um...let's see...pregnant, knocked up, with child, um...in a motherly way," she quipped. "What part don't you understand?"

"I'm saying, though, I don't understand how you go down south and come back pregnant," I replied.

Shelby exploded out her chair, rain across the room, leapt the coffee table, and launched into a hormone-fueled tirade.

I had a flashback to second grade and covered up.

"What the fuck you mean, 'come back pregnant'? Nigga, I left here pregnant!" she screamed.

"But we only did it that one time," I reasoned.

"That's all it take, dummy." She slumped down beside me and began to cry.

"Don't worry, ma…I mean, ma like—you know—not 'cause you pregnant, ma, but…well, you know," I stammered. "I'ma take care of you and the baby."

"David, I'm sixteen! I am not having no baby. I'm going to college! I am going to be a doctor," Shelby said plainly.

"Well, here," I said sadly, extending a wad of cash.

"What's this?" she asked while flipping through the bills.

"It's your cut from all the shows I did over the summer," I replied.

"My cut?" she said dubiously.

"Yeah, your cut. I gave Day his already. If I eat, y'all eat," I said emphatically. "It was supposed to be for you to go school shopping, but I guess we gotta use it for the abortion."

"Shit! Abortions are free at the clinic. I'ma shop with this," she exclaimed, smiling for the first time.

We made plans to hook up and hit Fordham Road later in the day. Of all the shopping districts in the Bronx, Fordham had the best selection. I left Shell to get some rest and walked straight into more drama.

"A-yo, whoever this Maria chick is, you need to call her ass right now!" my mother demanded as soon as I walked in. "Broad keep calling here night and day with her smart mouth. She must not know I'll whip her ass for her."

"I really ain't tryina talk to her, Ma, especially since Shell's home," I replied.

"Then you need to let her know, 'cause she gonna stop calling my house," my mother fumed.

"A'ight, Ma. I'ma call her later," I agreed.

"Later my ass! You gonna call her now," she shot back.

"Okay, okay." I surrendered and grabbed the phone. Reluctantly, I dialed Maria's number while my mother looked on.

"Aye, papi, I miss you," Maria purred seductively when she answered.

"Look, you can't keep calling me like this, ma. My moms is pissed!" I said, making eye contact with my mother.

"Shit, you ain't called me in months. I been tryna tell you I'm pregnant," she said, becoming agitated.

"Well, congratulations. My girl back, so, um…" I said firmly, hoping she got the hint.

"Congratulations?!" Maria screamed. "Motherfucker, you—"

That was all she got out before I hung up on her. Of course she called back, and she called every day afterward until my mother finally changed our number.

I didn't believe for a second that the kid was mine, but there was a nagging, *What if…?* in the back of my mind.

Once she did have the kid, I made my way over to her house to put the issue to rest one way or the other. As I raised my hand to ring the bell, I got caught up in the jazzy soca rhythm emanating from the apartment.

Immediately, I began to pull words and phrases from Spanish class, and a song was born. I'm not sure how long I stood there rapping before the door suddenly pulled open.

Both me and the beautiful Spanish lady who opened the door gasped in surprise. I had never met Maria's mother before, but I could tell right away who she was. She was an older—though not that much older—version of Maria. Except for the few years' difference and the hips of childbirth, they were dead ringers for each other. "Can I help you?" she asked sweetly, breaking me from my spell.

"Um, yeah, I'm…uh, I'm here to see Maria. I'm Lite…uh, I mean David… David Light," I stuttered.

"You're David?" she asked doubtfully. "You're the baby's father?"

I could only shrug my shoulders at the question because I didn't know the answer. I was curious at the woman's incredulous demeanor. *Perhaps she was expecting the father to be Latino,* I surmised.

"Come in," she ordered suspiciously. "Have a seat. Maria, come out here… and bring David!" She stared at me, scrutinizing my face as we waited.

I was so uncomfortable that I was on the verge of checking her odd behavior.

Finally, Maria walked in with the baby. The jet-black infant looked like a mini Joe Frasier.

I now understood her mother's odd demeanor. One look at me with my light complexion, and she knew I wasn't the father.

Before Maria and I could say a word, her mother flipped out in Spanish.

I don't know what she said, but Maria burst into tears and ran from the room.

"I'm sorry my daughter got you involved in this," her mother said apologetically.

"A'ight," I said, jumping to my feet and heading out the door. "Peace out!"

CHAPTER 6

The rest of high school was a blur. By the time I looked up, we were seniors, set to graduate in a week's time.

Desean had a storied high school basketball career. He broke Clinton's scoring record that had been set decades earlier by Lew Alcindor. He also shattered the city's assist record and shot a phenomenal 68 percent from behind the arc. As a result of his accomplishments, he was heavily recruited by every college program in the land. He decided on the University of Atlanta, who would have a good shot at winning it all with him as their premier point guard.

Shelby was a straight-A student, class president, and class valedictorian. She accepted a full academic scholarship to a prestigious all-girl college in Atlanta. She had her pick of any school she wanted, but her mother insisted on an all-female student body.

As for me, my moms blew a gasket when I told her I intended to stay in New York and pursue my music. She finally convinced me with an offer I couldn't refused: "If you don't go to school, you can't live here," she explained casually.

"Dang, Ma! You gonna put me out?" I exclaimed.

"No. I'm going to kill you. Like I said, you can't live here," she offered.

"But I didn't even apply for no schools, so I ain't gon' be able to go first semester anyway," I said smugly. I was quite pleased to have a way out, but Ma Dukes had a remedy for that too.

"I knew you would try that, so I already spoke with your Aunt Betty, and she talked to them at the University of Atlanta. They want Desean so bad we got them to take you too," she said, matching my smugness.

* * *

Coming from where we came from, graduation was a big deal. A good number of our classmates from PS 129 were dead or in jail—a number that would only increase as time marched on.

Since all graduation ceremonies took place on the same day, we weren't able to cheer each other on. As a consolation, our parents planned a celebration dinner at New York's fabled Tavern on the Green restaurant in Central Park.

The real festivities of the night took place at the city-wide graduation party hosted by Wild 101. One had to present a diploma to enter. Since my mentor, Wayne, was DJ-ing the party, I was the headlining performer among all the talented graduates set to perform.

Shelby drove her brand new car that her father had presented to her as a graduation present. She had gotten her license and had been driving during her trips south, and she drove like a pro.

Desean and I had recently acquired our licenses as well, but I was the only one who was whipless. Somehow, Aunt Betty came up with enough money out the blue to buy Day a brand new SUV with all the trimmings. We all knew it came from the school indirectly, but nobody cared.

We all ended up in Shell's car and headed uptown to Harlem, where the party was being held. We had to to park several blocks from the venue as a testament to how packed it was.

Shelby kept looking back at her new car as if she hated to leave it. "You sure it will be okay here?" she pleaded desperately.

"Yeah, ma. It's right in front of a busy diner. Ain't nobody gonna steal it," I said, hoping I was right.

As soon as we entered the ballroom, Day took off in search of prey.

I, too, had to go backstage and get ready to go onstage. Plus, Wayne said he had a present for me. "Daddy gotta go do this thing," I told Shell and planted a kiss on her cheek.

"Well, do the damn thing then, Daddy." She laughed.

"A-yo, son, where you been?" Wayne asked urgently.

"Tavern on the Green," I bragged. "Had to do the dinner thing with the fam'."

"Did you try the calamari?" he asked, indicating that he'd been there before. "I got some people here to see you, so you don't take no prisoners! Wreck that shit, fam'!"

"A'ight, B. Who here?" I asked offhandedly.

"Only the owner of New York Records!" he replied. "I've been making some moves with dude, so you in if you impress him."

I was in my zone backstage, pacing back and forth like a caged lion. I was so focused I didn't even hear any of the opening acts.

It wasn't until a trio of pretty girls walked past that I realized I wasn't alone. Actually, I only really took notice of one of them. All three were fine, but only one was my type. Of course she was light-skinned, with long hair and well built. Her ass! Her ass was the roundest, most perfect ass in the world. The announcer introduced them as Galaxy, and the name fit. They were all stars with heavenly bodies. The two dark-skinned girls, Egypt and China, were dual bookends to lead singer Asia. They were supposed to be a rap group, but they couldn't really rap. It wasn't until they sang their hooks that their potential came through. Those girls could sing!

"Good show," I said, congratulating the girls as they exited the stage.

"Thank you," they sang in unison.

I ignored the chocolate ones and zeroed in on the light skin. "D-Lite!" I said, extending my hand.

"Asia," she said flirtatiously, holding my hand longer than necessary. "These are my girls, Egypt and China."

"Hey," I said, never averting my gaze from Asia's green eyes.

When the announcer said my name, the crowd erupted. Asia nodded appreciatively at the response.

"Well, if you guys will excuse me, I gotta go tear this shit up." I chuckled.

As planned, Wayne started the beat, and I came out swinging. I ran through a medley of my songs from Wayne's mix tapes. The way the crowd rapped along, I felt like Jay or somebody.

When I came to the scheduled end of my set, I began giving shout-outs, but the crowd wasn't trying to hear that.

"Give 'em one more," Wayne said over the music.

"A'ight. I'ma give 'em a freestyle," I agreed. "Cut the music. I'ma give it to 'em raw." I turned toward the VIP section and said,

"THERE HASN'T BEEN A LYRICIST LIKE ME IN A LONG TIME…

MY RHYMES PUT YOU IN A MIND OF PAC IN HIS PRIME…

'SON GOT MAD SKILLS' IS WHAT YOU'LL SAY…

PLUS, LADIES LOVE ME LIKE LL COOL J…

IN THIS GAME, YOU'RE ONLY AS GOOD AS YOUR LAST RHYME…

SOME SAY NAS AIN'T BEEN THE SAME SINCE HALF-TIME…

TONIGHT D-LITE IS AS RAW AS HE'S EVER BEEN…

A NEW JACK, BETTER THAN A LOT OF VETERANS…

Y'ALL SICK OF SOFT NIGGAS TRYINA ACT HARD…

AND FUCK A BIG FACE, I'M TRYINA ROCK A BLACK CARD…

TURN ME LOOSE AND I'MA BLOW UP THE BOOTH…

IN A COUPLE OF BARS, YOU'LL SAY GOD IS THE TRUTH…

A-YO, Y'ALL LABELS BETTER KEEP IT REAL…Y'ALL SEE THE SKILLS, NOW LET'S

MAKE A DEAL!"

With that, I dropped the mic and walked offstage. I knew Wayne was going to chew me out about dropping his mic again, but I was trying to catch that chick Asia.

I was looking all around the backstage area with no luck. While I was looking for her, Wayne was looking for me. "Fuck you doing, B?" he called out when he spotted me.

"I know, I know. Stop dropping the mic," I replied. "I'm tryina find that girl."

"Dude! Son from the label wanna holla. Let's handle our business," Wayne demanded. He practically dragged me to the VIP section.

When we entered, a large white man with quite a bit of bling stood to meet us. His jewels wasn't that gaudy 'hood shit—just chunky with clusters of brilliant diamonds. "Bravo, bravo, bra-fucking-vo!" he exclaimed with a hard clap. "Is this the fuckin' guy?" he said, extending his large hand. To me, he looked like a young Tony Soprano.

"Rocco, this is the guy," Wayne said as I shook his hand.

"Pleased to meet ya," Rocco said enthusiastically. "Great fucking show! You'se gotta bright future ahead a ya."

"Thanks," I replied, feeling slightly intimidated by the man's presence. His heavy Italian accent, jewels, and demeanor screamed MOB! Not that I gave a fuck. I would have signed a deal with a devil had that been necessary. *Hell Fire Records presents...D-Lite!*

"I want you to give me a call," he ordered as he handed me his business card.

"We will," Wayne answered. "We will."

After the brief meeting, I ran backstage again to find that girl, but she was long gone. Once I accepted that fact, I went to find my friends.

Shelby had promised me some ass for graduation, and I was eager to collect. Saying she was stingy with the booty would be a gross understatement. Since our pregnancy scare a few years earlier, she very rarely put out, and when she did, it was condoms, foam, diaphragms, fucking National Guard. If it wasn't for my steady supply of groupie love, I would have been ass out of ass.

It took a while to track Desean down, but we found him coming out of a supply closet with a girl.

"Un-uh! I know you wasn't screwing that girl," Shelby said, disgusted.

"Nah. She's a basketball fan," Desean said plainly.

"And?" Shell laughed at the weak explanation.

"And, she likes ball, so I showed her mine," Day said, cracking up.

"You are so nasty." Shelby frowned.

"Speaking of doing the nasty," I whispered, reminding her of her promise.

"Boy, I said I would," she said as if it was a chore she wasn't looking forward to.

The three of us chatted as we made our way back to the car. We all silently prayed that the new car was still there. We heard the sound of people coming up behind us, but we didn't make much of it until my name was called.

"What's up now, Lite?" someone yelled.

When I turned to see what the problem was, I saw Ace and a couple of goons rushing toward us.

"Go to the car!" Day ordered to Shell.

We intended to stay and fight until Ace raised a pistol and opened fire.

We could hear and see bullets hitting the ground and wall as we ran. When we turned the corner, I banged my arm on the wall, and it went numb instantly.

Ace and company rounded the corner in hot pursuit, but there were so many people around the well-lit diner that they turned on their heels and left.

We piled into Shelby's car and chirped out, not knowing if we were still being chased or not.

"Y'all cool?" Day asked from the backseat.

"Yes," Shelby answered, the fear obvious in her voice.

"Yeah, I'm cool. Banged my shit on the wall though," I replied, wincing from the pain.

"Oh, baby, you're bleeding!" Shelby screamed when Desean turned on the dome light.

I could clearly see a small hole just below my elbow. "A-yo, that nigga shot me!" I exclaimed. That was when the pain set in. "Shit! I'm shot!"

Shelby blew through stop signs and traffic lights as she navigated to the closest hospital. It was just my luck that the closest hospital was Lincoln, where my mother worked—in the ER, no less.

"Hey, guys! What are y'all doing here?" my mother asked brightly. Then she saw the blood. "Oh my God! What happened?" she asked, near panic. You would think that after so many years of working in a south Bronx emergency room, she would have been immune to the sight of blood, but I guess it's different when the blood is coming out of your own child.

I was in a good bit of pain, but I had one thing on my mind. "A-yo, Shell, you still gonna do that?" I asked as I was wheeled toward surgery.

"Do wha...baby! Are you serious?" she asked, incredulous.

"I'm sayin' though," I reasoned.

Since my mom worked there, I was fast-tracked into surgery before the other gunshot victims. They removed a 380-caliber bullet from my arm and stitched me up. The doctor said I was lucky because the projectile didn't hit any bone or arteries. That was funny; I didn't feel so lucky.

I was feeling real groovy from the anesthesia. I was absolutely floating when the detectives came to interview me.

It is standard procedure for hospitals to notify law enforcement about all gunshots, and so many cats got shot up around there that they now stationed an officer at Lincoln to handle the volume.

This time, my mom was present while I was questioned.

I was high as a kite from the blunt I'd smoked backstage and whatever was in the IV.

"Who shot ya?" the detective asked so politely I thought I heard a trace of compassion.

It was futile, 'cause as soon as I heard, "Who shot ya?" the song by the late Great B.I.G began playing in my mind. I was halfway through the song before being interrupted.

"I think he's still groggy from anesthesia," my mom offered.

"If he can just tell us who shot him, we can be on our way," the detective said in frustration, creeping back into his tone.

My mind replayed the shooting, and I could clearly see Ace busting his gun. "Shit ain't have nothing to do with us," I lied.

My mother, who had heard at least a million of my lies by then, recognized it and frowned.

"Niggas started beefing. We ran when they started shooting," I added.

"So you caught a stray?" the cop asked eagerly, since a stray bullet needed no investigation.

"Yeah, a stray," I agreed.

The police thanked me and went on his way.

* * *

"Rap artist injured. Up-and-coming Bronx rapper D-Lite was shot last night after a performance. He was released from the hospital after surgery to remove a bullet from his arm. D-Lite claims he does not know who shot him or why, and police have no leads on the shooter."

"Read it again," I demanded for the third time.

"Boy, no," Shelby replied. "I still don't understand why you didn't tell them that fool shot you."

"No can do, ma. That ain't gangsta," I replied.

"You ain't gangsta," she shot back, stinging my ego. She sensed my injured pride and snuggled up close. "I'm sorry, baby," she purred, causing an instant reaction.

"I'm saying, though, I don't get no rain-check?" I asked, nibbling on her earlobe.

"Are you up to it?" she said, sounding concerned.

"Yep. See?" I laughed, opening my robe.

* * *

My mother insisted on attending my meeting with Rocco over my vociferous objection. We met at the world-famous Halima's Soul Food on Eighth Avenue.

"Wow! Look at you! Got ya stripes," Rocco said, standing to greet me.

"Yeah, our baby took one on the wing." Wayne chuckled, standing as well.

After the introductions were made and courteous small talk was out of the way, we got down to business.

"Let's cut to the chase. We want you," Rocco said plainly. "Wayne, here, tells me you got quite a following in the Bronx."

"He got the BX on lock. After that, Harlem…and then the world," Wayne said dramatically.

"We want you. We want to sign you," Rocco said emphatically.

"Bet! Where do I sign?" I said, having heard enough.

"Not so fast, David. Let's hear the details," my mother chided, patting my hand. "What does the small print say?" she asked, looking between Rocco and Wayne.

"It's all pretty standard," Rocco said, and then he laid out all the terms and conditions.

I didn't hear one word. All I knew was that I was getting a deal.

After Rocco's spiel, Wayne jumped in with more details. "I should have you in the studio in a month or so. In the meantime, we'll keep doing the shows to generate your buzz—start a movement. And I'll be managing him, Mrs. Light, so—"

"Davis," my mother corrected sharply. "My name is Davis, Ms. Davis."

"Uh, okay, Ms. Davis. He'll be in good hands," Wayne explained.

"Well, he better be, 'cause I know where you live," my mom said evenly.

Wayne, Rocco, and I all chuckled at the remark until we noticed that she didn't.

"My main concern is school. David starts college in the fall," she said, dripping with pride.

"Not a problem," Rocco chimed in. "We will work around his schedule."

"That's right, Mrs…er, uh, Ms. Davis. He can fly up for studio sessions on weekends, and since he'll be in Atlanta, he can build a fan base down there as well," Wayne added.

"Oh yeah," Rocco said, reaching into his jacket. "Besides the points, there's this." He tossed a stuffed envelope on the table.

"What's that?" I inquired, never taking my eyes off the envelope.

"Signing bonus. Ten stacks, if you want it," Rocco said.

My mother and I looked at the money, then at each other, then back to the money before she spoke up. "Son, get your money off the table," she ordered.

* * *

I may have picked up the money, but Ma Dukes controlled it. She drove me down to the auto auction in Pennsylvania, where I copped a used Maxima for $4,000. The miles were high, but it had a system and rims to compensate.

I cracked for two stacks to get this necklace I'd had my eye on, but that was obviously the funniest thing my mother had ever heard. I was able to finagle another G out of her for school clothes.

Of that, I gave Shell $300 for her pocket. She had to fly down to Atlanta to attend an incoming freshmen orientation, which meant she would be gone most of the summer. I harbored mixed emotions when she left. On the one hand, she was my boo, but on the other, there were the spoils of war. *Bring on the booty!*

Desean showed his ass at Rucker, and his stock rose by the day. Pro scouts were at every game, taking notes. Agents sent their agents, who would give Day a yard just to take a business card.

At the same time, I was busy tearing New York City a new one. Wayne had me opening for everybody. I was doing four and five shows a week, but since it was all promotions, I only got a $250 a week stipend. Still, that was big money for a kid like me, and, truth be told, I would have done it for free. I loved being onstage. The shit made my dick hard. Shit, I would have paid them. I was ten feet tall onstage.

When I had a show in Brooklyn, though, I felt a new sensation: fear. It wasn't stage fright—never that. This nigger Ace had me shook. To keep it all the way real, I am no thug, and I never claimed to be. Sure, I had a couple fights coming up, and I was always pretty nice with my mitts, but the dude shot me... with a gun!

"Dude, you ain't high?" Day asked as I lit a new blunt with the roach off the first one.

"Huh? Oh, yeah, I'm cool," I said, trying to at least appear cool.

"A-yo, B, you know I'm down for whatever," he said reassuringly. We'd known each other our whole lives, and Desean knew the deal.

"Son shot me, yo!" I exclaimed. "Tried to murder me."

"What the fuck, Light? You doing a reggae show?" Wayne asked as he entered the cloudy dressing room.

"What up with security?" Desean demanded.

"Security for what?" Wayne asked curiously. "Hold up. You ain't worried about that clown Ace, are you? That nigga locked up on a gun charge, three to five. Breathe easy."

I did. Wayne left, and I outed the blunt before I smoked myself silly. Me and Day were chilling until female laughter slipped through the cracked door. I made a move toward the door, but Day, being the athlete, beat me to it.

"A-yo, Dunn. That's them chicks from the graduation party," he informed me.

I darted out past him and confronted Asia. "What's good, ma?" I called out to get their attention.

"What's good with you?" Asia replied seductively. "You told me to wait for you, and then you ain't show up."

"Yeah, niggas got into some beef, yo," I began as Desean moved on Egypt. I knew China was more his type, but she had some dude with her that was either her boyfriend or her bodyguard.

"I heard. They say you got shot," she said, maintaining eye and hand contact.

"Word! Some Harlem niggas stepped to me and my man. We had to bang it out with niggas," I lied.

Desean struggled to keep a straight face as I went on with the highly embellished version of how I got shot.

"Yeah, five-o was sweating 'cause they say my hammer got bodies on it, and—"

Luckily for all, Galaxy got called onstage before the shit got any deeper.

"Son, you funny." Desean chuckled.

"What?" I laughed.

After the show, me and Day took Asia and Egypt to the nearest motor lodge and gutted them. They let us hit them in the same room with the lights on. Even when Desean yelled, "Switch!" indicating that we change partners, they didn't protest. I, on the other hand, did.

A dark-skinned chick can't do nothing for me but introduce me to her light-skinned friends. Don't get me wrong: Egypt was a dime—just a dark one. Besides, I was feeling Asia. Shorty smoked weed, rapped, sang, and was mad ambitious. She woulda been the wifey type, if not for Shelby.

Asia and I began seeing each other as often as our schedules would permit. Since we were performing on the same amateur circuit, we did a few shows together, after which we hit the nearest motel and sweated up the sheets.

Desean got with Egypt once or twice after the Brooklyn show before losing interest. I kept on seeing Asia, even after Shell came home.

* * *

The whole summer passed, and I had yet to record one line. I hadn't even stepped foot inside a recording studio.

Every time I complained to Wayne about it, he told me to talk to Rocco. Getting in to talk to Rocco was like getting in to talk to the president.

When I did speak to Rocco, he always threw me a bunch of excuses and an extra yard or two to placate me. It always worked; I'd just take the money and go on my way.

Rocco and Wayne seemed to have a lot going on, but none of it appeared to be music related.

CHAPTER 7

School was a week away when our three-car convoy headed south. The thirteen-hour drive flew by for me. I had a beat CD from producer Adam Salaah and freestyled the whole way. At one point, I rapped for two and a half hours straight. Even when the CD changed tracks, I flowed a cappella until it caught up.

Our first stop in the A was at Shelby's school. We helped her unload her belongings and take them to her dorm room. Actually, I did all the work because Desean was too busy getting phone numbers. "A-yo, Shell, I'ma be here e'rry day," he exclaimed happily.

"Mm-hmm. I bet you will." She laughed.

"You know I'ma be here e'rry day too," I said, attempting a little snuggle.

"Oh, I will be far too busy for that," Shell said flatly, pulling away. "We maybe can chill on the weekend, but my class load is bananas!"

We left Shelby's school and headed across town to ours—in the vicinity anyway.

I could only presume it was the school that provided the two-bedroom townhouse that we were staying in. The place was huge. It was set up in what's known as a "roommate floor plan," with both bedrooms being exactly the same.

Me and Day had planned to fight over who got the big room, but since that issue was moot, we fought over who got which room.

The three of us explored all the tourist attractions by day and the nightclubs once the sun set. Hot 103 was the sister station to our Wild 101, and they filled us in on what was hot.

Atlanta is a party town! There are several clubs and party options every night of the week. The clubs are always packed, and you are sure to see a star or two. In my first week there, I saw T.I., Big Boi, Jeezy, and Ludacris…oh, and JD. He seemed to be everywhere we went.

Everyone in Atlanta is in the music business in one capacity or another. Everyone is a rapper, singer, producer, videographer, choreographer, engineer, clothing designer, manager, photographer, model, DJ, agent, A&R, songwriter, promoter, dancer, or knows somebody who is.

There are also open mics and/or battles everywhere, but Wayne forbid me from doing any of them since I was under contract already. All I could do was watch from the sidelines.

* * *

When classes began, I rarely saw my friends at all, and I was miserable. Shelby was right: Her class load was bananas. She had class all day and labs at night, followed by studying in the library all weekend.

Even though me and Desean lived together, I hardly saw him either. His hands were full with classes, tutors, and the team. I only saw him coming or going, usually with a different girl in tow.

I was pretty much just going through the motions at school. I went to all my classes and completed all my assignments, but my heart just wasn't in it.

I still couldn't get inside a studio and wasn't allowed to perform without Rocco's consent. The label flew me up top a couple times a month to do shows, but I was miserable nonetheless. After a few months, my stipend abruptly stopped, as did my contact with Wayne. Try as I did, I couldn't get Wayne or Rocco on the phone. I left message after desperate message, but I got nowhere. By December, the phones were off, and I was lost.

Since I was broke, Shelby and Day ended up paying for my ticket home for Christmas break. Shelby and I flew up while Desean stayed behind. His team was in a big tournament, and he was all hot and heavy with some chick from the girls' team, so he stayed in Atlanta playing love and basketball.

When our plane landed at JFK, we took the first thing smoking into the city. My destination was West 43rd Street, home of New York Records.

"It's not the end of the world," Shelby said compassionately as we stood in front of the empty office of the now-defunct record label.

"For me it is," I said, tasting the salt of my tears as I spoke. My dream was over before it even began. I couldn't even qualify as a has-been; I was merely a never-was.

As it turned out, New York Records was a record label in name only. Its primary function was to launder drug proceeds. I was only signed to legitimize the company; at least they could show acts on their roster.

Both Wayne and Rocco were looking at "from now on" in a federal pen. As for me, I was sentenced to a life of obscurity.

I was in a funk for the whole Christmas break. The only consolation was Shelby loosening the pussy embargo to cheer me up.

My mother had a few encouraging words to offer, but I knew she was relieved it was over. "At least you can focus on school," she said on more than one occasion.

Slowly, I began to accept defeat. Then I embraced it. I decided to finally pick a major, sports management. Desean would be my first client, and I would build from there. Of course, that dream was short lived as well.

* * *

A couple of days after Christmas, I came home to find my mom and aunt on the verge of hysteria.

"A-yo, what's wrong with y'all? They closed the all-you-can-eat buffet?" I teased, hoping to lighten the mood. I knew from experience that those two could cry over a broken fingernail.

"It's Day!" Aunt Betty wailed before my mom wrapped her up in her arms.

"Is he...dead?" I asked, assuming the worse. I knew firsthand that Atlanta is a dangerous city. People flock there from the worst cities on the planet, like New York, Detroit, and L.A., only to find that some areas of Atlanta are just as bad as where they came from. Scores of people go to the southern Mecca in search of a better life, only to find a shorter one.

"No!" Aunt Betty frowned, disturbed by the thought, but at the same time realizing that anything short of death was far less serious. "It's just his...his knee," she said, regaining her lost composure.

"Oh, he cool. His knee been bothering him all summer," I said, letting a sworn secret slip. Desean had been having pain for months, but he still played. It was his time to shine, and he was not going to be denied.

"He blew it out, baby," my mother sorrowfully interjected. "It's...well, it's over."

The two women picked up where they had left off in their sobbing, and I went to call Day.

"What's good, son?" Desean asked cheerfully upon answering the line. "I guess you heard the news."

"Yeah, I heard, B. You a'ight? You don't sound bad. Your moms and my moms over here freaking the fuck out," I said.

"I'm cool. Shit don't look good, B. Might not be able to play no more," he replied casually.

"A-yo, you sure taking this shit well," I said, feeling worse than he sounded.

"I mean, it is what it is. Feel me? I wanna play, but if God's will is that I don't, then I won't. Shit, I'm still winning," he said.

"Winning?" I asked, the victory escaping me."

"A-yo, these niggas wanted me so bad my scholarship is good whether I play or not. The whip, the apartment...I'm good," he explained.

"I feel you," I lied. I was still crushed about losing my deal. Then, Plan B, to be Day's agent, blew up with his knee. *It's all bad. Fuck I'ma do now?*

* * *

Shelby and I decided to cut our visit short and hang out with Desean. We made our way back to JFK on New Year's Eve for the flight back home.

As fate would have it, we got bumped from our flight and had to wait a couple hours for the next departure. The airline upgraded us to first class to compensate us for our delay.

Shell bullied me out of the window seat and into an aisle one. When the plane reached cruising altitude, the seatbelts came off, and the laptops came out.

We were watching a Will Smith movie on the overhead monitors when I took notice of the guy directly across the aisle. He had a set of professional headphones attached to his laptop. I surmised it could only be a music program he was working on since he was nodding his head to his work.

I craned my neck, trying to get a better view of what he was doing.

"David, sit down," Shelby ordered through clenched teeth.

I was too far gone to heed her command and tapped the dude on the shoulder. I don't know which irked him more—my disturbing him or tapping his shoulder.

He gave me a pained expression in reply.

"What's that, B?" I asked, ignoring his obvious frustration.

"Pro-Tools," he said curtly. "I'm *trying* to finish a track." He stressed the word "trying" to let me know I was disturbing him, as if I couldn't tell by the annoyed look on his face.

"David!" Shelby snapped, trying to get me to leave the man alone.

I fell back in my seat to watch the movie, but only for a few seconds. Son was disturbing me. He was nodding so hard, like he was listening to the funkiest shit in the world, and I had to hear it. "A-yo, B," I said, tapping his shoulder again.

Again I was met with the same angry look.

"Can I hear it?" I asked, trying not to laugh at his obvious frustration.

"Here!" He sighed, shoving the headphones toward me. I guess he assumed if he gave in, I would leave him alone. When I placed the expensive headphones on my ears, he tapped the spacebar and filled my head with music.

"Shit's hot, son!" I said way too loudly, causing Shell to mean-mug me. The beat playing was some ol' slow-flow, jazzy-type shit, and I couldn't resist.

"D-LITE GOT THE SKILLS TO PAY THE BILLS WITH…
I AM LEGEND, SO NIGGAS CALL ME WILL SMITH…
FASTEST DRAW YOU NEVER SAW MEANS I PULL QUICK…
RUN YOUR LIPS, AND I'MA HIT YA WITH A FULL CLIP…
FUCK WITH THE LITE AND I'MA—"

"David Light! Are you crazy?" Shell screamed, pulling the plug on my impromptu concert. "I'm so sorry," she announced to the occupants of the first class section.

Everyone was looking, but dude was the only one smiling. "You're D-Lite?" he asked enthusiastically.

"Yeah...in the flesh," I replied smugly, giving Shell a *"See? Everybody knows who I am"* kind of look.

"Dude, I'm a fan," he said, pulling one of Wayne's mix tape CDs from his bag. "I'm Bliz," he introduced, extending his hand.

"Bliz?!" I exclaimed. "Dude, *I'm* a fan," I said, pulling his mix tape CD from my bag.

Bliz was the hottest DJ on the planet at the time. His mix tapes had launched the careers of the top rappers on the charts. He was the reason Atlanta rapper B-Bop was number one with a bullet.

"We gotta link up," Bliz suggested, handing me his card. "Give me a call, yo?"

"Now?" I asked, feeling silly when I heard it slip from my mouth.

"He'll call you." Shelby chuckled, patting my hand. "You can count on it."

CHAPTER 8

I took a long pull of my blunt, then tried to pass it to Desean. I knew he would decline, but at least I offered.

"I'm cool, yo. They got me on some shit way better than that," he said, waving off my attempt.

"So what them doctors talking 'bout? You gonna be able to walk again or what?" I joked.

"Yeah, I can walk, nigga!" Day chuckled. "But it's 50/50 whether or not I'll play again."

"Damn, that's fucked," I lamented bitterly.

"Fucks with you and all this doom-and-gloom shit, yo?" he said, becoming agitated.

"Our shit is all fucked up, B. Everything is falling apart," I whined.

"Son, we from the fucking slums. Now we in school, phat-ass crib, bitches! Nigga, we winning," he exclaimed.

"How we winning, yo?" I asked, becoming agitated myself. "I had and lost a record deal before I got to record one word."

"You mad ungrateful. You got ten stacks, a whip, did mad shows, and your name still ringing back home," he reasoned. "Shit, if anyone got the right to complain, it's me. You can still rap. I may never play ball again."

The atmosphere got thick instantly with the gravity of his statement, so I decided to try and lighten the mood. "Now who's being ungrateful?" I said, pretending to be upset. "You got a free ride to school, an apartment, and a new truck. Then the school send you all them tutors, and all you do is fuck 'em! Me?

I gotta go out and hunt my pussy down like a goddamn caveman."

My tirade succeeded in cracking us both up. We needed a good laugh, and in the end, Day was right: We had a lot to be thankful for.

* * *

Bliz was one of those people who never answered his phone, and I was one of those people who never left messages. The way I figured it, somebody would see I called. If they wanted to know what I wanted, they could either hit me back or answer the damn phone.

Those personality quirks meant it took weeks to get hold of Bliz. When I did, he wanted to link up right away, but I put it off until the weekend, as I was newly devoted to school.

The directions Bliz gave led me to a plain storefront location off of Cascade Road in Atlanta's west end. While the building may have been nondescript, the cars out front were anything but.

I pulled my suddenly plain-looking Maxima between a new Lexus and an old school box Chevy. I bet if you tallied up all the etcetera on the classic, it cost more than the Lex'.

I tried in vain to peek inside the blacked-out windows of the studio as I knocked. I could feel the music radiating through the glass and doubted anyone could hear me. I knocked a few more times before calling Bliz from my phone.

"Where you at, son?" Bliz asked immediately upon answering.

"Out front, beating on your door," I replied.

"My bad, yo. I'ma send my mans out now," he shot back and hung up before I could reply.

A few seconds later, locks were turned, and the door swung open. A young dread with a mouthful of gold teeth stepped aside, allowing me to enter. "'Sup, shawty?" he asked in a heavy Southern accent.

"Chillin', B," I answered as I walked in.

The front room was sparsely furnished with a small desk and a few chairs. I was not impressed. I followed the dread into the next room, where three other dudes were playing *Madden* on a huge TV. They all had dreads, gold teeth, or both. Not one of them looked up to acknowledge my presence.

"Bliz in there," the door opener said before he sat back down.

I tapped on the door and walked in. A dense cloud of weed smoke met me, and I inhaled deeply, enjoying the aroma. I had been broke lately and hadn't smoked in days.

"What up, B?" Bliz inquired without looking up from the large mixing board he was working on.

"Chillin'," I replied as I made my way over to him. I took a seat and watched yet another gold-toothed dread in the booth. Son was spitting some straight-up bullshit as Bliz tweaked knobs and buttons.

I let my gaze wander around the room, taking in the racks of machines blinking in sync with the thunderous beat coming out of the monitors. Another wall had keyboards of different shapes and colors, and, I could only assume, functions. The walls were covered with pictures of Bliz and every rap star known to man. Obviously, one had to go platinum to take a picture with Bliz. As I took in the pictures of Bliz alongside rap royalty, I suddenly wondered if I wasn't out of my league.

The music stopped, and Bliz leaned over to press a button on the board that allowed him to talk to dude in the booth. "That's a rap, yo," he told the dread, who responded by taking off the headphones and exiting the booth.

He came in and took a seat on the other side of Bliz. "How was that, shawty?" the rapper asked eagerly, as if he desperately needed Bliz's approval.

"Son, that shit was fire!" Bliz exclaimed rather dramatically.

Fire? That shit was shit. Somehow, I had missed what made him so-called "fire." Son dedicated a whole song to selling drugs, killing niggas, and his rims. The nigga said "nigga" so many times I actually tried to count them, but I lost count. *What a waste of a beat! I would murder a track like that—climb right onboard and ride that shit like a horse.*

"Sho nuff," the rapper replied, standing to reach into his pocket. The dread pulled out a large roll of cash and began peeling off hundreds. "Four for four," he said, handing Bliz four crisp bills.

"That's *your* price, shawty," Bliz said, looking around stealthily. "Keep that on the low!"

Now I knew I was in over my head. I was living on $100 a week, and there was no way I could afford $100 an hour.

The rapper and Bliz exchanged pounds and confirmed their next session, then said their goodbyes.

"That was hot, B," I said, trying to be courteous.

"What? That?" Bliz exclaimed. "That was some bullshit, but it keeps the lights on. Feel me? Yo, twist up," Bliz said, passing me a Ziploc bag and cigar.

The bag contained a couple ounces of the prettiest, fruity-colored weed I'd ever seen. "Damn, son, this shit is…beautiful!" I said, marveling at the red, orange, and purple hairs.

"Yeah, that's purple Buddha. I copped it up in Harlem for half a grand an ounce," Bliz replied.

"So how does this work?" I asked as I rolled a fat blunt. You know niggas always roll the fattest blunts when it's other people's weed.

"Well, those machines over there," he began, pointing at something that looked like several VCRs stacked on top of each other, "are ADATs, eight tracks a piece. The four of them make thirty-two tracks. Then I control each track from the mixing board…"

I let him go on and on about the process because I knew nothing about it. My real question pertained to the mix tape business.

We then passed the blunt back and forth as Bliz educated me on the ubiquitous business.

"It's essentially a marketing tool," he exclaimed. "That's why the big boys do them and why their labels tolerate it. Not only does it keep an artist relevant between releases, but it can also help new artists. Think Jeezy, T.I., and a bunch of other cats. All blew up behind mix tapes. I put B-Bop on the map with the one we did. I like to put one or two new niggas on. If you can shine alongside them, you're pretty much assured a deal.

"So the labels pay you to put out mix tapes?" I asked naïvely.

"The labels? Pay me?" he repeated. "Them niggas don't give me shit but a hard time—always bitching about using one of their artists or tracks without permission, sending them damn 'cease and desist' letters, threatening to sue."

"Sue you?" I asked, dubious that a billion-dollar record company would sue a small-time DJ.

"Hell, yeah, they will sue you," he exclaimed. "They got the feds running up in nigga's offices with machineguns and shit."

"Okay, so how you get money out of it?" I asked.

"Shit, I sell my joints for ten bucks a pop. Fuck the label!" He laughed. "Last time out, I did a little over 20,000 units with nobody on it. This time, I'ma do 50,000 or better with B-Bop, Mr. Red Clay…and you. I'm calling it *Atlanta Live*, since ain't nothing but ATL cats on it, so you gotta spit something about the city to keep the theme going." He told me about his plans to travel outside the region to promote and sell his CDs. The way he made it sound, he could easily sell 50,000 CDs, for half a million dollars.

While we spoke, the studio door opened, and in walked two works of art. The leader was a tall, dark-skinned girl with weave down her back. She was followed by a short, light-skinned girl who made my heart skip. She was well built, standing on pretty, slightly bowed, caramel legs. She was five feet tall at best, but she had enough ass for a six-footer.

"Hey, baby," the dark skin called to Bliz as she made her way over to him. When she bent over to kiss him, her short skirt rose, allowing me a full view of her thonged ass.

"A-yo, this my girl Tosha…and that's Tanisha," Bliz said formally.

"Hey, Lite," Tosha said in a rather friendly way, while her friend ignored me; light skin sat down without so much as a glance in my direction.

"Y'all just in time. We about to record Lite's verse," Bliz said, to my surprise.

"We are?" I asked. I had no idea he meant we'd be working that very day. I hadn't heard the track and didn't know too much about Atlanta to rap about.

"Yeah, B. Shit going to press in a few days. If you wanna be down, it's now or never," he said. "Roll up while we get this done," Bliz told Tosha, handing her the sack of weed.

I was relieved when Bliz pulled up the track I'd heard on the plane. The shit was so hot it had been playing in my head ever since. Mentally, I'd already been spitting to it for weeks. My relief was short lived when I found out my verse was in the middle of B-Bop and Red Clay. Talk about being in the middle of a rock and a hard place! Those dudes were monsters.

We smoked the next blunt as Bliz made adjustments to the track that only he could hear. Engineers are like that: They got dog hearing or something, always asking, "Hear that?" *Hear what?*

"Let's get it," Bliz announced after "fixing" the track.

I made my way to the booth, still trying to think of something to say, but nothing came to mind. I was frantically searching my memory banks for enough rhymes to string a verse together. When Bliz gave me my mark, it came and went without a peep from me.

"You a'ight, son?" Bliz asked, stopping the track.

Tanisha shook her head like I was just sorry, but Tosha looked embarrassed for me.

"A-yo, B, if you ain't ready, maybe you can be on the next joint," Bliz offered.

"Naw, I'm good, son. Run it back," I demanded. As it played, I flashed back to King-Stan winning a battle by name-dropping. I glanced around at the pictures on the walls and recalled what I'd seen of Atlanta as my mark came up. I watched Bliz through the glass as he counted me in.

"FOUR…THREE…TWO…ONE…!"

"YOU MAY CATCH ME IN MAGIC CITY, CHILLIN' WITH LUDA LUDA…
OR UP IN STROKERS WITH BIG BOI, PUFFING PURPLE BUDDHA…
I'MA GET HIGH WITH T.I., THEN GO PICK A FIGHT…
ME AND T-PAIN MAKE IT RAIN EVERY OTHER NIGHT…
WHEN I'M WITH JD, THE LADIES RUSH TO GET TOUCHED…
TIME TO GET MY EAT ON UP IN JUSTIN'S WITH PUFF…
MY BAD, NOW WE JUST CALL HIM 'DIDDY'…
TELL KASSIM REED I'MA NEED A KEY TO THE CITY…
SO I CAN ROAM FROM ZONE TO ZONE…
ALWAYS HANG ALONE, THAT'S WHY I TOTE THE CHROME…
I LOVE THE A, BUT ROCK NY ON MY FITTED CAP…
D-LITE IS THAT NIGGA, SO YOU BETTER GET WITH THAT…
I HEARD A LOT OF OTHER CITIES THAT SIMILAR…
I STILL REP THE BX, FUCK AROUND, I'M KILLING YA."

I knew I killed that shit, and so did Bliz and obviously Tanisha, who suddenly noticed I was present. "How was that? I can do something else if you want," I said as I exited the booth.

"Something else?!" Bliz exclaimed. "This fucking guy! You hear this guy?"

Tanisha, who wouldn't look at me an hour earlier, couldn't take her eyes off me now. We played eye tag with each other while Bliz added spices to my vocals.

After he added a few effects to my voice, it sounded even better. Bliz played it over and over, singing my praises each time. "Son, you on a track with two heavyweights, and you shining," Bliz said seriously. "A-yo, son, you dope!"

When I finally stood to leave, I felt like I was ten feet tall—fucking King Kong! Bliz was right: I'd held my own on a track between two beasts.

"Ain't you forgetting something?" Bliz asked as I floated toward the exit.

"Oh yeah," I said, turning to Tanisha. "Come on, ma. Let's bounce."

"My name ain't no 'ma'!" Tanisha exclaimed, and she grabbed her purse and stood up.

"I meant your copy of the song, but that's what's up." Bliz chuckled.

I left with a blunt of the fruity in my ear, a CD in one hand, and Tanisha's hand in the other. *Now how is this shit not supposed to go to my head?*

CHAPTER 9

"Get the fuck outta here! This ain't no freestyle," Desean swore when he heard my song.

"That's on Ma Dukes—one take!" I swore back.

"Do you, my nigga," Day replied proudly. "Told you you would bounce back."

"So, how you, B? What them doctors talking about?" I asked. I saw my best friend's demeanor change when he heard the question. The difference would have been imperceptible to everyone else on the planet except for me and maybe Shell. I bet his own mother would not have caught it.

"Shit's good, yo. Knee is getting stronger. I'ma be back soon."

He said it confidently, but all I heard was *"Shit's fucked up. Can't play no more."*

"Okay…so tell me about honey you bagged at the studio," he asked, apparently eager to change the subject.

"A-yo, lil' mama is right, son!" I exclaimed, happy to switch gears as well. "She's a solid dime piece, and she might just have the best pussy in America— North and South America!"

"So why you ain't call her back? Who you tryna be, me?" Desean chuck-led.

I searched for an answer but couldn't find one. Tanisha was mad cool. The night I took her home from the studio was perfect. We smoked a blunt, watched a movie, and she hooked up a meal from the scraps we had in the fridge. Then, the sex was outrageous—any way I wanted it, as much as I wanted. I probably could have gotten some head if I'd tried, and thinking back, I should have tried.

"A-yo, Lite, you with me?" Day asked, breaking the spell.

"Word life, shorty would have me open, B," I confessed.

"I feel you. Last thing we need is another Maria episode." He smirked.

"Had to go there?" I said, trying not to laugh…but failing. I filled my friend in on what I had learned about the music biz in general and the mix tape hustle in particular. Instantly, I could see the wheels turning in Day's head.

"A-yo, B, we can do that shit ourselves, son!" he said excitedly. "Son, we move1,000 units at ten bucks, that's a quick ten stacks. We can do this shit, Lite."

"Who is 'we' and 'us'?" I asked.

"Me and you, nigga! Same 'we' and 'us' it's always been," he replied sharply. "Matter fact, I might change my major and be your manager…and I ain't gonna charge you but 30 percent."

"Thirty! Try 20!" I shot back.

"Twenty? That's a bet. I woulda did it for 15 though." He laughed.

"A-yo, B, we gotta get a contract," I said, wanting to make it official.

"Contract?" Day asked, incredulous. "Son, if 'we' can't trust 'us', then 'we' fucked."

* * *

I called Shelby to fill her in on our plans, but as usual, she didn't have time for me. I doubt if I got a whole minute out of her. Our conversation consisted of, "Mm-hmm…That's nice…Can you call me later?" Even when I told her I loved her, she simply said, "Me too."

I felt rejected and knew just to person to heal a bruised ego. The conversation with Tanisha was equally short but far more productive. I said, "This is Lite."

She said, "Come get me."

I went down to my car and struck out toward Decatur. I exited I-20 on Candler Road, and two turns later, I was heading down the hill in the Eastwyck Apartments complex.

A feeling of guilt overtook me as I got closer. I loved Shelby, and I understood her situation, respected her hustle. She was working her ass off for our future, and I was fucking around. Just the last weekend, Shell had blown everything off and spent the whole time with me. She was probably extra busy making up for that excursion.

We had mad fun too. Even a simple trip to the video store became an adventure. We couldn't get any new releases, so Shelby suggested we hit the black cinema section. As we browsed the shelves, the music began playing in my head, and a song was born.

"Okay, let me hear it," Shelby asked knowingly.

"Hear what?" I said innocently.

"Yeah, right! You nodding and smiling. I know you're in there rapping." She laughed, tapping my forehead.

"Okay. You wanna hear it? Here it go," I said. I began freestyling, pointing to the various DVDs as I went.

"I WAS GOING UPTOWN SATURDAY NIGHT WITH CLEOPATRA JONES...

SAW SHAFT WITH THE PREACHER'S WIFE AND TOLD HIM TO TAKE HER HOME...

THEN WENT TO THE BARBERSHOP AND GOT A FRESH FADE...

BUT THERE'S VAMPIRES IN BROOKLYN, SO I CARRY A BLADE...

SHE WENT TO THE BEAUTY SHOP AND GOT HER ROOTS DYED, THE COLOR PURPLE...

THERE'S GONNA BE HELL UP IN HARLEM IF SHE'S OUT PAST HER CURFEW...

THAT BABY BOY IN HER BELLY COULD BELONG TO ANY ONE OF THEM BOYS IN THE 'HOOD...

CLAUDINE SAW HER IN ROSEWOOD, AND SHE WAS UP TO NO GOOD...

HER HUSBAND'S A MENACE TO SOCIETY WITH DEAD PRESIDENTS ALL LAID OUT BY HIM...

'CAUSE HE'S FROM SUGAR HILL, WHERE BOTH LOVE AND BASKETBALL ARE PLAYED ABOVE THE RIM...

THEY SAY IT'S A THIN LINE BETWEEN LOVE AND HATE...

CAN I EXHALE NOW, OR DO I STILL HAVE TO WAIT?...

I'M GOING TO BIG MOMMA'S HOUSE ON FRIDAY TO SEE HOW SHE'S DOING...

SO IF I DON'T SEE YOU THERE, I'LL CATCH YOU AT THE NEXT FAMILY REUNION."

"Yo, you mad ill," Shelby said, standing in her b-boy stance.

I laughed at the fond memory and prepared to turn my car around and go home. Then I saw her!

Tanisha was standing on her front porch wearing a tiny pair of shorts and a matching half-shirt that showed her belly piercing. To make matters worse—or better, depending on how you look at it—she was vigorously working over a Blow Pop. "Hey, boo," Tanisha cooed as she slid into the passenger seat.

"What's good, ma?" I replied, accepting the peck on the lips that she offered. Her lips were soft and sticky-sweet from the lollipop, causing me to lick my own to get it all.

Any thoughts of returning home alone were long gone. I pulled the car around and headed back to Candler Road. Tanisha spied me envying the Blow Pop and went into overdrive. She was really giving it the business, sucking it, slurping it, and twirling her tongue around the head…er, I mean the top. "Watch out!" she screamed as I almost hit the car in front of me. "So busy sweating my lollipop."

"I wish I was a lollipop," I said seriously.

Tanisha threw the sucker out the window on I-20 and granted my wish.

* * *

When I met with Bliz, he was excited about our plans to do a mix tape. "That's what's up, my nigga. Your name gonna be ringing from my joint. All you gotta do is slide in behind me," he explained.

"Yeah, my only problem though," I began, then paused for a more dramatic effect, "is I can't afford no $100 an hour."

"Man, don't worry about that, yo. I'll do your shit on the strength. Just bring the weed," he offered.

"Dude, I can't afford that rich-nigga weed you smoke," I confessed. He was used to kush, hydro, and purp', but all I could afford was Reggie Babbitt.

"Damn, nigga! Can I get a Fish Supreme then?" he laughed. "Bring a nigga a two-piece whiting and fries then."

"I think I can handle that." I laughed with him, wondering if I could stand it.

"I got hundreds of beats, son. You can use them for the low," Bliz offered.

"Probably just need a couple. I got some heat from Adam Salaah, Kimani Brown, and the Word Chemist," I said, hoping to put my people on too.

"A'ight, B. Only thing, we gotta get started ASAP 'cause I'm about to hit the road," he warned.

"You got back at Tanisha?" Bliz asked offhandedly.

"Matter fact, shorty was with me yesterday," I replied.

"Humph," Bliz groaned with a disconcerted look.

"What? Ma good people. She got a good head on her shoulders," I said defensively. I was digging her.

"That's what I heard," Bliz joked, but I wasn't amused.

CHAPTER 10

The recording process turned out to be far more tedious than I'd ever imagined. Performing is a piece of cake compared to that. Onstage, I was in my zone. There was no room for error there, so I didn't make any.

Bliz kept stopping the track and making me start over, each time with a different command. "Stop moving! More feeling! Less feeling! Enunciate!" was all I heard for the first two hours.

I had written a song to my black cinema freestyle and was lacing one of Bliz's tracks. Writing a song to a track is a lot easier than trying to fit them together. Sometimes they just don't fit.

I was in the booth feeling frustrated until Tosha and Tanisha walked in. Eager to get out there to her, I laid the whole song on the next take.

"I see you work better with your little buddy around," Bliz announced when I came out of the booth.

"Whatever!" Tanisha and I said in unison, surprising even ourselves.

"Damn! Y'all synced up and everything." Bliz laughed.

"A'ight, a'ight," I demanded, trying to change the subject. Tanisha had me open, and it bothered me; it bothered me more that people were starting to notice. "Same time next time?" I asked, standing to leave.

"Yeah, I'll see y'all next time," Bliz said, really enjoying himself. "Oh, yeah…have your radio on tonight. We debut on the *Top Eight at Eight*."

"Say word?" I said eagerly, wanting to hug him.

"Word!" Oh, and y'all performing it on Tuesday at the release party," he added casually.

At that point, I did hug him.

Once we got outside and in the car, Tanisha was going on and on about what she was going to wear for the show, until she caught my reaction. "What?" she asked in response to my raised brow.

"A-yo, you know my girl gonna wanna come with me to the show," I said firmly.

"Oh, yeah. I keep forgetting you got one of those," she quipped. "That's cool. I'll just go with some of my girls."

"I'm saying though," I warned with the same look pasted on my face.

"What? Boy, ain't nobody gonna put you on blast," Tanisha said unconvincingly, then went back to planning her outfit.

After dropping Tanisha off, I swung by and scooped Shelby up. She was genuinely excited to hear my song on the radio and agreed to come and share the experience with me. She even agreed to use her credit card to buy me an outfit for the show.

Desean was already at the apartment when we got there. He was with the most beautiful woman I'd ever been in the same room with. She looked to be East Indian, from Trinidad or somewhere, with her light complexion and long black hair. Ma was about five-nine or ten, and the body of a Victoria's Secret model. The girl was so stunning that she stopped both me and Shelby dead in our tracks, causing Desean to laugh.

"Come on in. She don't bite." Day laughed before making the introductions. "Lite, Shell, this my girlfriend Veronica."

Shelby and I shot each other a quick glance, shocked by the word "girlfriend." For as long as we'd known him, Desean had never had a girlfriend.

"I'm Shelby, and this is my boyfriend Dave," Shell said, shaking the girl's hand.

"Hey, guys. Nice to meet y'all. Call me V," she said in a slight Caribbean accent.

As for me, I said nothing because I couldn't. Veronica took my breath away and left me speechless.

Our song debuted on the bottom of the show, but the DJ gave me props, saying I was the best new rapper out. My friends congratulated me before we adjourned to our rooms.

That night, I made love to Shelby's body, with Veronica's face in my mind.

It wasn't the wild sexual Six Flags ride like Tanisha, but making love to a person you love is incomparable.

The next day, Shelby and I hit Lenox Mall in search of an outfit worthy of my Atlanta debut. That was easier said than done. I dragged that poor girl from store to store, coming up empty. Everything I liked was too expensive, and everything she liked was too gay. Skinny jeans? Fuck I look like in some skinny jeans? We finally settled on a gray jean set from Avirex. I matched it up with gray Tims and a fitted cap.

"A'ight, let's grab me some jewels and be on our way," I said, detouring toward a jewelry store.

"You better be talking about a Juelz Santana CD," Shelby shot back. "You need to be buying me some jewels, Mr. Rapper."

I was trying on different chains while Shelby fussed over wedding rings.

"Ooh, baby, look at this," Shell squealed from across the store.

I grudgingly returned the diamond necklace I was modeling and walked over to her.

"I love this ring," she said, actually bouncing up and down. On her finger was a stunning three-carat rectangular solitaire. Both Shell and the sales lady were beaming with pride.

"How much?" I asked, even though I couldn't afford three carrots at the moment.

Shelby passed the ring back to the sales lady, who viewed the attached tag.

"It's only $15,000," she said casually.

"Only?" I laughed to myself. "You want it?"

"Hell yeah, I want it," Shelby said, a whisper below a shout.

"By Christmas," I promised, meaning every word. I had absolutely no doubt that I would blow up by then, and I had absolutely no doubt that Shelby was the one.

"Lite?" Shelby sang, using my stage name—something she rarely did. "You do know that's an engagement right, don't you?"

"Yes," I answered stoically to tease her.

"Well, you never asked me to marry you," she sang sweetly.

"Ma, when I buy you that ring, *you're* gonna ask me to marry *you*," I replied smugly.

"If she don't, I will," the sales lady said seriously.

Sa'id Salaam

* * *

Before I could blink, the night of my first show in the ATL was upon me. It would be my first time sharing a stage with a major artist. I had opened for plenty of stars in New York, but never on the same stage or with the same song.

I dressed meticulously in front of my full-length mirror. Even in the cheap mirror, my reflection looked like a million bucks! I tugged my jeans down to achieve the right amount of sag and admired myself some more. When I finished primping and posing, I ran through my verse, using my hairbrush as a mike. I practiced several times using different tones and facial expressions, which amused Shelby immensely.

"Do ya thing, Daddy." She chuckled from my bed.

Desean tapped on the door before sticking his head in. "Yo, me and V 'bout to bounce. We common folk got to wait in line," he said with an air of levity, but I knew he was a little salty about not being on the guest list. He left just before 10 p.m., hoping to beat what was sure to be a long line.

The party was being held in a midsized club on Peachtree Street, in the heart of downtown Atlanta. Ever since silly niggas shut down the Buckhead District with a bunch of shootings, stabbings, and fighting, downtown had regained its spot as the place to be.

Bliz insisted we meet at the studio and all roll out together. He mentioned a limo and got no objections from me. My only problem now was getting Shelby out of the bathroom. "Baby, come on!" I whined for the umpteenth time.

"Boy, don't you rush me. As long as you took to get ready?" she yelled through the door.

I sat on my bed, pouting for a few more minutes, until she finally emerged. The finished product was well worth the wait.

"Well?" Shelby asked provocatively, posing against the door. "You like?" The low-cut Prada dress left one arm bare and exposed the top of Shelby's breasts. It stopped mid-thigh, set off by a lovely pair of Jimmy Choo heels. "Well?" Shell asked again, alerting me that I hadn't answered her the first time.

"You straight, yo. Let's go," I demanded, heading toward the door.

"I got your 'straight', punk." Shelby laughed, falling in step behind me.

* * *

I pulled Shell's Accord into one of the few empty spots at the studio. I texted Bliz to alert him to my presence so he could let us in.

Shelby coughed as we entered the smoke-filled outer room. The room was full of people, and the mood was festive. The regulars greeted me warmly, causing me to think back a couple of months, when they had ignored me.

I greeted everyone as I led Shell by the hand into the studio's inner sanctum. There were only a handful of people, but the smoke was just as dense.

"What's up, my nigga?" Bliz asked, jumping to his feet.

"Ready to go catch some wreck," I replied before exchanging pounds and hugs.

As we embraced, I noticed Tanisha and another girl sitting on one of the sofas. I pretended not to see her and introduced Shelby to Bliz and Tosha.

"Hello," Shelby said sweetly to Tanisha and her friend.

The friend spoke back, while Tanisha only glared at me.

Shelby raised a questioning brow when Bliz passed me a blunt. She had seen me high before, but she'd never seen me get high.

"A-yo, son, let me show you something," Bliz announced and headed toward the booth.

I didn't budge. There was no way I was leaving Tanisha alone with Shelby.

"Come on, B," Bliz urged upon seeing I haven't moved.

"Go on, boo. I'm okay," Shelby said, as if she sensed my apprehension.

Reluctantly, I followed Bliz into the sound booth. He showed me the new mike he had bought and began expounding on its technical abilities.

As soon as we left, Tanisha made a beeline toward Shell.

I didn't hear one word Bliz said. I was trying in vain to make out what my two women were saying to each other. They were chatting it up real nice, laughing and the whole nine.

"Playing it close, ain't you?" Bliz laughed at my dilemma.

"You think she blowing me up?" I asked in a near panic.

"Naw. She fucking with you though," he replied.

As if on cue, Tanisha looked dead at me when she pulled her cell phone from her purse. I couldn't stand it anymore and rushed back inside. When I reached them, it was too late; they had exchanged phone numbers.

"Have you met Tanisha?" Shell asked, ready to make the introduction.

"We haven't met," Tanisha lied, extending her hand.

I took her hand and glared at her a Shell made the introduction.

"Say, shawty, y'all limo out there," a gold-toothed dread announced.

"Okay. You and your girl riding with me and Tosh," Bliz said, shutting down the equipment.

Outside, everyone piled in their cars and followed the limo.

If Shelby was impressed by the limo, I couldn't tell. In fact, she looked right at home. As for me, I was freaking the fuck out. I was in a limo, 'bout to perform with two of the hottest dudes in Atlanta. *This is the life,* I thought as I poured glasses of champagne as Bliz lit yet another blunt.

Shell wasn't much of a drinker, but she accepted the glass and downed half of it in one swallow. "Blow me a gun." Shelby giggled when the weed made it to me.

"Yeah, right," I said until I saw she was serious. I put the lit end of the blunt in my mouth and blew a soft, steady stream.

To my surprise, Shell inhaled it deeply and tried to hold it. After a few seconds, she coughed it out. She took another slug from her glass to soothe her throat, then asked for another gun.

We all drank and smoked our way to the venue. We were all lifted by the time we pulled up, especially Shelby, who was all smiles and giggles.

I decided to take advantage of her condition and ask her what had been eating at me since we left. "A-yo, what was that girl talking about?" I asked casually.

"What girl?" Shell giggled.

"At the studio—the girl you was talking to," I urged.

"Oh! The little cute girl? Nothing…hair, nails, girls' stuff," she replied, to my relief. "She like you though."

"Huh? She told you that?" I asked.

"Didn't have to. Girls know girls, and that girl likes you," Shell said matter-of-factly.

"Let's do this!" Bliz exclaimed when the driver pulled the limo doors open.

There was still a long line waiting to get in, and all eyes were on us.

"Oh my God! Look at all these people," Shelby said, clinging to my arm. "And they all staring at us!"

"They staring at you, ma, and I can't blame 'em either, 'cause you a bad bitch," I teased.

"Bitch?" Shelby asked through the smile pasted on her face. Before I could reply she caught a glimpse of herself in the glass window. "I am a bad bitch!" She giggled.

"I gotta get you high more often." I laughed.

Bliz had a table reserved in the VIP section like I was a real star

"Ooh, look, babe!" Shelby announced upon seeing my name on the place card. "I'm keeping this," she whispered, slipping it into her purse. Shell seemed to be enjoying herself, pointing out the different celebrities in attendance.

A waitress came over with a bottle of champagne and glasses.

"Oh, no more for me," Shelby pleaded, but she still drank from it when it sat in front of her.

The hostess of the show introduced the first of many opening acts just as Desean and Veronica arrived at the table. I hadn't seen what V had on when they left the house, but ma was killing it. The middle of the designer dress was cut away to reveal a six-pack and the majority of her breasts. The small dress would not allow a bra, and Veronica's nipples could clearly be seen through the fabric. Her long hair was in a bun, except for one long curl cascading down her face.

"Damn!" Shelby exclaimed loudly.

Again, I was speechless.

Shelby switched seats with Day so we could talk while she and Veronica chatted. I assumed they were talking about me because V was staring at me the whole time.

"Big night, player," Day said, giving me a pound.

I just nodded and scanned the club to take it all in. The view from the elevated VIP section was spectacular. I could see the whole club. Everywhere I looked, all I saw were beautiful people. Women openly flirted when our eyes met. They knew I just had to be somebody to be in the VIP section.

I saw Tanisha and her crew out on the dance floor, working up a sweat. She must have seen me first, because she was already looking at me. When our eyes met, she screwed up her face and backed her ass up against the wannabe player she was dancing with.

Dude's eyes lit up, and he started gyrating even harder. I can't front: The sight bothered me. I had grown close to Tanisha over the past few weeks.

"Okay, y'all, we gotta surprise for you!" the hostess announced as a mediocre group finished their average performance. "All the way from New York City!

These ladies just signed to Third Eye Records, and their single 'Dreaming' is already blowing up the charts! Y'all give it up for Galaxy!"

Desean and I looked at each other like *"Naw!"* then turned to the stage.

Sure enough, out walked Egypt, China, and Asia. They had wisely abandoned rap and signed a deal as an R&B group—a deal with Third Eye Records, the biggest urban label in the country.

I had been hearing the song on the radio, but I'd never made the connection. We had all lost touch when we'd left for school. Me and Day watched the girls perform with silly grins on our faces.

"You like what you see?" V asked Desean sharply.

"Y'all sure are sweating them," Shelby cosigned.

We played it off, turning our attention back to our girls, stealing occasional glances at the stage. Galaxy did the one song and were quickly whisked out of the club.

"Finally, the moment we've been waiting for!" the hostess yelled as Bliz appeared center stage. "Atlanta Live!"

I excused myself to go wait side stage for our song. B-Bop gave me a pound, but Red Clay just nodded a *"What's up?"*

After Bliz cut and scratched a medley of his previous songs, he threw our track on.

B-Bop ran out and went straight into his verse. I almost hated to have to go behind him the way he rocked the crowd. Since I had no choice, though, when my verse came up, I went out swinging. To my surprise, the whole club was rapping my verse along with me. It was at that moment that I knew I had arrived. Red Clay came out and did the damn thing as well. The crowd loved us!

"A-yo, you killed that shit, son!" Day exclaimed when I returned to our table.

"You did your thing, baby," Shelby congratulated as well.

Even Veronica gave me a hug and said something in my ear that I couldn't quite make out. It was either *"I'm lucky"* or *"Fuck me."* I just thanked her to be polite.

"You really liked it?" I asked in Shell's ear.

"No...I loved it! Matter fact, you gonna get you some booty, mister!" She giggled.

"A-yo, Day, we out!"

CHAPTER 11

I finally took Desean to the studio with me to meet Bliz and get involved in the whole process. When I made the introduction, I sensed the slight friction that comes from introducing old and new friends.

"Yo, you killed that shit, son," Bliz said seriously.

"Thank you, thank you," I said, pretending to be humble.

"On the strength, B, you was up there with multi-platinum niggas and shined," he stressed. "You need to get your joint done while your name is ringing. Y'all song getting picked up all across the country."

"So how much publishing my man getting?" Day asked suddenly, making Bliz uncomfortable.

I had no idea what "publishing" even was, so I looked at Bliz, too, waiting on the answer.

"Well, he ain't got no publishing on this one," Bliz stammered.

"A-yo, what's publishing?" I asked naïvely.

When Bliz didn't respond, Desean began to explain, looking at Bliz as he spoke. "Son, every time your lyrics get played on radio or video, you get paid—well, at least you are supposed to." Desean had taken his role as manager seriously and done his homework. He went on to fill me in about the entire publishing aspect of the business while Bliz nodded in agreement.

"Your man's right," Bliz said to me, looking toward Desean. "But on this one, I get the dough. You get the exposure," he said to me. "Performing alongside B-Bop and Red Clay is shit you can't buy. What's that worth?" he asked Day.

"Shit's priceless," Desean answered, and the building tension vanished in an instant.

"Besides, once you get your mix tape out, you will be seeing all the dough," Bliz said, becoming animated. Son, I'm up to 3,000 units already, and I ain't even start grinding yet."

"Damn, B, that's thirty large!" Desean said, quickly doing the math.

"Not quite, yo. After the salesperson, store, or distributor gets theirs, I see $5 to $6 on each one," Bliz explained.

"That's still fifteen stacks, minimum," Day shot back without missing a beat.

Bliz was talking numbers, and that was Desean's language. They were throwing figures back and forth as I slipped inside the booth.

I ended up recording two more songs during that session, which was good work—but it was not enough.

"How many is that?" Desean asked as Bliz tweaked my vocals.

"That, uh…what, twelve?" Bliz asked me.

"Thirteen," I corrected. "Seven more to go."

"You putting twenty songs on a mix tape?" Desean asked.

"Yeah, 'cause niggas don't mind paying ten bucks for that much music," Bliz reasoned.

"Makes sense," Day agreed.

"Not only do you gotta get the rest of your songs laid, but mixed and mastered too," Bliz said. He saw the confused looks on our faces and began to explain. "A-yo, I'm a producer, but I can record. I can mix, too, if I have to, but it's better to let a pro do it with a fresh set of ears. The mix engineer gonna make your voice pop, make the bass boom, highs sparkle…feel me?" For a demonstration, he played a song from his mix tape from ADATs, then again from a finished CD. The difference was plain as day. "I'ma give you the names and numbers of the people I use. They will take care of you," Bliz said, shutting his equipment down. "Mention my name when you hit 'em."

"That's what's up," I said, preparing to leave. Shelby had agreed to take a few hours off to catch a movie with me, and Day had plans with V.

"A-yo, I got a party we can hit," Bliz announced as we stood to leave.

Me and Day looked at each other, then shook our heads. We told him of our plans to chill with our girlfriends, and he understood.

"That's what's up. Probably gonna be boring anyway." Bliz sighed. "One of them industry things for that group Galaxy."

Desean and I looked at each other and said, "On second thought…"

"What?" Bliz asked, confused at our sudden change of heart.

"We used to bang them chicks back home," Desean explained.

"Word up! I used to hit Asia, and Day had Egypt," I bragged.

Bliz gave us the information, and we all agreed to meet up later.

* * *

Shelby had no problem with me standing her up. In fact, she seemed relieved. "No problem, babe. I got a ton of work anyway," she said without emotion.

Knowing she was out the way for the event, I planned on bringing Asia home and rocking her for old time's sake.

Desean, on the other hand, was catching pure hell from Veronica. I noticed her Caribbean accent becoming more pronounced when she was upset, and, boy, was she upset! "How you gonna blow me off for some party?" I heard V say, even from my side of the apartment.

Every time Day tried to say something, she cut him off. He made excuse after excuse, but he still wasn't excused.

I laughed my ass off when Desean came to tell me that Veronica was going with us to the party. "Son, you mad pussy-whipped." I chuckled.

He kept trying to explain, and I kept cracking my invisible whip. "Whoop-pshhh!"

We rode in Veronica's SUV in virtual silence. Desean was brooding about having to take his girl, but I was loving it. Every time he looked back at me, I cracked my invisible whip again and cracked up.

* * *

The party wasn't a party in the conventional sense. It was more of a get-together where the movers and shakers of the industry moved and shook. It was definitely a classy affair. Third Eye Records pulled out all the stops for the function. They rented space at the Georgia Aquarium and spared no expense. Three separate caterers provided exotic dishes from every kind of cuisine. There were champagne fountains around the room, spewing the world's best bubbly.

I located Bliz shortly after we entered and left Day and V at a table. We instantly posted up by one of the fountains and indulged. Bliz and I knocked off flute after flute, until we were good and tipsy.

The room fell dark, and a short film featuring Galaxy played on multiple screens. It showed a lot of behind-the-scenes footage of the girls making their album and culminated with the premier of the new video for "Dreaming."

When the video ended, three spotlights cut through the still, dark room, allowing the girls to make their entrance.

"Ladies and gentlemen…Galaxy!" the DJ announced as Asia, Egypt, and China walked into the room.

I watched how the girls graciously worked the room, greeting everyone with smiles, hugs, and cheek kisses. I knew Asia was going to freak out when she saw me, so I hung back and let her do her thing. Meanwhile, me and Bliz tried in vain to empty the champagne fountain we were working.

Desean was miserable over there trying to watch Egypt and listen to V at the same time. He looked at me helplessly, and I almost felt bad for him—almost, but not quite, so I cracked my invisible whip again and laughed at him some more. He'd finally had enough and made his way over to us. Since that was obviously too far for him to travel alone, V followed closely. "A-yo, I'm out. If you see *E*, give *him* my number," Day ordered.

"E? Who E?" I asked, fucking with him.

I guess he didn't find it funny, because he just turned to leave. As he did, Veronica mouthed something, but I couldn't make out what she said.

"What the fuck was that?" Bliz asked, having seen V's move.

"What?" I asked, as if I didn't catch it.

"Nothing, yo. I'm buggin'," he said.

"Must be," I replied sharply.

Asia and another woman headed straight for me, so I posted up, trying to be nonchalant. I pretended not to see her, then did a double-take.

"Asia! What's good, ma?" I smiled, expecting a big reunion.

"Oh, hey, um…?" she replied curiously, like she couldn't remember my name.

"Lite," I reminded her. "The Bronx." I started to say, *"Remember? I fucked you backstage at Summer Jam,"* but I didn't.

"Oh, yeah. Lite! How are you? Are you still doing your little rap thing? That's nice. Nice to see you. Bye," she said and bounced.

I stood there with my mouth agape, in total shock. "No she didn't just play me," I said to no one in particular.

"A-yo, don't sweat that, B. It's part of the game," Bliz offered in condolence.

"Son, I would never let success go to my head," I vowed solemnly.

"Sure you will." Bliz chuckled. "Like I said, it's part of the game."

CHAPTER 12

I managed to get the rest of my songs recorded before Bliz hit the road. My next step was to get my songs mixed and mastered.

I called the number and set up studio time for the weekend. I was initially quoted a price of $45 and hour, but mention of Bliz's name got the rate cut to $30.

When I got to the Blue Studio, I was initially skeptical that the long-haired hippie knew anything about hip-hop. Mickey, the engineer, looked like one of the Beatles, but the gold and platinum plaques adorning the studio walls vouched for him. "Yeah, you definitely worked with Bliz, judging by these dinosaurs." Mickey laughed as I handed over the ADAT tapes. "He has got to be the only one left in the city using these. The room had a ton of machines and gadgets, but Mickey bypassed them all and went straight to a computer. "This is pretty much the standard," he explained as the dual monitor Mac G-5 began to boot up. He loaded the ADAT into the one he kept more for nostalgic reasons and transferred all the data to the Pro-Tools program via Lightpipe.

Since Bliz had done a premix and arrangement, it only took about an hour to mix each song. Mickey had me take it out to my car and listen. Of course it sounded great in the $1,000 studio monitor, so a cheap car stereo would expose any flaws. There were none; my shit sounded great!

I ran back into the studio and hugged Mickey tightly. "A-yo, my bad son," I said, embarrassed by my effrontery.

"No problem." He laughed. "I get that a lot."

At an hour a song and with my limited resources, it took over a month to get the mix right. The finished product was hot, but it would be even hotter once it was mastered.

Bliz's name got me a $10-a-minute rate at the mastering house. I realized then that who you know is more important than what you know.

As I spoke with the mastering house on the phone, I repeated the price aloud so Day could do the math. When I terminated the call, he gave me the grisly news.

"That's at least $800, yo…and we tapped," he said somberly.

"Well, the appointment is for next week. So we gotta get it up," I replied.

"Son, where we gonna get $800 in a week?" Day asked.

Good question.

Shelby shot me down when I asked her, and Tanisha was always broke. Bliz said he had it but couldn't get it to me for a couple of weeks. He was still on the road and up to 13,000 CDs sold.

"A-yo, that's like eighty stacks!" Desean said after his mental multiplication. "Son, we gotta get this money."

Utter desperation led us to call our mothers and hit them up for the money. I tricked Day into calling first, and Aunt Betty shot him down so quickly I almost didn't want to try my own mother. I ended up taking the phone in my room so Desean couldn't hear me grovel. I was prepared to cry if need be.

"I ain't got no money for none of your rap crap!" my mother announced loudly upon answering my call. "Your Aunt Betty told me you was about to call me," she said, answering my pending question.

"Rap crap?" I laughed. "See, Ma? You rhyming too!"

She didn't find the pun the least bit amusing and launched into one of her world-famous tirades. "Boy, I pay for your food, books, gas, and spending money, and you still want more. You are so ungrateful. All I hear out of you is 'rap, rap, rap'! It's like you have some obsessive-compulsive disorder. You need Jesus!" she screamed, taking a pause to breathe.

I used the opportunity to slip in a little freestyle.

"I got obsessive-compulsive behavior…

Jesus Christ with a mic rap's lyrical savior…"

My mother was still not amused. "Ugh!" she screamed and hung up.

Undeterred, I called right back.

She picked right up where she left off. She chewed me out some more before unknowingly stumbling upon the answer. "Boy, you lucky I made you put that $5,000 into that CD, or you woulda run through that too," she said.

"That's it! The CD!" I exclaimed, as if I had hit the lotto. In a sense, I had. "Thanks, Ma. I love you."

"Boy, you better n—" was all she got out before the line somehow cut her off.

* * *

The mastering house had so much electronics equipment that they could probably have launched a space shuttle mission from there. Again, I saw walls full of gold and platinum plaques from every genre, and that served as a standing résumé.

I returned the next week and picked up my retail-ready masters. I paid a little over $800 for the service and thanked the engineer profusely.

He gave me a number to a company that could press up my CDs at a good price. "Tell 'em Rodney sent you," he advised, reminding me again that it's not what you know, but who.

Disco-Tech was a small CD and DVD duplication company just south of Atlanta in Clayton County.

I was quoted a price of 1,000 CDs for $1,000. I had hoped I could do a little better by ordering 3,000, but the price breaks didn't begin until 5,000 or better. The price did include all print work and 100 posters to boot. I shopped around a bit before realizing they were the best deal, so I went ahead and placed my order.

A week later, I drove down to Jonesboro and picked up my order. It was a good thing Day went along, because I neglected to add sales tax and was short $75.

The CDs came in 15 boxes of 200. The load barely fit in the car, and Desean ended up holding a box on his lap. "A-yo, Dunn, we moved all these for dolo. That's thirty Gs!" Desean said.

"Yeah, your cut comes to, like, six stacks," I added.

"I know!" Desean laughed, having already done the math.

"Only question now is where to begin," I pondered aloud.

CHAPTER 13

M e, Desean, and Shelby all started out selling CDs to people we knew at school. Shelby being as antisocial, as her schedule demanded, and only sold 25, while Desean, being the Big Man on Campus, moved close to 500 in the first week.

I was getting a name for myself by making the rounds to all the open mics and battles around the city, and I was able to get off a couple hundred as well.

Our families supported my efforts and bought and sold a few. All told, I sold a little over 2,000 CDs in a month.

Desean did his manager thing and got me shows around the city and in surrounding areas. At first, we paid them to let us performed, then we performed for free, and finally, they paid us. It was only $100 here or $250 there, but the exposure was priceless. I sold the remaining CDs in a week.

I had over $20,000 in cash, and nobody could tell me nothing. That was the most money I'd ever seen in my life. I sent my mom a couple bucks, and she had some fly shit to say. I wouldn't have expected nothing less.

Shelby was ambivalent at best. She was happy about my success, but she said I should quit while I was ahead. When I told her about my plans to double up, she balked and called it "a gamble."

Bliz, on the other hand, urged me to press more CDs and hit the road. "A-yo, B, I sold 40,000! You ringing now. Get that money!" he exclaimed.

"Scared money don't make no money," Tanisha advised when I asked her opinion.

Desean was wide open, ready to add to the easy six stacks he made.

I decided to go for broke and called Disco-Tech. They gave me a price of $7,500 for my 10,000 unit order. The price included 10,000 flyers and 500 posters.

Desean spent some of his own money and had some t-shirts printed for additional promotions. Bliz gave me his exact route and contacts in every city.

We contacted every club, radio station, record store, and weed man between Atlanta and Houston. Desean blitzed Facebook, Twitter, and MySpace, promoting our little tour.

I tried and failed to get Shelby to go along. She had registered for summer sessions and would be tied up with classes and studying. Tanisha jumped at the chance to not only spend a couple of weeks with me, but also get out of the city for a minute. Veronica forced Desean to take her along.

I rented a luxury van at $500 a week so we wouldn't be cramped. We loaded up the CDs and our personal effects and hit the road. Both me and Day took spending money because the plan was to deposit every dollar from every CD every night. When we left town, I had exactly $3.42 in my account.

After a few minor detours in northern Georgia, our first stop was Nashville, Tennessee—or, as the locals called it, Cashville, Ten-a-key. To my surprise, Nashville had a vibrant hip-hop scene.

The radio had added Bliz's song featuring me, B-Bop, and Red Clay, so I got love on arrival. The DJ at the local station put me on air for a couple of minutes and set me up at a show.

We hit all the 'hoods, malls, barbershops, and car washes in the city. We solicited any and every one we came in contact with. It didn't matter if they was old, young, black, white, or blue, we tried to sell them a CD.

Tanisha and V were our biggest assets. We could let them out of the van with their little outfits and big bodies, and dudes would flock.

Desean was salty about seeing so many dudes hound his girl though. Whenever they came back to the van, he searched her for phone numbers. As for me, I knew Tanisha was fine and used it to sell CDs. I couldn't be mad.

Day worked the phones and Internet to augment the resources Bliz gave us. He set up shows in every city on the list.

The next stop was Alabama, then Mississippi, all over Louisiana, and Arkansas, and then we hit Texas—Dallas, Fort Worth, Austin, San Antonio, and finally Houston.

It was dead of night when we reached our last stop. I had been making daily deposits but resisted checking the balance. We had three boxes of CDs left, and with the big hip-hop convention in town, we would have no problem moving them.

For the entire trip, we'd booked separate rooms, but all of the hotels were booked solid, so we were forced to take the last double in town. Desean crashed out immediately upon entering the room, and Veronica rushed in the bathroom to get her shower. She came out a few minutes later wearing nothing but a towel.

I tried my best not to look at her, but ma was fucking gorgeous. Her long, black hair framed her face perfectly.

She made a big show of applying oil to her mile-long legs. Then, V pulled a pair of lacy panties from her bag and held them up, either to inspect them or show them off. When she caught me looking at her through the mirror, she let the towel fall.

"Do you fucking mind?" Tanisha fumed.

"Oh…my bad." V giggled before ducking back into the bathroom.

"That bitch done lost her mind," Tanisha said loudly.

I'm sure Veronica heard her because she came out of the bathroom while the words were still in the air. She had on a t-shirt and panties, with a scarf tied around her head.

"Come on," Tanisha ordered forcefully as she stood to take her shower.

"I'm cool. Go ahead," I teased, knowing she wouldn't leave me alone with V. It was an unnecessary precaution because there was no way I would ever fuck with my man's girl.

"Boy, I know you better come on," Tanisha said angrily through clenched teeth.

Knowing when to quit, I followed her into the bathroom. I tried my best to fuck Tanisha in the shower, but she wasn't hearing it. She was still hot about Veronica's exhibition.

"That bitch on my last nerve," she fumed. "Lite this…Lite that…stay staring at you!"

We showered, then went to our bed to get some sleep. As soon as we slid under the covers and Tanisha's hot skin touched mine, I was hard again.

"Boy, stop." Tanisha giggled halfheartedly when I put the wood on her back.

"They gonna hear us," she said, eager to be talked into.

She was right too. No way could we get busy without being heard. Tanisha and I didn't just "make love" or "have sex." We fucked! It was a loud, mutually aggressive sexual slugfest.

When I kept persisting, she slipped under the covers to offer a compromise. As I lay back to enjoy Tanisha's hot mouth, I noticed Veronica propped up on her elbows, watching. I usually broke off eye contact with V when she stared at me, but that night, I couldn't.

The combination of her eyes and Tanisha's throat brought me to a climax quickly.

V ducked back under when Tanisha got up to go spit and gargle. "I'm better," Veronica said flirtatiously as soon as she cleared the room.

Tanisha must have heard something, because she rushed back into the room, looking back and forth between me and where V had ducked back under the covers. Finding nothing, she frowned and returned to her task.

The next morning, we ate a big breakfast before setting out to work. Bliz had warned us that Houston was really big, and we saw that firsthand. We could drive for an hour and still be in the city. We hit all the spots Bliz had suggested and were selling CDs like crazy. H-town really supports independent artists. No wonder them cats are doing the numbers they are!

By six that evening, we called it quits. We still had one box of CDs left, but I had to get some rest. I don't know how he pulled it off, but somehow Day managed to get me on the bill of the big concert after the convention.

After a few hours of sleep, we headed to the club. Tanisha and V set off with the last box, while me and Day went backstage to mingle.

As fate would have it, B-Bop was one of the headliners, so instead of being one of many obscure opening acts. I would hit the stage in prime time. Me and B-Bop did our song from Bliz's mix tape. Then, I got to do one of my own on his time.

When I left the stage, Tanisha and V proudly displayed the remaining twenty or so CDs. As a show of gratitude, I began passing the remaining disks out for free.

Everyone gladly accepted them except for one middle-aged man dressed in a suit. "I do not accept unsolicited material," he said smugly.

"Whatever!" I laughed and shoved my last CD in his pocket.

The next morning, I returned the van to the airport location and sprang for airfare home. The $2,000 the airline taxed me for the last-minute tickets was far cheaper than the long drive back to Atlanta.

Back in the A, I put Tanisha in a cab to Decatur and shared another cab with Desean and Veronica. Shelby was at the apartment waiting on me. The last month had been great, but I was ready to see my Shell.

With Shelby looking over my shoulder, I went online to check my account balance.

"Oh my God! Is that right?" Shelby exclaimed as the zeros filled the screen.

"I...I...uh...yeah!" I stammered. "I mean, I think so."

"That's $85,000!" she said slowly. "You did it, baby!"

After we did it, I left Shelby sleeping and set off to handle my other business. My first stop was the bank, where the teller talked me out of withdrawing the fifty stacks I wanted. Instead, I opted for several cashier's checks and just $6,000 in cash.

I swung by Tanisha's house and gave her $5,000 for her assistance. I gave her cash so she wouldn't try to cash a check at one of the local liquor stores and get robbed. She tried to pull me inside so she could "thank" me, but I turned down the offer. Even when she sweetened the deal with a little lollipop action, I still declined. I promised I would return later, even though I knew I wouldn't. That would be the last time I would see Tanisha; her chapter had ended.

My next stop was Lenox Mall and the jewelry store.

"Ready for your ring?" asked the clerk, who obviously remembered me.

"As a matter of fact, I am," I said, placing my debit card on the glass.

The bank had to approve the $15,000 purchase before I left with the goods. I hit up the local Fish Supreme for dinner for four and headed home.

Everyone must have been pretty hungry, because there was none of the usual banter at the table. Niggas just got their eat on. Besides, when Fish Supreme is on the table, there really ain't a whole lot to talk about.

"Oh, yeah, son...before I forget," I said, sliding Desean a cashier's check for $20,000.

"That's what's up!" He laughed at the sight of the check. "Dis 20 percent?"

"A little more actually. We ain't see $100,000, but it's all good," I replied.

"Yeah, all them '2 for $15' deals probably," he said, explaining the shortage.

"And for you, Ms. V," I said, pushing Veronica a check for five stacks.

"Thank you," she said so seductively that both Day and Shell frowned.

"Um, excuse me," Shelby inquired, holding out her hand.

"None for you, ma. Remember? You ain't wanna come." I laughed as Shell poked her lip out. We both knew she knew she had something coming.

Back in my room, Shelby still had her lip poked out as she cuddled up against me. "You really didn't bring me nothing?" she whined.

"Have you been good?" I teased.

"Yes, yes!" she sang excitedly.

"Okay. Close your eyes and hold out your hand," I instructed.

Shelby frowned curiously when I pushed her right hand away and picked up her left. Her whole body tensed as she felt a ring slide onto her index finger.

"Okay. Open up,": I said, waiting to see her reaction.

"Oh my God! Oh my God! Oh my GOD!" Shelby yelled over and over, jumping up and down.

The commotion brought Desean and Veronica to my door. "What's up?" Day asked, watching Shelby jumping around.

"Look! LOOK!" Shelby answered, flailing her hand around as if it was on fire.

"You gotta stop moving," V said, grabbing her hand. "Dayum! Does this mean…? Are you guys…?"

"I don't know. She ain't asked me yet," I replied.

At that, Shelby dropped to one knee to uphold her end of the deal. "David Light, would you do me the honor of becoming my husband?" she asked sincerely.

"The honor is all mine," I answered, pulling her to her feet. As we began to kiss, I heard my bedroom door close behind me.

CHAPTER 14

I had my contact information printed on the CDs, so the calls began to pour in. Since Desean and Shelby were back in class, I was left to field the calls myself.

I had decided to blow off school and go full steam ahead with my music. I pressed up a few more CDs just to eat off of and began writing for the next mix tape.

A lot of calls were from other rappers, either wanting to work with me or for me. I got a lot of calls from my female fans, wanting to hook up, but since me and Shell were engaged, I was chillin'.

Tanisha called ten to twenty times a day. Her messages went from sweet to pleading to enticing and then moved to just flat-out nasty. Those got deleted too.

I heard from quite a few independent labels who wanted to sign me, but Bliz assured me I would be helping them more than they could help me. I had a small movement steadily gaining momentum.

Several months later, I got one message that intrigued me so much I played it several times to be sure I had it correct: "This is Samuel Jennings. I'm with Third Eye Records. We met down in Houston a few months back. I would like to meet with you again at your earliest convenience to discuss your future." He left an Atlanta number and urged me to call him.

I racked my brain trying to remember meeting him but couldn't. I played the message for Day, but he didn't recall meeting any Mr. Jennings either.

Bliz flipped out when I told him about the message, and he made me play it for him a few times, just to confirm. "Son, Samuel Jennings ain't 'with' Third Eye. He *is* Third Eye!" he exclaimed. "Quit playing and call him."

I still stalled a few more days to weigh all my options. My name was ringing, and I knew I could go back on the road and sell more CDs.

Bliz moved over 50,000 and made north of 300 grand. Son had a new Benz, jewels, and even moved his studio equipment into the current century. I thought about what he'd said about labels taking a year to pay versus getting mine's now.

He also told me his girl Tosha told him that Tanisha was trying to send me messages through them. I reminded him about my engagement and that I wasn't messing around.

I decided to include Shell on my decision and made a date for dinner. Shelby was notorious for being late, so I was pleasantly surprised to see her already at my apartment when I pulled up. "Hey, babe!" I called out cheerfully as I walked in.

Shelby just waved and continued the conversation on her cell phone. "Oh, girl, that's awful!" she said, looking like she wanted to spit. "No he didn't! What, guuurl?"

I came back from dressing and found my girl in the same position, still yapping away. I gestured with my hands for her to come on, but I only got a finger for a reply—not the middle one, but the pointer, telling me to wait.

Shelby covered the phone for a second to reply to my demands. "Wait, baby. I'm talking to Tanisha," she whispered.

I almost ran. Instead, I sat by as Shell commiserated with her competition. A few minutes later, she ended the call, but not the conversation. "Niggas ain't shit!" she fumed.

"What's wrong, baby?" I asked, looking at the door in case I had to make a break for it.

"Some lowlife got Tanisha pregnant and now won't even take her calls," Shell said hotly. "I told her she need to tell his woman."

My mind flashed to the road trip, when Tanisha and I had sex every day for over a month with no sign of a period.

Just then, my cell vibrated on my hip, and I knew without looking at the caller ID who it was. "What's good, son?" I asked when I took the call.

"Oh, so now I'm your son?" Tanisha chuckled. "More like carrying your son."

"I hear you. I'ma have to look into that, B," I said as Shell looked on.

"I know you can't talk now. I know ya girl there, so just swing by after she leave. I don't wanna have to run up in Justin's and show my ass," Tanisha said before hanging up.

I was so caught up in thought that I barely touched my meal. *How could she be pregnant? What happened to her implant or pill or—*

"Okay, let's have it," Shell demanded with a sigh.

"Have what?" I snapped, irritated at being pulled out of my head. "My bad, ma," I said, apologetic for my outburst. "Just got a lot on my mind."

"Well, I'm here for you, baby," she offered sweetly, patting my hand. "There's nothing you can't tell me.

Wanna bet? For a split second, I entertained the idea of coming clean and telling Shell. Then I had a vision of her coming over the table and shook it off. "Man, what the fuck was you thinking about?" I scolded myself for not using protection.

"Huh?" Shelby asked, alerting me to the fact that I was thinking aloud.

"Just thinking about what to do about the label situation," I lied.

"Is that it?" Shelby laughed. "That's so simple. Just call them. If they make you a better offer than what you're doing now, take it."

"Simple?" I asked. "Just call them?"

"That simple, baby," she reassured.

* * *

When Tanisha opened the door and saw me standing there, she leapt into my arms. She wrapped her legs around my waist and smothered me with kisses. "I missed you so much," she pleaded desperately.

I was .38 hot about her calling Shell and neither responded nor returned her affection.

"What's wrong, boo?" Tanisha cooed, as if she had no idea.

I peeled her off of me and took a seat in a chair to distance myself from her before I spoke. "How you know it's mine?" I said, reciting probably the most asked question in the history of mankind.

"Boy, stop. You know it's yours," she replied nonchalantly. "You know I had my period right before we went out of town. I sucked your dick in the car, remember?"

She was right. I had come over a day or two before the trip, trying to hit it, but she was on her period. *Damn! It is mine!* "What are you doing?" I inquired as Tanisha began to undress.

"Look, Lite, we gonna have a baby. We gonna have to deal with each other even after you get married, so we may as well enjoy it," she said, now completely naked.

"May as well," I agreed, removing my own clothes as quickly as I could.

CHAPTER 15

"We have been expecting your call," the receptionist at Third Eye gushed when I gave my name. I was taken aback at how eager she was to set an appointment. After a brief hold, she told me I was to meet with Mr. Jennings, the company president, the next day.

I had expected to talk with an A/R rep or maybe even the head of artist repertoire, but not the president himself.

Desean and I pulled into Third Eye Records, into the underground parking lot, an hour before my scheduled meeting. He was telling me what I should accept and what I should demand. Day had done so much research that he sounded like a real pro—to me anyway. "Okay. Publishing. Make sure you keep all your publishing," he stressed as I half-listened.

I was too deep inside my own head to hear anything he was saying. I had signed a deal before, but this was the big time. This had a whole different feel to it. They were so eager for me to come in.

"Okay, okay. If Rocco could give you ten grand, they can do at least twenty." Desean went on, a mile a minute. "Video...yeah, you're gonna need a video."

"It's time," I said stoically and got out of the car. "Let's get it!"

Inside the elevator, we exchanged pounds and a hug before riding up in silence. The doors opened inside of the reception area.

"You must be Mr. Light," the beautiful receptionist said as we entered.

"Yes he is," Desean answered for me, as I was too busy marveling at the office.

The place spoke of money—lots of money. It was adorned in glass and chrome, with rich black leather everywhere. The carpet was brilliant white, with the Third Eye logo, and the walls were full of plaques, proving their ability to produce platinum acts.

The receptionist hit a button on her phone and announced my presence.

"Send him up," a voice replied instantly.

"This way, gentlemen," she said, escorting us to yet another elevator.

After a short ride, the elevator opened in the middle of an office, the office of the president himself.

"Welcome, gentlemen. Good to see you again, Mr. Light," Mr. Jennings said, reaching to shake my hand.

As I shook his hand, I shot a glance at Day to see if he recognized him, but a shrug of his shoulders told me he didn't. "I'm sorry, sir, but I don't recall meeting you in Houston," I admitted once we were seated.

"A month or two ago, at the conference," he replied, trying to jar my memory.

"Un-uh," I said with a shrug.

"You forced your CD on me." He laughed, picking up my mix tape from his desk. "Shoved it in my pocket when I refused it."

"Oh yeah!" I laughed as his face came back to me. "You're Mr. I-don't-accept-unsolicited-material, right?"

"That would be me." He laughed good naturedly. "I almost chucked it, but I have too much respect for the game. I know what it takes just to put a demo together."

"Well, I'm glad you kept it," I said appreciatively.

"It ended up in my bag, and my ten-year-old son got a hold of it. I swear, with all the money I pay these A/R people around here, he picks hits better than any of them. Of our ten releases last year, that boy accurately picked the ones that blew up and the ones that flopped. I could have saved a few million dollars listening to him. Now I run everything past him. Screw what my A/R people think! So anyway, a couple weeks ago, he comes running to me with your CD, going on and on about it. He says you're…um, what was the phrase he used?"

"I'm the shit?" I offered, helping him along.

"Yes, yes, as a matter of fact, that may have been exactly what he said. So I listened and had to agree. You're a very talented young man. I asked my A/R people about you, and no one had a clue, so I called myself. This is now my project."

"Um, okay. Thanks?" I stammered, trying not to blush.

"Let's cut to the chase, Mr. Light. I want you on the team. You can have whatever you want," Mr. Jennings said, leaning forward in his chair.

"Okay. I'm down," I replied eagerly. "Where do I sign?"

"Not so quick," Desean said, speaking up for the first time. "Let's discuss his terms, budget, what kind of advance you're talking about, promotions, publishing—"

Mr. Jennings just chuckled and held up his hand, stopping Desean. He leaned back in his chair. "Like I said, he can have whatever he wants." He hit a button on his phone and leaned in to speak. "Mr. Ketchup, can you come in here for a second?" he ordered.

"Sure. Be right there," an unfamiliar voice replied.

Day and I shot each other a childish glance and chuckled at the unusual name.

Moments later, a well-dressed, light skin with good hair came in. Son looked like El DeBarge.

I was about to crack a joke but noticed that dude was kinda diesel, and nobody wants to get their ass kicked by El DeBarge.

"This must be Mr. Light," Ketchup said upon entering the room.

"That's me. Just call me Lite," I said, offering my hand. I was hoping he was gonna say, *"Just call me K or KP or EL,"* but he didn't.

"Well, I'm Mr. Ketchup, VP of A/R," he said.

"Lite is coming aboard. Give him whatever he wants," Mr. Jennings advised his underling.

"Sure thing, Mr. Jennings," he said before turning back to me. "Follow me, guys."

We followed him down the hall to his office and sat in front of his desk.

"I'm sorry, but I didn't get your name," Mr. Ketchup said to Desean.

"Oh. I'm Desean Salaam, Lite's manager," he replied.

"Manager?" Ketchup asked, furrowing his brow. "Um…okay. Well, we'll get to that." He turned to me. "Okay, Lite. The boss said to give you whatever you want, so what do you want from Third Eye?"

Me and Day looked at each other, wondering if he could possibly be serious. We decided to see and began throwing stuff out there.

"How 'bout an advance, say, twenty stacks?" I said, testing the waters.

"Naw, B, like fifty Gs." Desean laughed.

"Let's make it $100,000." Ketchup chuckled, getting in on the act.

"Oh, oh…and a whip. My man need a new whip," Desean said excitedly.

"You like Escalades?" Ketchup offered.

"Naw, son. Let me get a Range, yo Canary yellow," I shot back.

"Navigation, B. Don't forget the navigation," Day threw in.

We were having a good time until Mr. Ketchup hit his intercom button. "Excuse me, guys."

"Yes, Mr. Ketchup?" the receptionist said, answering her summons.

"Carla, call Davis down at Elite and have his people deliver a canary yellow Range Rover with navigation—all the bells and whistles."

"Right away, sir," she replied quickly.

Mr. Ketchup sat back in the chair and suddenly became serious. "What else can we get you?"

"You for real?" Day asked, sounding ten years old.

"Lite, you're the future of this company. We know we will make a ton of money together," he said frankly, then explained my terms. "It's a two-album deal, standard points with a 10 percent bonus per million units. Tell your client how much cash that translates to," he said directly to Day. There wasn't a trace of sarcasm, but it was obvious he wanted to make a point, and he managed to make it. "It's a dollar a record to start," he told Day.

"We getting six now," Desean shot back proudly.

"Yes, but you can't press two million CDs to launch an album. You can't get into all the stores. You can't get radio, video, or overseas. We can," he said plainly. "We have a system that's tried and proven. You will sell four or five million records, no problem."

"Where do I sign?" I asked again.

"Hold up, B. What about his publishing?" Day asked defiantly.

"It's yours," Ketchup said quickly. "Tour support, the best producers, engineers, managers—whatever you want. At least a million on production, promotion, the works."

"Okay. Where.do.I.sign? I asked emphatically.

"Well," Ketchup began, then turned to Day. "Would you mind if we spoke alone for a minute?"

"No problem," Day said, rising to his feet. "I'll be out there with that sexy receptionist."

"That's fine." Ketchup chuckled. "That's unless Lite wants her too."

"Let me be frank. I know he is your friend," Ketchup began.

"*Best* friend," I interjected so dude would understand what sort of territory he was entering.

"Okay, best friend, but he is not a manager," he said plainly. "You're going to need a manager who knows the business, has the contacts, etc. Trust me, once the thing gets rolling, you're going to need your best friend to be your best friend." He offered to buy Day out as manager and put him on payroll as an assistant. "You think $20,000 will ease the pain?"

"What pain?" I laughed, knowing I'd just sold my man out.

"We took the liberty of preparing a contract," Ketchup said, producing a rather thick document. "It's all pretty standard—recoupment, retention of masters, blah…blah…blah. Feel free to take it with you and have your lawyer review it if you like."

"Here you go," I said, sliding the signed contract back to him.

He signed the document as well and hit his intercom again. "Carla, have accounting cut Mr. Light a check for $100,000 and another in the name of Desean Salaam for $20,000…oh, and have Davis deliver the truck to 1583 Peachtree."

"Right away, sir," the receptionist replied.

"What's the address?" I inquired, wondering where they were sending my Range.

"Well, 1583 Peachtree is the address of your new condo," he said, presenting me with a set of keys bearing the Third Eye logo. "Welcome to the family, Lite."

"I'm saying, though, since we fam' and all, do I have to call you Ketchup?" I laughed.

He looked like I might have pissed him off for a second, then smiled. "Corey. You can call me Corey."

"On second thought, I think I like Ketchup better."

When I got back to the lobby, Desean was leaning over, whispering in Carla's ears. Her face, like the phone on her desk, was lit up like a Christmas tree from all the calls she was neglecting. He bolted upright when he saw me.

"So, how did it go?" he asked eagerly.

"Done deal," I said proudly.

"You did it, kid!" Day replied, scooping me up in a bear hug as Carla clapped.

"*We* did it," I corrected. "I couldn't have done it without you."

"Excuse me," a middle-aged white man with "Accountant" written all over his face said as he entered the lobby. "Which one of you gentlemen is David Light?"

"That would be me," I said, extending my hand.

"And Mr. Salaam, I presume?" he said, handing a check to my confused friend.

"I'll explain later," I said in response to the puzzled expression Desean was wearing on his face.

* * *

"A'ight, what's the check for?" Desean demanded as soon as we got back to the car.

"For your management contract," I said somberly.

"Contract? We don't have a contract," Day questioned.

"I know, so a $20,000 buyout for something that doesn't exist is the ill come up," I explained. I then went on to tell him about his new position as my personal assistant. I could tell he was slightly wounded, but it was not about him; it was about me. Son would be getting paid to do what he'd been doing for free his whole life: for hanging out with me. "A-yo, B, we going out tonight," I offered, trying to lighten the mood. "Call what's-her-face. We gonna celebrate."

"You really ain't feeling V, huh?" Day asked in a serious tone.

"What makes you think that?" I replied, wondering if I'd been that obvious.

"Let's see, uh…'what's-her-face' uh, 'that chick'—not to mention that whenever she walks into a room, you bounce. You act like you scared of her. You hurting her feelings, B."

"Ma got a funny vibe about her," I admitted honestly.

"You ain't right." Desean pouted.

I'd never seen playboy so caught up over a chick before. Dude was in love, and I had to fuck with him. "Man, you ol' sucker-for-love-ass nigga! Don't let me find out you soft. Y'all gonna be wearing matching outfits in a minute. Ol' his-and-hers-ass nigga!" I laughed.

"A'ight. Don't get me started on yo ghetto-ass girl Tanisha," he ribbed back.

"Whoa! Whoa! Don't be talking about my baby-mama," I replied.

Desean cracked up until he saw I wasn't laughing. "Say word?" he demanded. "Son, you did not get that broad pregnant! You buggin', yo!"

"Ain't like I tried to. Shit happened," I said defiantly.

"A-yo, Shell is gonna fuck you up," he said with fear in his voice.

"She don't know, and she ain't gonna know," I replied.

Later that night, I took the whole crew out to celebrate my contract. No one knew about the condo yet, so even Day would be surprised.

Of course Shell had all sorts of financial advice on how I should spend *my* 100 grand—talking about stocks and IRAs.

I told her, "I'm gonna get an IRO—I'MA RUN OUT and fuck this money up as soon as humanly possible. I got more coming, so why not?"

I even had one of those horse-drawn carriages on standby when we left the restaurant. "Uh, 1583 Peachtree Street please," I said to the driver.

"Right away, sir," he responded, setting us in motion.

A few minutes later, we pulled up to a brand new high-rise building that even surprised me. I didn't know what I had expected, but it wasn't that!

"Who stay here?" V asked as we dismounted the carriage.

"Good dude. Y'all gonna love him." I chuckled, leading the way.

We walked into the luxurious lobby, where we were met by a rather snobby little man. "How can I help you?" he inquired, inspecting us.

"Yeah, I'm David Light. I—"

"Ooh! Mr. Light! We have been expecting you," the concierge gushed. The little man's demeanor changed in an instant.

My friends frowned from the confusion, but I said nothing.

"Please follow me," our host said, leading the way to the elevator.

We rode up to the fifteenth floor in silence and followed his lead down the plush hallway. The concierge produced a passkey and opened the door of a corner unit. "Welcome home, Mr. Light," he announced, taking a step aside.

Nobody moved. We just stood there for what had to be several minutes before someone finally spoke.

"Th-thi-this is *yours*?" Shelby managed to stutter.

"I'm not sure. I think so," I replied, unsure myself.

We eventually ventured inside and wandered around in a daze. The condo was a fully furnished, three-bedroom, three-and-a-half-bath masterpiece! When I say "fully furnished," I mean fully furnished! We're talking Natuzzi leather sectional, plasma TVs, and the whole nine yards.

"Oh.my.God! Would you look at this kitchen?!" Shelby said, sending Veronica scrambling toward her.

I walked into the master bedroom and shook my head. "Would you look at this shit?" I asked my reflection in one of the huge mirrors.

"What the fuck have you gotten yourself into?" the reflection asked back.

I saw a set of keys on the dresser; they sported the iconic Range Rover logo. "That's what's up!" I said, sticking them in my pocket. I almost cried when I saw all that black marble in my bathroom—almost. I'm a man, and there wasn't going to be no crying. "Okay, one more surprise," I announced once we all gathered back into the living room.

They all followed me down to the building's underground garage. In my own personal parking spot sat a brand spanking new canary yellow Range Rover Sport.

"A-yo, B, that shit got navigation?" Desean asked, beginning to cry.

"Yeah, Dunn," I said with tears streaming down my face.

* * *

Over the next few days, me and Day moved our stuff into the condo. Both Shelby and Veronica managed to slip in enough stuff for extended stays. Shelby was at school most nights, but it seemed V was always there.

I moved Tanisha into our old apartment so she would be close by. Things were pretty much back to the way they had been between us, not to mention that the sex was incredible. Tanisha gave it to me when I wanted it, where I wanted it, and how I wanted it. We even made up a position we called "the pogo stick." She would do a headstand, I would climb between her legs and…well, y'all don't need to know all that.

CHAPTER 16

A couple of weeks after signing my deal, I was summoned to the office to meet my new manager. I already had a mental chip on my shoulder about my boy Day not being my manager, but it got worse when I got to the office.

"Lite, my boy," Donnie sang as he forced a hug on me.

I took an instant dislike toward him. For one, he seemed phony, and for two, the dude looked gay. "'Sup, B?" I said, squirming from the embrace. I took in his immaculate dress, arched brows, and *Wait…is that lip gloss?*

"Pleased to meet you, Lite. Loved your mix tape," a white girl said, stepping forward. "I'm Amy. I'll be your publicist and assistant."

Amy was cute in a college coed kind of way, with her blonde hair and bubbly personality. I almost expected her to break into a cheer. *"Give me an L-I-T-E!"*

"Thank you, I said, trying to remain humble and take compliments gracefully.

"Yes, it was fan-tastic!" Donnie said rather flamboyantly, making me wonder if he was about to break into a cheer as well.

"Well, thanks, Don. I—"

"Un-uh! It's Donnie. Don-*nie*!" he corrected.

I was proud of myself for not laughing.

"As I was saying, we loved the CD. It shows your creativity. However, we want to go in a slightly different direction on your album," Donnie explained.

"Is that right?" I asked dubiously.

"Yeah. We want you to be more street," Amy chimed in.

"Street? Which street?" I asked, confused.

"Oh, what street? That is rich!" Donnie laughed girlishly.

"You know…street, 'hood, um…gold grill, bling…maybe some dreads or braids. Braids are in, you know," Amy said white girlishly.

This time, I had to laugh. In fact, I cracked the fuck up. I laughed so hard that Donny and Amy started laughing with me. "Look, guys," I said, trying to regain my composure, "I appreciate the input, but leave the rapping to me. I'ma do me."

"Yes, by all means, do…you," Donnie agreed. "Just do it a little edgier."

"Yeah! Hardcore!" Amy cheered.

"I am not a hardcore rapper," I insisted.

"Oh, no, I disagree," Donnie cut in. "I know your pedigree. You're a battle rapper. You come up in the trenches of South Bronx!"

His remarks hit me dead in my ego, and he now had my full attention.

"We're not trying to change you," Amy said sympathetically. "We just need you to conform to what's hot. Face it, sex and violence sell."

"So you want me to be one of them studio gangsters?" I asked with fake enthusiasm. "I can take pictures with a gun…a machinegun. No…a bazooka!"

"Exactly!" Amy practically shouted, obviously missing the sarcasm. "And with your murder arrest, then subsequent shooting, I know we can pull it off."

"Lite, you are an intelligent guy," Donnie began. "We are not trying to take away from that. All we are saying is that we have a proven, successful program. We just need you to get with it."

This nigga jus told me to get with the program.

Donnie and Amy tag-teamed me, throwing ideas back and forth.

"Think sex and violence," Amy offered.

"Yeah, take a few weeks and listen to the radio. That's your competition. Do what they do—only do it better," Donnie said.

"And the name of your album can be—get this—*Rapper's D-Lite!*" Amy said, cheering again.

"Get it?" Donnie clapped. "Like the old-school group. We want to release your album sometime third quarter. I know nine months seems like a long time, but trust me, it's not."

"Remember…sexy. Think sexy for your first single," Amy advised. "Something for the ladies!"

"So get busy with that pen. You're in the studio in two weeks," Donnie said.

* * *

Those couple of weeks went by so quickly that when my first session was scheduled, I hadn't written one word. I had spent most of the time at the old apartment with Tanisha.

The first session was more or less me meeting the engineer and getting acquainted. I was supposed to listen to some beats and pick a few to write to.

Third Eye Records built a massive studio complex off Howell Mill Road in Atlanta. It boasted several full recording facilities to support its growing roster. There were always a few projects going on simultaneously.

I was scheduled for Room B, which would be my home away from home for the next few months. Room B was several rooms, to be exact. Of course there was the main control room, complete with the latest Pro-Tools setup, running on multiple wide-screen monitors, and the booth was lined in custom foam to dampen extra noise. Another room had sofas, TV, and a wet bar. I guess they wanted me to be comfortable while I worked. The last room just had a bed and a recliner.

I was greeted by a middle-aged white man sporting a low grey crew-cut. After my experience with Mickey at Blue Studios, I knew not to underestimate white guys when it came to hip-hop. "You must be Lite," he said warmly, extending his hand.

"What's good, son?" I said as we shook.

"My name is Guy. Come on and make yourself at home," Guy said, taking a seat in front of the mixing board.

I looked at the plush leather sofas on the wall, then opted to sit next to him near the action. "Well, they tell me they want sexy for my first single." I sighed.

"Let's see what we can find," Guy said and began pulling up different tracks that he had on file.

We listened to hundreds of beats over the next couple of hours, but nothing moved me. They had quite a few bangers, but nothing I would have thought of as sexy.

"Don't fret. We'll find something," Guy said, addressing my growing frustration.

I was only half-listening as my eyes began to wander around the room. I was intrigued by all the computers, and an idea formed in my head.

"A-yo, you got that song 'Computer Love'?" I asked.

"The ZAP song? Yeah," Guy replied before pulled it up on the computer. "This has been done before…a few times."

"Not the way I'ma do it," I shot back. I played around with a few lines in my head as we listened to the classic song. "Yeah, I can run with this," I announced.

"Okay. Gimme a sec' to replay it, 'cause samples are a bitch," he said, moving to a keyboard. As he pulled up and played the bass line, he explained the whole sample and sample-clearing process, and it was a bitch. A couple minutes later, and the bass line was re-created. "How you want the drums?" he asked, pulling up a drum kit on the keyboard." I can do it like the original if you like."

"Naw, I need more space. I don't wanna compete with drums. I wanna get in there and ride them real sexy like. Feel me?" I asked.

"Um, yeah, and it's kinda creepy." Guy laughed.

I liked Guy right away. That was good, since we would be spending so much time together. He had an old hippie vibe to him, though, so I had to try him. "You told me to make myself at home. How literally did you mean that?" I inquired.

"I don't follow," Guy said, but I think he did. He just wanted me to lay it all out, so I did.

"I'm saying, though, when I'm at home, I smoke weed," I said plainly, "a lot of green, sticky weed."

Guy shot a conspiratorial glance around the room before speaking. "Light that shit up!"

We passed the blunt back and forth as he loaded the tracks from the keyboard into the computer. The whole while, lyrics ran through my brain, slowly forming a song.

"Ready when you are," Guy announced, having completed his task.

For a response, I got up and entered the booth.

"Who would have known a chance encounter on MySpace…

would lead to love and sleepless nights at my place?…

NOW YOU'RE ONLINE ALL THE TIME, SO YOU CAN BROSE MY BOD…
DELETE THEM OTHER DUDES AND DOWNLOAD ME IN YOUR IPOD…
D-LITE IS KNOWN TO KICK RHYMES AND PLACE HOOKS…
TIME TO UPDATE BOTH YOUR TWITTER AND YOUR FACEBOOK…
MY DOT.COM IS THE BOMB, BABY. CLICK ON MY LINK…
PERUSE THROUGH MY PAGES AND TELL ME WHAT YOU THINK…
UPGRADE YOUR MEMORY SO YOU WILL ALWAYS REMEMBER ME…
AND WE CAN LIVE OUT THEM DIRTY TEXTS YOU BE SENDING ME…
YOUR FULL-SERVICE PROVIDER, YOU'LL NEVER NEED ANOTHER…
WWW-DOT-D-LITE, YOUR COMPUTER LOVER!"

When I exited the booth, guy was nodding with approval. "That was very… interesting. I love the analogy," he said.

"Thanks. Let's smoke another blunt so I can think up my next verse," I replied.

Two blunts and two verses later, I had my first song. We fooled around with a hook for a while before deciding to get a singer to come in and lace something. Guy threw a rough mix on it and burned a copy for me to take with me.

Even though our first session was for us to get acquainted, we ended up getting a lot done. Guy put it best when he said, "What better way to get to know someone than making a song?" I concur.

It was after 1 a.m. when I left the studio, but I was high and horny when I did. Shelby owed me a booty call, but she was sound asleep when I called. Likewise, Tanisha had been sick, so she wasn't shaking nothing either. I thought about hitting club, but that meant changing clothes, and I really wasn't up for that. I finally gave up and steered the truck toward the condo.

"Hey, Lite!" Veronica sang cheerfully when I walked into my unit.

I was shocked and pissed to see her since Day was in California with the team. He couldn't play anymore, but he often traveled with them anyway. "What are you doing here?" I asked sharply, not bothering to hide my contempt. "Where's Day?"

"He went with the team," she said, removing the wet towel from her head. It was similar to the one she had wrapped around her body. "He said you wouldn't mind."

But I did mind. The way her wet hair fell around her beautiful face pissed me off…and turned me on.

"He told me you was going to the studio. How'd it go?" she said sweetly.

"Cool. I got a song done," I replied without stopping.

"Ooh! Let me hear it! Please!" she begged, springing to her feet. Her whole body shook, and I was hard instantly.

"Here," I said, quickly taking a seat so she wouldn't see the bulge growing in my pants.

"'Computer Love'? I love that song!" she exclaimed when the familiar bass line came on.

I wanted to get up and go to my room, but when she began swaying to the music, I was stuck. I was mesmerized as I watched her body move in sync with the beat. I was so hard I felt my dick straining against my pants. The only thing I could do was light yet another blunt, hoping to calm myself.

When the song ended, I jumped up to run to my room, but V cut me off. "I loved the song," she said, giving me a hug. She felt how hard I was and pressed her body up against me, and I couldn't even stop her. I wanted to say something, but she slipped her tongue in my mouth, and I couldn't stop her.

I made up my mind to leave, then changed it again when the towel hit the floor. Veronica and I made love, then fucked, then we made love some more, and then I fucked her a couple more times.

The next thing we knew, it was morning. We agreed that it had to stop, then did it one more time, and I knew it would not stop.

Desean was right: Veronica did have the best pussy in the whole Western Hemisphere.

CHAPTER 17

When I returned to the studio a few days later, I took Tanisha with me. I warned her that I might be there all night, but she begged to go along anyway.

When I went to pick her up, she was looking good, as usual. The tight dress showed off her figure and growing belly. Tanisha made even pregnancy look good. Her face was fuller, and her breasts were huge.

Guy was already hard at work by the time we got there, causing me to check my watch.

"Am I late?" I inquired as I entered.

"No, no, not at all. Just had a few ideas in my head I wanted to try out," he said, playing with the track. "Oh, you must be Lite's girlfriend he speaks so highly of," Guy announced when he finally looked up and noticed Tanisha.

"No, I'm his chick on the side," Tanisha shot back, taking a seat.

"Oh. I'm sorry." Guy blushed. "I…I didn't know…um..."

"It's cool." I laughed. "At least she know her position."

After listening to the song over the last few days, I'd come up with several changes I wanted to make. I had done some research on computers and wanted to update some of the jargon.

"How about a little stimuli before we begin?" Guy said, producing a joint from his shirt pocket.

After getting a buzz, I stepped into the booth and did my thing. I ended up re-recording most of the song and laid new adlib tracks.

"We hungry!" Tanisha demanded when I emerged from the booth. She was rubbing the baby bump for emphasis.

"Go ahead and take lunch," Guy suggested. "We got the singer coming to do the hook at 2."

With that settled, Tanisha and I headed over to east Atlanta for the best pizza in the city. Desean had put me up on the spot. He raved about it so much that I wasn't at all surprised to see him and V leaving as we arrived.

Day greeted Tanisha, and I said, "What's up?" to Veronica, but the girls ignored each other. I knew Tanisha didn't like her from the road trip, and knowing she had more access to the condo than her just added to it.

V went to the car, and Tanisha went inside, leaving me to face my friend.

"Veronica told me what you did for her while I was gone," Day said without a trace of emotion.

I could only assume he wasn't talking about me eating her pussy, so I just shrugged my shoulders. "Don't mention it."

"She told me you were very nice to her—even let her hear the new song," Day said happily.

"Oh, that," I said with a sigh of relief. "Man, my pleasure."

"Okay, 'cause I'm going to Colorado next week. Promise you'll do it again," he asked.

"You have my word," I replied emphatically.

After smashing a large pizza covered with spicy jerk chicken, Tanisha and I headed back over to the studio. As we rode, my cell vibrated, and Shelby's name appeared on the screen. "Hey, Shell," I said upon answering, looking sternly at Tanisha.

She sucked her teeth and crossed her arms but remained silent.

"Guess what," Shell said, as if I possibly could. "I got the assignment done early, so I'm yours all night."

"That's what's up. I'll be home in a few hours," I replied.

"You said you were spending the day with me!" Tanisha shouted as I closed my phone.

"I am spending it with you…right now. Then I'm going home," I said hotly.

We arrived back at the studio thirty minutes later, and the singer was already in the booth. Dude looked like Trey, Neo, Bobby, and Whitney all rolled into one and sounded like shit.

"Fuck is son doing?" I asked Guy as we took our seats.

"Um…I'm not quite sure," Guy replied.

"Why he gotta make them faces?" Tanisha asked.

He did look like he was in pain as he belted out the new hook I wrote. He recorded a few more takes before we finally had enough. We thanked him profusely, swearing it was just what we needed. As soon as the door closed behind him, we all cracked up.

"Where the hell did you find him?" I asked.

"He's the lead singer of the group working up in Room E," Guy said, shaking his head.

"Lead? In a group?" I laughed.

"Stranger things have happened," Guy replied.

In the middle of our revelry, Donnie walked in, causing the laughter to die. "D-Lite, my boy!" he announced cheerfully.

I just glared at him. That "my boy" shit got real old real quick.

"What we got going?" Donnie asked, turning to Guy.

Guy didn't speak either. Instead, he hit the spacebar on the keyboard to start the track.

Donnie listened to the song with an occasional smile or nod of his head. At one point during playback, he checked out Tanisha, looking her up and down. When their eyes met, she rolled hers and went back to her magazine.

When the track came to an end, we all eagerly awaited his reaction.

Donnie seemed to enjoy the attention and dragged it out. "Hmmm. I like it," he said, nodding. "A little tame, but love the concept. Clever analogies. Album filler, maybe."

I was hot about the "filler" remark and sat up to say so, but Guy caught my eye and called me off with a slight headshake.

"Let me hear it again!" Donnie ordered with a snap of his fingers.

This time, I had to call Guy off with my own headshake.

"Stop! Right there!" he demanded when the song came to the hook. "That's the missing link." He winced. "The hook is all wrong. I'm not feeling it at all."

"We're not digging it ourselves," Guy said, coming to my defense.

"We can use the original," I offered naïvely.

"NO!" Don said, practically screaming. "No, samples cost too much, and they are a bitch to get cleared—nothing but problems."

"Just use a girl," Tanisha said from across the room, solving the problem without even looking up from her magazine.

The room was silent until Donnie snapped his polished fingers again. "I know! We can put a female singer on it," he suggested, as if he'd thought of it himself.

Tanisha sucked her teeth as me and Guy laughed.

"Maybe we can get Mary," I said, thinking automatic classic.

"Mary's great, but I may have a better idea," Guy said, heading for the door.

"Better than Mary?" I asked in disbelief. Even I knew Mary plus rapper would equal a hit. I pulled out a blunt, but Guy stopped me from lighting it up.

"As much as I could use it after that prick, let's wait until he's gone for good," he said.

A few minutes later, Donnie reappeared with his usual fanfare. He stuck his head in the door and announced that he had a surprise. When he felt the suspense had built high enough, he stepped aside, and in walked Asia.

Donnie was about to do the introductions, but when Asia saw me, she rushed over to greet me. "D-Lite!" she squealed as we embraced.

"You guys know each other?" Donnie asked, ignoring the obvious.

"We go way back," Asia explained as we separated.

"Yeah, we used to do shows together back home," I added.

"Lite, here, has just been signed," Donnie interjected, eager to take back control of the conversation.

I saw Asia's mouth water when he called me "the next big thing."

"We need you on this hook. We are thinking of making it a single," Donnie said.

"I'm down, but he gotta come up and spit on the remix we're working on," Asia said.

"It's settled then. You guys will get a copy of each other's songs, and we'll record in a couple days," he said. Donnie began guiding Asia toward the door.

She broke free and came back to me. "It really is good to see you again," she purred. "Call me." Then Asia gave me a hug, as well as her personal info.

Tanisha was fuming, having witnessed our exchange. "Take me home… NOW!" she demanded when Asia and Donnie walked out.

"Well, we're done here." Guy spoke up as if her tone frightened him.

I gave him a pound and a hug and bounced out.

Tanisha refused to speak to me on the way home except to demand Fish Supreme. I'm saying, though, I only went for it because she was pregnant. After grabbing her a three-piece whiting meal and twelve shrimp, I took her straight home.

She dropped the attitude as soon as I pulled in front of the apartment. "You coming in?" she asked sweetly, rubbing a hand on my thigh.

Knowing Shelby was waiting on me was the only thing that gave me the strength to resist. We had recently invented a new sexual position called "the clapper." That's where you…well, again, y'all ain't ready for that.

I walked into the condo and saw Desean and V hugged up on the sofa—the same sofa I'd beat her back out on just days earlier. For some odd reason, I felt a little jealous.

They greeted me in unison.

"Where's Shell?" was all I could think of to say.

"Right here," Shelby said, appearing from my bedroom.

After some cursory small talk, Shelby and I retired to my room. Physically, I made love to Shell, but mentally, Veronica was the one I was inside of. Afterwards, my girl said it was the best sex we'd ever had.

* * *

I was glad Tanisha opted to go shopping with her allowance instead of coming backing to the studio. That allowed me to spend a little more time with Asia.

Guy was hard at work, pressing buttons and turning knobs. When I walked in, he paused long enough to give me a pound and a hug. It was a testament of how quickly we had bonded. "What's up, B?" he asked seriously.

"Chillin', fam'," I said, holding back the giggles. Guy was as white as a man could get, and hearing him speak slang cracked me up. I liked Guy and could tell he was fond of me as well. Furthermore, we respected each other.

We shared a solid work ethic and sought perfection. We smoked our first blunt of the day and carefully scrutinized the song. We were looking for a way to improve it but found none. The shit was already hot.

"All we need now is the hook, and this one is in the can," Guy said.

As if on cue, Asia tapped on the door and stuck her head in. "You guys ready for me?" she asked, making even those few words sound like a song.

Guy invited her in and greeted her with a handshake. I, on the other hand, got a kiss; it was only a peck on the lips, but it was a far cry from her not remembering my name.

Asia was looking good, too, in her Gucci sweat suit with matching sneakers. I made a mental note to cop the same outfit for Shelby. *While I'm at it, may as well grab one for my baby-mama too.*

"Ready to get to work?" Guy asked.

"Sure am," Asia replied. "By the way, I love the song. You so crazy!"

Asia hit the booth and got straight down to business. I could tell she had practiced in her spare time. She began adlibbing, ooh-ing and ahh-ing to the rhythm.

"That's how she sounds when you hit her from the back," I said to Guy and laughed.

"You're a regular Casanova, aren't you?" Guy replied.

"Don't be no hater!" I laughed.

After the adlib track, she laid the main hook, then backed herself up and was done. "How was that?" she asked anxiously as she entered the room.

"Super!" Guy exclaimed with a round of applause.

"Yeah, that's dope, ma," I cosigned, clapping along with Guy.

"Thank you, guys," Asia said sweetly. "Now, when you gonna return the favor?"

"Ready when you are," I replied eagerly. I had written a killer verse for their remix and couldn't wait to spit it. The original version of the song was burning up the charts, and that meant instant airplay for the remix.

"The film crew coming Saturday to film footage for the video, so you may as well come then. You can be in it," Asia suggested. "Matter fact, you need to come do it at our show, 'cause they filming that too."

"I'll clear my schedule and do both," I said, as if I really had a schedule to clear. Out of the corner of my eye, I saw Guy stifle a laugh.

"You so sweet," Asia said, rushing in to hug me. This time, I got a little tongue with the peck.

"Schedule?" Guy laughed when Asia walked out. "Casanova!"

CHAPTER 18

I was happy to catch Day home alone. It had been ages since we'd been able to kick it. Of course, I wanted to talk about me, but all he wanted to do was talk about V.

"Chick really got you open?" I finally asked.

"I know you ain't talking," he said seriously. "You got a baby on the way, and you engaged to somebody else. Don't be surprised if I ain't right behind you."

"Right behind me?" I yelled, horrified at the thought that V might be pregnant. "Please tell me that chick ain't expecting!"

"Naw, not that I know of. I meant about getting engaged," Day said brightly. "Son, I'ma marry her."

I was feeling sick to my stomach, so I changed the subject. "Son, I'ma do a verse on Galaxy's remix to 'Holla' and be in the video," I said.

"Say word? Son, put me down!" he exclaimed.

"Most of the video is already shot. The film crew just trying to get some studio footage, but I'ma be laying my verse for real. That, plus what they shoot at the show gonna be edited in with the rest," I explained.

Desean was silent, but I could hear the wheels turning in his head. "A-yo, B, that's what we need to do. Film everything!" Day announced. "Son, we shoot you in the studio, doing shows, plus just everyday shit. Then, after your album drop, we drop the DVD."

"*We*? No. *You*? Yes," I advised. "Son, that will be *your* project. I'ma focus on my music."

Desean went out that same day and picked up all the equipment he would need for the task. He bought two professional HD cameras, lights, tripods, mics, and the whole nine yards. Then he signed up for classes on how to run it all.

* * *

When we arrived at the studio, the film crew was getting set up. Desean made a beeline to the director, ignoring everyone else. I had hoped something would pop off between him and Egypt to get V out of the picture, but Day was more interested in learning the film business.

The director, Jamal Finkley, from Black Tree Media, told us to pretend to have a conversation so he could get some footage. Since we were all old acquaintances, the conversation was natural, and the laughs were genuine.

When my moment arrived, I went into the booth and laid my verse. I nailed it in one take, but the director had me pretend a few more times for the sake of the video.

After the sessions wrapped, we all headed over to Buckhead to eat. Over dinner, the girls filled us in on their accession to the top of the R&B charts.

"Lite, Mr. Jennings told us we could have whatever we wanted if we signed," Asia said, incredulous.

"Meant it too," China spoke up. "Bought us all BMWs and a big-ass condo."

"Mm-hmm, and Corey—I mean, Mr. Ketchup," Egypt said, catching herself, but not before making it obvious that they were fucking. "He been there for us every day."

"For you maybe." Asia laughed, confirming it.

The girls had sold over four million records to date. The remix was the final push for the album, followed by another tour.

"Then we start on our next album," China said.

"Baby, we got publishing checks for a million dollars," Asia said, like she couldn't believe it herself.

"A piece!" Egypt shouted.

Desean and I just looked at each other. The magnitude of everything was really sinking in. The shit was both real and unreal at the same time. I used to beg Wayne to let me rap, and now I was on my way to getting paid millions to do it.

We walked the girls to China's X-5, and I slobbed Asia down shamelessly. I had never fucked a millionaire—not yet anyway.

* * *

Desean had the cameras rolling as I dressed for my performance with Galaxy. This time around, I had use of a company credit card, so gear would not be a problem. I went to the mall and loaded up, courtesy of Third Eye. I settled on a pair of black Armani slacks and a matching shirt. A pair of black crocodile loafers with a matching belt completed the outfit.

He set up a camera on a tripod to film us as we smoked a blunt and hammed it up. We were having a good time until Veronica walked out and stopped time. V had on a sheer dress that left nothing to the imagination—not that I hadn't seen it all before anyway. Her breasts and rock-hard abs were clearly defined, but a slightly thicker material obscured her crotch.

After the shock of her entrance wore off, time was about to start again, and then Shell walked in. Ma had on a black mini-dress and six-inch Manolo Blahnik heels. Her bare shoulders were covered by her cascading curls.

"Hello!" Veronica said, restarting time again. "Y'all ready?"

"Dang, David, you act like you ain't never seen a dime before." She laughed.

I had gotten so used to the sweat pants and t-shirts that had become her daily uniform that I had forgotten how fine Shell really was. After we all complimented each other, we set out for the club.

When we pulled up, the line was wrapped around the corner. Galaxy was selling out arenas. There was no way all those people were getting in.

We entered through a side door reserved for VIPs and made our way to the VIP section. I ordered a couple bottles of champagne off the top, hoping to get Shelby drunk. V was the designated driver, so she just sipped a Coke. I had to perform, so I nursed a beer. Meanwhile, Shell and Day were tossing back flute after flute of bubbly. I was dying to spark up a blunt, but it wasn't that type of club.

Desean tapped me discreetly and pointed out Tanisha with a crew of hoochies. She saw me and stuck her tongue out. I winked my reply and turned my attention to Shell.

Shelby and Desean graduated to vodka and were getting tipsy.

"Okay, remember what happened last time you got drunk?" I whispered in Shell's ear.

"Oh no! Not the pogo stick." She laughed way too loudly.

The DJ began playing songs from Galaxy's album. Halfway through the second song, the girls came out and finished it live. They did a couple more songs as the crowd sang along.

When the lights grew bright, I knew the cameras were about to roll. I kissed Shell and gave Day a pound before heading backstage.

"Do your thing, Daddy!" Shelby slurred behind me as I left.

We didn't rehearse anything, so I planned to go out, spit my verse, and bounce. The director said we had such great chemistry that it would play better unscripted.

When my part came up, I swaggered out and did my thing indeed. As I rapped, the girls all danced around me like I was a stripper pole.

Shell was all smiles until Asia slid up against me, grinding her crotch against my side. She did a dip and let her hand run down my chest, stomach, and crotch before shimmying back up and dancing off.

After my verse, I stayed onstage, doing a little two-step until the song ended.

When I got back to the table, Shelly was fuming. "A-yo, son! What the fuck was that?" she demanded when I took my seat.

Desean and V turned away, trying not to laugh. That was the flipside to getting Shelby drunk: It brought out the freak in her, but she could be a mean drunk. I never knew what I was gonna get, fuck or fight.

"What?" I pleaded innocently. "It's for the show. We just shot a video!"

"Oh, so I'ma hafta see some bitch feeling my man up every time I turned on the TV?" she spat.

"Man, they probably won't even use that part. You buggin' over nothing," I said sternly.

"Whatever, nigga. I got your buggin'!" she retorted.

"Hey, girl," Tanisha said sweetly, giving Shell's neck a hug.

"Hey yourself, lil' mama," Shelly sang, rubbing her large belly.

Desean and Veronica looked at Tanisha, then Shell, then each other, and finally at me.

I just shrugged my shoulders.

"Nice show, Lite," Tanisha said to the side of my head.

"Thanks," I replied without looking.

"Well, call me," Tanisha said to Shell while looking at me.

"I will," Shelby slurred before draining the glass of vodka.

"Let's bounce," I commanded, rising from my seat.

Day and Shelby were both pissy drunk and had to be helped to the truck. We put them in the backseat and headed home.

Veronica had to wait with Shelby while I struggled to get Desean upstairs. I half-carried, half-dragged him all the way to his room and into his bed.

Back at the truck, I scooped Shell up and carried her upstairs with V in tow. "You know I'm still gonna hit it," I teased Shell, who replied by throwing up on me. I took her to the shower and stripped us both down before using the handheld showerhead to hose us off. When I finished, I dried her off and put her to bed.

Since I was still awake, I decided to smoke a blunt and watch a movie. A few minutes into it, there came V in a t-shirt—Day's t-shirt at that. She sat on the other side of the sofa and watched the movie. Without looking at her or speaking to her, I passed her the blunt.

We watched the movie and smoked the blunt in silence. About halfway through the movie, V called my name. When I turned to look, she lay back and spread her legs.

At first, it pissed me off, and I started to check her. My girl was in the next room, and her man—my best friend—was in the other. But Veronica slid a finger inside of herself and pulled it out, glistening wet. Next thing I knew, I was pounding away inside of her.

It got so good I wanted to try out a new position called "the MacGyver," but I didn't have a spatula or jumper cables, so I put her in a "Hammer time" and gave her the business.

She was moaning so loudly that I thought we might wake our mates up—if not from her moans, then from the sound of our bodies banging together or the splish-splash of her vagina.

We climaxed together, then lay there trying to catch our breath. Once we gained our composure, we got up without saying a word and joined our sleeping mates.

CHAPTER 19

I had a meeting with the label so Donnie could check on my progress. Since I was the president's personal project, they intended to micro-manage me. We met in Amy's office and listened to the completed version of "Computer Lover."

"It's great—not a single, but good work nonetheless," Amy offered.

"Not a single? This shit is dope!" I said, feeling wounded.

"Dope indeed," Donnie chipped in, "but too tame. He shook his head and wrinkled his nose, as if the track had a bad odor.

"Man, y'all said sex, and I gave you sex," I demanded.

"Nah, not really. You skirted around the issue. You didn't say 'pussy' or 'dick' or 'bitch', 'ho', nothing," Amy complained.

"Remember what we said about sex and violence?" Donnie chided, as if I were a child.

"Check this out, B," I said, growing agitated. "You signed me on the strength of my mix tape. Ain't no sex or violence on that, so, uh—"

"Look, Mr. Jennings told you that you could have whatever you wanted. Now you need to return the favor and give him what he wants," Donnie snapped.

"Sex. Sex! You do know what sex is, don't you?" Amy asked.

"Naw, tell you what. Why don't you suck my dick, and I'll rap about that?" I shot back, turning my publicist beet red.

"Okay, okay. No need to be crass," Donnie said calmly. "Look, Lite, we are a very successful company. We have a formula for success, and we know it works. If you follow it, you blow up. Here, take this." Donnie handed me a CD with beasts from all the top producers. "Now, give us sexy!" With that, he excused himself, leaving Amy and I to discuss matters of my image.

There was an awkward moment of silence as a remnant of the blow-up lingered in the air.

"Um, I saw a rough cut of the Galaxy remix video. You look great, and the verse was so hot," Amy offered as a peace treaty.

"Thank you. They been playing it on the radio all day," I replied.

"People love Asia, and now they love you," Amy began, then paused. "So imagine how they might feel about Asia and Lite…together."

"Can't answer for 'they', but my girl ain't going for it." I chuckled.

"No one's asking you to break up your home," Amy said soothingly. "We're talking photo shoots, a few joint interviews, and performing together, of course. Think Jay and B."

"Hov, huh?" I said, excited about any similitude to dude. "I'm down!"

"Look, Lite…" Amy said, coming around from her desk. She sat on the sofa beside me and placed her hand on my knee. "We—I—am committed to your success. I will do *anything* to make this project successful…even that," she said sincerely.

"Even what?" I asked.

"You know…what you said," she answered, sliding her hand up my thigh.

By the time she reached the wood, I was rock hard, and yes, it did help. I was rapping to myself the whole time she blew me.

* * *

"They said what?" Shelby snapped when I told her about my meeting. Of course I left out the part about the blowjob. "How some suburban white girl gonna tell you what black kids want to hear?" she asked.

She had a point. "I'm just gonna do me. If they don't like it, fuck 'em. I'll do my own thing," I said defiantly.

"Whoa! Don't be too hasty," Shell said quickly. She was enjoying the benefits of the label and wasn't ready to give them up. "I got an idea." She smiled deviously. "Write something so nasty, so over the top, that they will just feel silly."

"Yeah, I feel that." I nodded, catching on. "They want sex? I'ma give 'em sex!"

"Just go crazy with it." She laughed.

"Okay, but I need some inspiration. Strip!" I demanded, going for my zipper.

"Boy, you know I have to go to class," Shelby replied and gathered her books to leave.

Shell was gone, but I still needed some inspiration, so I called Tanisha.

"Come get me," she said instantly when she answered.

When I got there, she rushed out to the truck. She had a little waddle in her walk from her growing belly, but she did look good in the Gucci sweat suit.

In the truck, I had been banging an Adam Salaah track that had caught my ear. The Range was on autopilot, 'cause the beat had my full attention. I was in that creative space in my head until Tanisha said something, jolting me back to the present. "Huh? What?" I snapped at the interruption.

"I said," Tanisha began, matching my tone, "when you coming to spend a night with me?"

"Soon, soon," I said curtly, trying to go back inside my head.

"Well, your coochie is getting lonely," she pleaded.

"Whose coochie?"" I inquired, not having paid attention to the statement entirely. All I heard was "coochie," and I had to investigate.

"It's *your* coochie," Tanisha assured me.

"That's it!" I announced, actually swerving the vehicle as inspiration struck.

"What?" she asked, puzzled my by outburst.

"That's the song!" I laughed. "'Whose Pussy Is This?'"

"Mmm, it's yours, D-Lite," she sang, and a hook was born.

I told Guy about my plan, and he loved it. "I can't wait to see their faces. He laughed as we loaded the track into the Pro-Tools program.

"I'll get it on tape," I replied as I prepared the camera to capture the session.

Desean had left a camera in the studio, already set up to catch footage, even if he wasn't available. Once Guy was ready, I hit record and hit the booth. I took Tanisha in with me for her contribution to the hook. It took some doing, but we finally got it right. Guy caught all her giggles and laughs to spice the track up.

Once we laid the hook, me and Guy smoked a blunt so I could go inside my head and find some lyrics.

Guy was at work spacing the hook out to allow me room for the standard sixteen-bar verse. We finished about the same time.

I WENT INTO THE BOOTH WITH EVERY CHICK I'D EVER BEEN WITH AND SAID,

"I GOT A SPANISH CHICK WHO SUCKS DICK TO WISH ME LUCK…

A REAL FREAKY SLUT. SHE CALLS ME 'PAPI' WHEN WE FUCK…

A CHURCH GIRL, PREACHER'S DAUGHTER FROM WAY DOWN SOUTH…

STINGY WITH THE PUSSY, BUT SHE FUCKS WITH HER MOUTH…

I GOT A PROJECT HO WITH ABSOLUTELY NO CLASS…

KID BE IN THE NEXT ROOM WHILE I'M TAPPING THAT ASS…

MY RICH BITCH DOES IT ALL AND LOVES TO BALL…

AFTER I DIG HER OUT, WE GO STRAIGHT TO THE MALL…

A WHITE GIRL WITH FOUR PRETTY PINK LIPS…

TWO ON HER FACE, AND TWO BETWEEN HER HIPS…

SHE LOVES TO CALL ME HER 'BIG BLACK BUCK'…

SO I MAKE HER APOLOGIZE FOR SLAVERY EVERY TIME WE FUCK…

MY RADICAL BITCH IS ALWAYS PREACHING BLACK POWER…

TOLD ME TO KEEP IT CLEAN, SO I FUCK HER IN THE SHOWER…

I FUCKED HOES AROUND THE GLOBE, ALL OVER THE WORLD…

THEN COME HOME TO THE A AND MAKE LOVE TO MY GIRL…

WHOSE PUSSY IS THIS?…

I DON'T EAT PUSSY. I BEAT PUSSY TILL ITS RAW…

WHORES BE SORE BUT STILL BEGGIN' FOR MORE…

WHOSE PUSSY IS THIS?…

THEY LOVE THE DICK. I GOT 'EM HOOKED LIKE CRACK…

THEY FIEN' AND SCREAM FOR ME TO HIT IT FROM THE BACK…

WHOSE PUSSY IS THIS?…

IT'S YOURS, D-LITE."

The shit was just crazy, way over the top. Me and Guy laughed so hard we were crying.

"That song is hot!" Tanisha said over our laughter. I knew she, of all people, would like it.

The next meeting was held in Donnie's office. Amy was already there and blushed the moment I walked in.

"Peace, people," I greeted. "I hope you guys like the new song. I hope it's sexy enough." It was all I could do not to laugh as Donnie scrambled to load the disk. I sat next to Amy on the sofa and waited.

"Good choice," Donnie said appreciatively when the beat began to play.

When the song started, both Donnie and Amy were expressionless. I hid my face in my hands so they wouldn't see me laughing. They listened to the entire song in complete silence and were motionless when it ended, like they were trying to figure out what they'd just heard.

"Well? What ya think?" I chuckled, with tears streaming down my face.

They looked at each other, then turned to me and lost it.

"I love it!" Donnie exclaimed. "This...this is what sells."

"Ladies and gentlemen, we have our single!" Amy cheered.

"I want this mixed and mastered ASAP," Donnie ordered. "We're going to release this to radio and clubs now."

"Right away," Amy complied. "The remix for 'Holla' is at the top of the charts, and the video is climbing quickly."

"Which reminds me..." Donnie said, reaching into his desk. He came out with a check and handed it to me.

"What's this?" I asked, questioning the $26,000.

"That's for the remix," Amy said cheerfully.

"Naw, I'm supposed to get $50,000 for that," I protested.

"You did. That's minus fees and taxes and stuff," Donnie explained.

"Don't fret, Lite. We got you ten more guest spots at $50,000," Amy said. "Justin, Mary, everybody wants you."

The thought of more money and all those guest appearances made me forget to ask for an explanation of "fees" and "stuff." I had already run through my advance. *Why sweat it though? I got more coming, right?* I had been spending a G a month on weed alone. Shelby got a nice allowance, and I was totally supporting Tanisha. It was a good thing I had use of the company credit card. I used that for everything from food to clothes to jewelry and even put twenty-four-inch rims on the Range. I wished the kush man took Visa. "Well, let's get it!" I exclaimed, ready to get at that money.

"I see Amy's talk helped," Donnie said.

"Oh yeah. Best talk I ever got. She got a good head." I chuckled. "On her shoulders, that is."

Donnie looked back and forth between me and a blushing Amy before he shrugged his shoulders. "Anyway, you have a photo shoot with *Beat Street Magazine*," he advised.

"Okay," I said, rubbing my hair. I had been trying to let it grow because Amy said braids were in.

"Don't worry. Your new stylist will be there," Amy said, noticing my dilemma.

"Well, folks, good work!" Donnie announced, standing to indicate that the meeting was over.

"A'ight. Hey, Amy, would you mind going back over what we talked about last week?" I asked my publicist once we were clear of the office.

"Love to," she said, leading the way to her office.

CHAPTER 20

The photo shoot was held in an artsy-type loft near the downtown area. An old industrial building was given new life as a residence. It had hardwood floors and exposed brick that set off the floor-to-ceiling windows.

"We gotta get one of these." Day marveled as we entered the large open space.

There were about twenty people milling about, all engaged in one aspect or another of the shoot. The caterers were fussing over a buffet, making sure everything was right.

"D-Lite! Pleased to meet you," a tall, pretty brown-skinned lady said, extending her hand. I'm Colleen Valentine with *Beat Street*."

"Pleased to meet you as well," I said, shaking the six-footer's hand. "This is Desean, my assistant and videographer."

"Asia is already in her dressing room, and your stylist is in yours, waiting on you. After you guys shoot, we'll do the interview," Colleen said.

I followed her to the area that was to be my dressing room.

"Raynard, this is Lite. Lite, Raynard, your stylist," she said, introducing me to a Little Richard lookalike.

Reluctantly, I accepted his outstretched hand and shook it. "What's up, B?" I said, pulling my hand from his clammy grip quickly.

"Hey, chile," Raynard sang, sounding like Little Richard too.

"Well, I guess I'll leave you guys to your work," Colleen said, obviously amused.

"Naw, it's cool. You can stay," I called out, but she was gone.

"Chile, what we gon' do with dis hair?" he said, fondling my miniature fro.

I was mad uncomfortable, but I kept my mind on the bigger picture.

"I wanted some braids, yo, but it ain't long enough yet," I replied.

"If it's braids you want, it's braids you gon' get. Ray Ray gon' hook you up," he sang. "I'ma hafta add a little hair."

"Hey, do you mind if I smoke?" I asked as I retrieved one of the ready-rolled blunts from my pocket.

"Un-uh. I don't mind at all—long as Auntie Ray can get a pull," he said.

"Better yet," I said, reaching back into my pocket, "you can have your own!"

When Raynard said he had to add a little hair, I had a no idea he meant weave. I sat there pissed off as he put extensions in my hair. By the time he finished, we were both pretty high.

"Sitting there with your lip poked out," Ray teased as he trimmed my hairline. "Chile, you gon' love it."

And he was right. I couldn't even tell he'd put weave in. I had an intricate display of cornrows running around my head. "Yo, this shit hot, son!" I said, admiring his handiwork.

"Tol' you Auntie had it going on," he bragged. "Now let's get you dressed."

We stepped over to a rack of clothes, so-called fashions. I tried on almost everything, but nothing fit. They had the size right, but none of it was me.

"Mm-mm-mmm," Raynard huffed. "Ain't none of this gon' work."

I started putting my regular clothes back on, and he got all excited.

"Stop! That's it right there," he exclaimed.

I looked in the mirror, and he was right again. All I had on were my One Ummah jeans and nothing else.

"We ready!" Raynard yelled up front, announcing that his work was done.

I took my place in front of the camera and waited on Asia. I don't know what took so long, because when she came out, all she had on was a robe.

"Sorry," she whispered when she took her place next to me.

"Ready, guys?" the photographer asked.

"Yes," Asia said and dropped the robe.

I dropped my jaw when I saw she was naked except for a thong.

"You like?" She giggled, amused by my reaction.

"You'll see how much I like after the shoot," I warned.

The plan was for us to pose together, with me using my hands to cover her breasts. Finally, he had us face to face, holding each other.

"I can feel you," Asia said about my erection pressing against her.

"No, that's not working. She's too short," the photographer complained.

"How's this?" Asia said, jumping into my arms. She wrapped her legs around my waist as I held her up by her ass.

"Great!" both the director and I yelled.

"This is how I'ma hit it," I whispered in her ear.

"Promises, promises," she said, nibbling on my ear.

The camera's clicked like crazy as we began to kiss.

"This is fucking great!" the photographer exclaimed, shooting the realistic scene.

After a few more minutes of making out and Asia grinding her wet crotch against me, I had had enough.

"Hey, where are you going?" the photographer yelled as I marched off with Asia. We didn't stop kissing the whole way back to my dressing room.

"Shoot's over." Desean laughed. He knew what time it was.

"Oh my!" Raynard squealed when I burst into the room. He saw what was about to go down and grabbed his purse to run out of there.

I never put Asia down. I just dropped my jeans and pulled her wet thong to the side.

By the time we finished, the crew had evacuated. The only people who left were Colleen and Desean. He was still laughing, and she looked like she was in shock.

Asia joined us after a quick shower, and the interview began.

"Um, I don't even know where to start," Colleen said, blushing. "That was, uh...quite a photo shoot!"

"The best I've ever had." Asia giggled.

* * *

I walked through Atlanta's Hartsfield Airport feeling like a million bucks. Desean and I were set to fly out to Cali for my third guest appearance in as many weeks.

Erv-G's people said he was really looking forward to working with me. *Ain't that some shit? Erv-G, Mr. Stupid Swag himself, looking forward to working with little ol' me.*

"Uh-oh!" Day exclaimed as we passed a newspaper stand.

"Oh fuck!" I agreed, looking at the cover of the new *Beat Street Magazine*. In the photo, I had Asia in my arms, and I was shamelessly palming her ass. My head was tilted back like I was in ecstasy as she licked my Adam's apple.

"A-yo, son, Shell is gonna fucking kill you," Desean said, looking at the picture.

"It's not so bad," I said, trying to convince myself.

"Yes it is," he said, opening the copy he'd just paid for.

It got worse with every turn of the page. First was the cover shot. Then, there was me sticking my tongue out and Asia sucking it. Another one showed us engaging in an intimate kiss. On top of that, they airbrushed her thong away to make her appear completely nude.

"A-yo, read it. I made it perfectly clear that we are not together," I demanded.

"Yeah, that will help, 'cause Shell gonna ignore the pictures and just read the words," Day said sarcastically.

"Hip-Hop's Newest Power Couple…

Colleen: So, Lite, let's start with you. That was quite a photo shoot.

Lite: Well, Asia and I are old friends, so it was natural.

Colleen: And you, Miss Asia, you seemed to enjoy it too.

Asia: Yeah, it was intense and had a happy ending. (giggles)

C: Lite, when can we expect the album? The world is waiting!

L: Soon, soon. We're putting it together as we speak. There was a little setback, 'cause my mic tested positive for steroids.

C: People are comparing you guys to Jay and B.

A: B is my hero. Just being mentioned in the same breath is an honor.

L: For real, though, I'm flattered. Jay is the man.

C: They could mean how evasive you guys are about your relationship.

L: What I can tell you is that I am very much in love.

A: Same here. The pictures speak for themselves."

"I'm dead," I said, stopping Day from reading further. They had twisted my words and copied and pasted what we said out of context.

My phone vibrated on my hip, and I was relieved to see Amy's name instead of Shelby's. "Did you see it? Did you see it?" she said, excited. "You guys look great."

"Looking at it now," I said solemnly. "My girl is gonna freak the fuck out when she see it."

"It's entertainment, Lite," Amy said plainly. "What about when you start doing movies? What if you have a love scene?"

"I didn't think of that," I confessed.

"It's Art, Lite. You are an artist," Amy said. "She will understand."

"I guess I'm about to find out," I said as Shelby beeped on the other line.

"Good luck," Amy said and hung up.

"'I'm very much in love'?" Shelby demanded, just short of screaming.

"Hold up, ma. Let me explain," I said casually.

"Explain? What's to explain? Page 89 says all that needs to be said," Shelby spat.

I flipped to the page and winced at the sight. It was a picture of Asia sucking my outstretched tongue. "It's art!" I demanded. "What about when I start doing movies? You gonna leave me every time I have to do a love scene?" By the time I finished twisting it around, she was apologizing to me.

"I'm sorry, baby. It's just that seeing you and another girl…" she said contritely.

"I know, I know. I'm sorry too. How can I make it up to you?" I asked gently.

"928!" Shelby blurted instantly.

"What's that?" I said, unfamiliar with what the numbers represented.

"928. That's the model Porsche I want," Shelby said happily.

"A'ight. That's what's up." I laughed, happy to get through that one. "My flight is boarding. Call you from Cali."

"Well? How'd it go?" Day asked eagerly when I hung up.

"We cool. I'ma buy her a Porsche. It's all good," I replied.

* * *

When we landed in California, we were met at the airport by someone from Erv-G's record company. I don't know what made me think he was coming himself to pick me up. "I guess we'll all hang out or something," I told Day.

"Yeah, or catch him in the studio," Desean consoled.

The session wasn't until the next night, so we got some rest at our hotel before hitting the L.A. night. We did all the tourist stops, then hit a few clubs before calling it a night.

The next morning, I did a few promotional stops that Donnie set up. "Whose Pussy?" was catching steam in the clubs, and radio was demanding a clean version.

When I got to the studio, I was crushed to find out that Erv-G wasn't even in the country. According to the engineer, we didn't even have to go out there to record. They could have e-mailed the track so I could record in our studio and e-mail the lyrics back.

"Fuck it, B. At least we got a free trip," Day said, sensing my frustration. "Go in there and rip that shit up so we can bounce."

And rip it up I did! I was so hot, and that came across in my delivery and actually helped. I sounded so angry that it played into the theme of the song. The track was called "Wet Work," and I sang from the perspective of a hit man. When my cue came up, I rapped,

"I DON'T KNOW WHAT YOU DID, BUT SOMEBODY'S PISSED…
YOU DONE FUCKED AROUND AND GOT YOUR NAME ON MY LIST…
CRY ALL YOU WANT, IT JUST DON'T MATTER…
I'VE BEEN PAID GOOD MONEY TO PUT YOUR HEAD ON A PLATTER…
THIS IS MY PROFESSION, AND THERE'S NO QUESTION I DELIVER…
YOUR HEAD GOES IN THE BAG AND THE REST GOES IN THE RIVER…
YOU BETTER TAKE A FEW SECONDS TO GET RIGHT WITH GOD…
'CAUSE IN A FEW SECONDS, YOU GONNA BE RIGHT WITH GOD…
I'M A HIT MAN FOR HIRE, A WALKING FIRING SQUAD…
INSTEAD OF BEGGING ME, YOU NEED TO HOLLA AT GOD."

"Great job! Erv-G is gonna love it," his people said when I came out of the booth.

"Whatever," I said, still hot about the snub. I didn't even bother to hang around to listen to the playback. Desean had to scramble to collect his camera equipment and catch up with me in the hallway.

CHAPTER 21

The next few months were a flurry of activity. Me and Guy were in the studio every night, frantically trying to get the album finished. Would you believe Shelby actually complained about me not spending enough time with her?

I had also done more guest appearances on other people's albums. As a result, I was on four top-twenty songs at the same time. Donnie had me doing free promo shows every weekend. I didn't complain about not getting paid because the guest spots filled my account.

Likewise, just about everyone I wanted on my album, Donnie made it happen. Ketchup's advice about having a manager with connections rang true.

Desean had finally gotten the news that his knee wasn't strong enough to play, and he took it in stride. He dropped out the next semester to follow me with his camera fulltime.

Tanisha was as big as a house, ready to deliver any day. I usually crashed out at the apartment with her. Besides a little lollipop action here and there, the kid was in a pussy slump.

With radio stations around the country clambering for a clean version of "Whose Pussy?" the label made it a priority. Guy did the radio edit, talking shit the whole time. "It makes no sense to record a dirty song when you know you gotta come back and clean it up," he moaned. "You know radio can't play it like that, and some stores won't even sell it." He had to painstakingly go over the whole song and edit or remove all the curses. There were so many that the radio couldn't keep up, and the song had taken off.

I went back into the booth to record another hook, saying "Whose coochie?" and changing a few of my verses.

"Don't they know this was meant as a joke?" Guy griped when I came out of the booth.

"Looks like the joke's on us. They are making this the lead single," I replied.

While we may have hated the song, the people loved it. It was in heavy rotation nationwide. Veronica said they played it three times in one night when she was in a club.

Donnie scheduled a video shoot and several shows to promote the horrendous song. The first time I had to perform it, I had a major attitude.

I was scheduled to go on at 1 a.m., so we pulled up around 12:30. We sat in the parking lot with Desean filming me chain-smoking blunts.

The promoter called me frantically at ten till, wondering where I was. He claimed the place was packed and the crowd was screaming for me.

"Keep your shirt on. I'm outside," I said curtly and hung up. "Let's get in here so I can kick this bullshit and be out."

"A-yo, B, you need to see this," Desean said as he peeked into the club from backstage. His serious tone caused me to rush over to investigate.

"Fuck!" was all I could manage to say.

The club was packed, and all I saw were women. The street team definitely did their thing, 'cause my posters and flyers were everywhere. At least 100 or so girls were wearing t-shirts bearing my name. Some had taken the liberty of cutting them into halter tops.

"A-yo, somebody's getting hit tonight," I exclaimed. I'd been so busy the last few weeks that I hadn't touched anything, and the drought was over.

After Day got his cameras set up, I alerted the DJ that I was ready. I told him I didn't want a whole lot of fanfare, just to do the song and split.

When I walked onto the stage, the crowd went wild. I hadn't expected that. I just stood there scanning the audience. After a few minutes, the cheers died down, and the club was silent. Still, I stood there. They were looking at me, and I stared right back at them. Finally, I lifted my mic and their spirits and said, "To all y'all chicks who like to put on for their city…on the count of three, let me see them titties!"

I didn't have to count to nothing before the crowd turned into a sea of breasts.

The DJ was right on time, and I went into the song.

I hated the song before I started, but when I got to the first hook, I loved it. When I asked, "Whose pussy is it?" the crowd thundered back that it was mine.

Right up front, there were two beautiful young light-skinned girls going out of their way to be noticed. One of them never even bothered to put her breasts away. I pulled them both onstage and let them dance around for the rest of my performance.

When the song ended, I tried to leave, but the crowd wouldn't hear it. I ended up blessing them with a few more songs before leaving under protest.

Desean saw that I had that look in my eye and gathered up his gear quickly so I couldn't leave him behind…and I would have.

The girls introduced themselves as Baby and Doll and claimed to be cousins. They jumped in the backseat, with Day riding shotgun. "A-yo, we gotta do this quick. V at the house," he whispered.

"I'ma swing this one dolo," I said, breaking his heart.

He looked like he wanted to cry, but that was gonna be my first threesome, and I knew he'd be all right. "What, you think you Charlie Sheen or somebody?" he grumbled lightheartedly.

"Take the truck," I said, pulling in front of the Marriott Marquis. I practically dragged the girls upstairs.

"Put on some music, and we'll dance for you," Doll suggested.

I really wasn't interested in seeing them dance, but I complied 'cause it gave me time to smoke another blunt.

It took the girls two seconds to strip, since all they had on were tiny shorts and cut-off t-shirts bearing my name. They danced around in their thongs until I couldn't take it anymore.

I outed the blunt and called the girls over to the bed. They both started kissing my face, moving downward and stripping me as they went.

"We're gonna have a blowjob contest," Baby announced.

"Yeah, and you gotta pick the winner," Doll said.

Me! I'm the winner!

* * *

The day of the video shoot for "Whose Pussy?" arrived, and I was excited. I had been in plenty of other people's videos from all my guest appearances, but this was all mine.

The other times, I'd roll up, shoot a few scenes, and push, but this was totally different. I had to be on set by 6 a.m.

Judging by the amount of people and equipment, it was a pretty big production. Donnie and Amy were already there waiting on me when I arrived.

"First things first," Amy cheered, producing a diamond necklace. At the end of it was a medallion with my name written in even more diamonds.

"Damn, son!" I exclaimed at the sight of the expensive piece.

"Every rapper needs a little bling," Amy said, on the verge of a cheer.

"You deserve it," Donnie said enthusiastically. "Everything is moving well. Everyone—from Mr. Jennings on down—is pleased."

Our meeting wrapped up just before Day pulled up with Shelby and Veronica. Desean had been a little distant since the Doll-Baby episode, but I figured he'd get over it. He had to understand that it wasn't about him, the basketball star, anymore. It was about me. It was my time to shine.

"Hell no!" Shelby exclaimed when I tried to get her to be in the video. "Won't make no video vixen outta me!"

V, on the other hand, begged to be in the video. Desean made me promise to put her down. She had an outfit that was just a stitch above naked, and was killing even the professional models.

The director called for the first scene, which was the mandatory club scene—the one with the artist chillin' in the VIP section, surrounded by pretty women, sipping Crys', everything in slow motion.

When he announced that he needed a couple of girls to sit by me, he caused a small stampede. Doll-Baby worked as a team and muscled their way to one side, while V shoved some girl down to get to the other. Shelby frowned, then laughed at the spectacle.

The filming began, and I lip-synced through the song. The chorus came, and all the women said the pussy was mine.

Shelby was so disgusted by Baby and Doll rubbing and kissing on me that she got up and left.

I took the stage for a mock performance in the next scene. Again, I was joined by a bevy of beautiful women. We shot the same scenes over and over, until the director finally called for lunch at 1.

With an hour to spare, I took Doll-Baby to my trailer so they could have a rematch. The last contest had ended in a draw, so they battled it out again, and again, I was the winner.

A rented Lamborghini was the set of my next scene. It would be pulled by a truck as I pretended to drive. I wanted Day by my side, but the director insisted on a woman.

Veronica had showed out so much in the earlier scenes that he chose her.

When the director yelled, "ACTION!" I lip-synced to the song as the car was pulled along. V was working it, dancing and rubbing and kissing on me. I caught a glance of Day, and son was .38 hot. When I got to the line about getting head in the whip, Veronica dropped her head into my lap. It was a good thing the car was being pulled, because when she kissed the wood through my pants, I wanted to pull off.

Finally, we shot endless takes in front of a green screen, changing clothes 100 times. The director explained that they would use computer graphics and put different backgrounds in place of the green screens.

It was almost 6 a.m. again by the time the shoot was wrapped—twenty-four hours of work, listening to the same song over and over and over again. Since Shelby had left them stranded, Day and V rode in the Range with me, and wouldn't you know that song was playing on the radio? Desean sucked his teeth and reached over to turn it off. The only reason I didn't say anything was because I was so tired of hearing it myself.

I pulled up to the front entrance so they could get out, and as soon as the door closed, I pulled off without a word. I wasn't in the mood for Desean's attitude or Shelby's bitching. They swore I was changing and letting shit go to my head, but they were the ones acting different. *My song moves up the charts every day, and do they give me props? Hell no!* "Fuck 'em," I said, steering the whip to a place where I knew I would be appreciated.

I fully expected Tanisha to be asleep when I slid my key into the lock. The plan was to slide in bed next to her and crash out. To my surprise, she was sitting in the living room watching TV. "What's good, ma? What are you doing up?" I asked as I entered the apartment.

"Your son is in here playing soccer," she said, rubbing her huge stomach.

"Son?" I replied, placing my hand on hers.

"If it's a girl kicking like this, we in trouble." She laughed.

I watched as she reached into the sardine tin on the table and extracted one. She placed the small, slimy fish in her mouth, then quickly followed it with a spoonful of butter pecan ice cream. "You are so nasty!" I laughed.

"Mm-hmm, and you like it," she said, laughing with me.

I laid my head on her lap and enjoyed the peace and adulation that I couldn't get at home.

* * *

"Hey, baby, time to get up," Tanisha purred in my ear while gently shaking me. "You said 8 o'clock."

I don't know how I got into the bedroom, but that was where I woke up.

"Go on and get your shower so you can eat before you go," she said, laying a freshly ironed outfit on the bed.

"Where I gotta go?" I asked, still groggy from the long sleep.

"Uh, to the studio." She laughed. "Remember? You s'posed to do the song with Signature and Red Clay today."

"Oh yeah!" I said, leaping from the bed, now fully awake.

I had been dying to do a song with either one of those cats, and Donnie got me both. Signature was another rapper from the Bronx with mad skills. He had just done a five-year bid stemming from a shootout with the Atlanta PD. Son got hit six times! Red Clay was from the Adamsville section of Atlanta, known for his fierce lyrical skills and a dangerous street rep'. He had just beaten a second murder charge, and his album was rushing up the charts. Donnie felt that me doing a song with the two bona fide street soldiers would bolster my street cred'. He and Amy played up my being questioned by police as a murder arrest and leaked it, along with the story of me getting shot. The results even fooled me; they made me a gangsta!

I rushed through a shower and quickly changed into my clothes.

Tanisha was in the kitchen fixing me a plate of fried chicken, macaroni and cheese, and collard greens. "Hey, boo," she said, sitting the plate in front of me, topping it off with a kiss on my forehead.

It was times like that when I had to reevaluate my relationship with Shell. I was treating her like a queen and Tanisha like the chick on the side. Truth be told, I got everything from Tanisha and nothing from Shelby. I realized I had some decisions to make.

I was an hour late getting to the studio, which was on time in my business. I pulled up and parked at the same time Red Clay arrived, pushing a brand new Bentley Coupe with the sticker still in the window. "What's good, fam'?" I said enthusiastically.

"Chillin', shawty," he replied, giving me a pound and a hug.

"I thought all y'all ATL cats pushed was Donks," I said, admiring the quarter-million-dollar whip.

"Got twelve of dem," he replied, "but I like that imported shit too."

As we spoke, a bubble Chevy on thirty-inch rims pulled up, banging Tupac. When Signature got out of it, me and Red Clay looked at each other and laughed.

Guy was already in place in front of the boards when we made our way into the studio. I greeted him, then introduced him to Red and Sig. We all turned our phones off and pulled out blunts, ready to get to work.

We finally agreed on a M'Tuni Brown track and began to write. Each of us separated with our pads and scribbled away furiously. The mood was festive, but mad competitive at the same time. We were doing the song together, but on the low, we were going at each other. No one wants to be outdone, especially me on my own song.

It was after 1 in the morning before we took to the booth. The name of the song was "Robbing Spree," an ode to armed robbery. We collaborated on a hook to be sung in the melody of Tupac's "Hail Mary." One by one, we laid our contributions to the chorus, then got down to business.

Signature went first and straight murdered it. He came out of the booth with a smug look on his face that said, *"Top that!"* It made me feel like tearing my verse up and starting over.

Red Clay went next and showed no mercy. He had the same satisfied look on his face when he came out. "It's all you, shawty, but careful…it's still hot."

This time, I did ball up the paper containing my verse as I hit the booth. *Live by the freestyle and die by it,* I thought as I put the headphones on. My cue came, and I said,

"I'M LIKE DEBO TO ALL Y'ALL FUCKIN' LAMES…

SEE ME COMING, YOU BETTER TUCK YOUR CHAIN…

OR I'LL HIT YOU WITH SOME SHIT THAT WILL TOUCH YOUR BRAIN...

I COULDN'T CARE LESS ABOUT WHAT YOU CLAIM...

COME OFF THEM JEWELS OR FEEL A RUSH OF PAIN...

DON'T LAUGH. THIS AIN'T NO TYPE OF FUCKING GAME...

Y'ALL BETTER ACT LIKE Y'ALL KNOW MY MOTHERFUCKIN' NAME...

INFER RED SIGHTS, SO I DON'T HAVE TO AIM...

YOU CAN GET IT AT ANY GIVEN TIME...

DON'T SPEND A DIME. I SHOP WITH THE NINE...

COME TO THE 'HOOD AND STICK YOU AND YOUR MANS UP...

BUST THE FIRST NIGGA TO GET BRAVE AND TRY TO, MAN UP...

SHIT, I'LL EVEN STICK MY OWN FANS UP...

MATTER FACT, Y'ALL GET YA MOTHERFUCKIN' HANDS UP."

Both Sig and Red Clay nodded in approval when I came out of the booth.

"We got us one, shawty!" Red said, giving me a pound.

"Stick your fans up?" Signature chuckled. "Son, you ill!"

CHAPTER 22

"Look at you!" Amy gushed as I walked into her office with my new jewels.

I had used the company card and copped a few new pieces. I bought a chunky diamond bracelet and ring to go with it. I also picked up a one-carat stud for my ear and a few trinkets for my ladies.

She was still admiring my new etceteras when Donnie stormed in. "Hot off the presses!" he announced, holding up the final edit of my video.

We viewed the finished product and were totally satisfied with the results. The shots filmed in front of the green screen allowed me to travel the globe.

I laughed as women from all over the world proclaimed that the pussy was mine. "Shelby's gonna love that." I laughed, anticipating her reaction. I did wince at the scene when Veronica dropped her head into my lap. "Oh, Day's gonna love that."

At my request, we watched the video several times before getting down to business.

"Okay. The video goes to all networks today, and it is already viral on the Web," Donnie announced. "Where are we with the album?"

"Almost done. Just waiting on Asia to come do her part on the last song," I advised.

Asia had come up with an idea for a song while she was on the road. She called me from her tour and sang it to me. It was so hot that I refused to wrap up until we included it.

"She will be back tomorrow," Amy advised.

"Well, get her into the studio so we can put this one to bed," Donnie demanded. "We are running behind. I want the product in the mastering house in a week and off to the presses after that."

"No problem. It will be done," Amy said, trying to soothe him. "How many are we shipping?"

"Two million." He smiled and turned to me. "You will be platinum in a week."

* * *

I was getting $5,000 a show now, but Donnie said that would double once the album dropped. He had me performing literally every night of the week, with two shows on the weekends. Atlanta is the type of city that parties every night.

I was onstage, giving it my all, when my new Blackberry vibrated on my hip. Since only one person had the number, I immediately knew what it was. Tanisha was in labor!

I finished the song, but not the set, and took off for the hospital.

When I got to the Maternity Ward, I was told that Tanisha needed a C-section and that I could only stay for a few minutes.

"Dang, baby, you look a mess," I teased as I entered the delivery room.

"You did it!" She pouted and tried to smooth her hair.

"Just me, huh?" I laughed, helping her with her hair.

We held hands and chatted it up until the nurses ran me off.

"I'ma have a scar." Tanisha pouted as I left the room.

"Look on the bright side. At least the coochie won't get stretched." I laughed.

"Get out, stupid." She chuckled as the nurses moved in.

* * *

"There go your daddy," Tanisha cooed to the small bundle in her arms.

My knees went weak, and I had trouble crossing the room.

"Come on and meet your son," she said triumphantly.

"My son," I repeated in awe as I took the baby in my arms. "What's good, B?" I chuckled, staring at my miniature face.

"He look just like you," Tanisha said proudly. "Look at his eyes."

Instead, I looked at his toes. My two middle toes are longer than my big toe, a trait my mom said I inherited from my father. "He got my toes, yo!" I laughed, seeing that I had passed that along to him.

* * *

Me, Shell, Desean, and Veronica gathered at the condo to watch the world premiere of the "Whose Pussy?" video.

I took the time to give Shelby the "It's just entertainment…" pep talk, and she didn't get upset. Instead, she made fun of Veronica and all the other hoochies. She really found the part where V dropped her head in my lap funny, but Day was fuming. "Girl, you gonna win a video vixen award," she teased.

"You just mad 'cause I went down on your man." V laughed back.

The girls were cracking up when Desean got up and stormed off to the patio.

Seeing my boy was clearly distressed, I followed him out. "What's up, son?" I said, lighting a blunt and taking a pull.

"Chillin', superstar," he replied curtly.

"A'ight, yo," I said firmly, "let's have it. What's wrong?"

"I think you fucking my girl," he said, taking the blunt.

"What girl?" was the best I could come up with.

"Nigga, you know what girl. V, nigga!" he spat angrily.

"A-yo, B, how you gonna say some foul shit like that?" I replied, feigning indignance.

"Just a feeling I get when she around you, and when you ain't around, it's 'Lite this' and 'Lite that'," he lamented.

"She just excited to be around a celebrity, B," I explained. "Y'all used to it 'cause y'all know me, but you see how people treat me now."

"Yeah, and I see how you take advantage of it," he spat.

"Nigga, I'm supposed to! I earned that shit!" I yelled. "Don't let me find out you jealous."

"I just want to know if you fucking my girl," he said, pleading.

"Son, I would never violate our friendship, but if you don't trust her, you need to cut her off," I said sincerely.

"I can't. I love her too much. I'm gonna marry that girl," he whined.

You can't imagine how bad I felt fucking Veronica that next day, but as soon as Day and Shell went off on their business, we went at it on the living room sofa. V showed me a new position she called "the sidewinder." The shit was off the hook. I couldn't wait to try it on Shelby.

* * *

The decision to wait for the duet with Asia proved to be a wise one. We dropped it as the second single, and it shot to number one.

My album release party was nothing short of spectacular. It was held in a new club in the same Atlantic Station area as my condo. From my window, I could see throngs of people lining up outside.

When I arrived, the party was in full swing. It was a virtual who's-who of rap music royalty. I was getting major love from the same artists I looked up to. Major rap cats were sending me congratulations and champagne.

Shelby looked stunning, as usual, but I could tell she felt uncomfortable in the skimpy designer dress. "My boob keeps trying to pop out," she complained as she adjusted herself.

"Let it out, ma. It's a party," I teased, earning a punch in the shoulder.

I had the best seat in the house and watched as the crowd danced to my music. Bliz was DJ-ing and vowed to only spin my songs.

I got a scare as Asia approached the able. "Hey, baby! Congratulations," she said, opening her arms to hug me.

"Thanks, ma," I said, standing to hug her back. As we embraced, I whispered in her hear, "This is my girl Shelby." We pulled apart, and I introduced Asia to the table.

"Oh, so you're the lucky lady Lite's always talking about?" Asia sang as she shook Shelby's hand.

Shell was polite, but her face said, *"Yeah, right."*

"Are you going to Belize for the photo shoot?" Asia asked Shell, already knowing she wasn't.

"No. I have class," Shell replied, but Asia missed the insult.

"Oh, that's too bad," Asia replied, stifling a smirk. "Well, it was nice to meet you."

"I know what you're up to," Shelby said as I handed her another glass of champagne.

"What?" I asked, afraid to know what she was talking about. I was, after all, up to a lot of different shit.

"Trying to get me drunk so you can have your way with me," she said, to my relief.

"Is it working?" I asked slyly.

"Mm-hmm. You gonna get some tonight," Shelby said seductively. "From the front, the back, the side—any way you want it."

I knew I would probably catch hell for leaving my own album release party, but as I hit Shell from the front, the back, and the side, that was the furthest thing from my mind. After making love, we cuddled up and kicked it for the first time in months.

"I love you. You know that, don't you?" I said, planting a gentle kiss on Shelby's forehead.

"Me and all the rest," she said lightly.

"I don't love them. I fuck 'em, then fuck them!" I laughed.

"I believe you," she said seriously.

"I'm just playing, ma. You know I don't mess with no one else," I said quickly.

"Boy, stop," Shelby said, getting up on one elbow. "Look, Dave, don't insult me. I'm not crazy. I know you fuck with other chicks."

"I don't know what you're talking about," I said innocently.

"Yeah, right! You be tryna twist me up in all these new positions. 'Turn this way…Lift your leg…' and what was that business with the spatula? No…don't even tell me," she said. "You getting that shit from somewhere."

I tried to say something in my defense, but she waved me off.

"I know with my schedule it's hard to spend time, so I know you fuck around. It was painfully clear at your video shoot."

"What about the video shoot?" I protested.

"Them two half-white-looking bitches. Don't give me that 'It's entertainment' bullshit either. Them hoes was way too comfortable. Oh, and that little bitch Asia." Shelby chuckled.

"Asia? You heard her, and—"

"Negro, puh-lease! You think I went for that shit. I started to get up and whoop her ass for playing with me," Shelby spat.

"Look, baby, I—"

"Come on, Dave. Don't lie to me," she said anxiously. "You ain't been lying to me. All I'm saying is, don't give me nothing, don't make no babies, and once we get married, no more!"

"I hear you," I said, neither confirming nor denying anything.

"I mean it, Dave. No second chances. You play me, and I'm gone," she said. "I don't ask you for much. Feed me when I'm hungry. Talk to me when I'm lonely, and fuck me when I'm horny."

"So I'm a piece of meat, huh?" I laughed.

"Yeah. So get that spatula and come on," she said.

CHAPTER 23

Tanisha was turning out to be an excellent mother. Every time I went over there, little Dave was in her arms, like she never put him down.

"He just like his daddy," I joked as she breastfed our son.

"You crazy." She laughed before changing expressions. "So, how long you gonna be down there?" Tanisha pouted.

"Just the weekend. It's a two-day shoot," I said to console her.

"I'm sorry I can't go with you, but I ain't leaving my baby with nobody," she stressed.

"Yeah, I feel you. Maybe next time," I said, relieved that she wasn't going. Asia had been talking real nasty on the phone, and I was gonna hold her to it that weekend.

Donnie wasn't bullshitting about going platinum in a week. By the time we left for Belize, three days after its release, the album passed gold. "Today's numbers!" Donnie announced gleefully, getting everyone's attention in the private jet. "People, we've hit 512,000 units! Gold in three days, ladies and gentlemen."

The occupants of the G-4 jet gave ourselves a round of applause. Only management and the artist took the private jet down, and the rest of the crew traveled in a chartered plane. Mr. Jennings was springing for a big-budget video.

When the plane touched down in Central America, a convoy of rental Jeeps whisked us away to our hotel. We were told to enjoy ourselves for the day and be ready to work bright and early in the morning.

Me and Day caught a water taxi out to one of the keys and went snorkeling, while Asia and her girls went sightseeing at some Aztec ruins. After a dinner of the freshest seafood and a joint of the greenest weed, I called it a night.

The cast and crew assembled for breakfast at 6 a.m. and got down to business. The treatment called for me and Asia alone in most of the scenes. A private beach was rented so we could folic in the white sand and blue water. We rapped and sang to each other, jet skiing, parasailing, and just walking in the surf.

That night, we shot a club scene using the locals as extras. It was after midnight when we finished shooting. Asia and I had been planning to hook up that night, but both our camps had meetings, so we couldn't pull it off.

The next day, we had to shoot a scene at the hotel pool, and since it was a love song, it required a love scene. I wondered how we were supposed to be romantic with fifty people milling about. Asia and I were both naked under the thin sheets.

The director told us, "Make it as realistic as possible." When he yelled, "AC-TION!" we began kissing and caressing as the song played in the background.

The excitement kept building until I somehow slipped inside of her.

Desean was the first one who noticed that we'd gone from trying to make it look real to really being real. "My nigga!" I heard him laugh before clearing the room. "E'rrybody out! We ain't making no porno." He ushered everyone out, but a few cameras managed to stay on.

Once the room was clear, we pushed away the covers and got to it.

* * *

Since my own tour wasn't scheduled to begin for a couple of months. I had no objections to finishing the Galaxy tour with them. They had ten shows left when I joined them in Kansas City.

I wasn't crazy about the $10,000 a show, but it was a quick 100 stacks—not to mention Donnie had over 100 dates for my own tour at $25,000 each.

Since Bliz was now my official DJ, he and Desean flew out to KC with me. We landed and had to rush straight to the arena, with no time to spare. As soon as we arrived, I was pushed onto the stage. I was not ready for what lay ahead of me.

I had been performing for years, so I was no stranger to an audience, but an arena? There I was in front of 30,000 people, all screaming my name.

Day turned the camera on the crowd as they changed, "Whose pussy! Whose pussy!"

I gave Bliz the nod, and he cued up the song so we could give them what they wanted. I did a few more songs, then stepped aside for Galaxy.

We both had separate after-party obligations, so Asia and I agreed to meet up at the hotel. Local promoters would pay to stop by a club and hang out for a minute, and it was a good hustle—a couple tax-free stacks cash to get a few drinks and a few freaks.

I stayed long enough for Bliz and Day to bag a couple honeys. They had one for me—or more because of me—but she was gonna be disappointed.

Egypt and China were still in Asia's room when I got there. We all kicked it for a while until Asia started dropping hints for them to leave.

"Y'all don't do nothing we wouldn't do," China said as they stood to leave.

"Ain't nothing y'all hoes don't do," Asia teased.

"We ain't making no porno tapes." Egypt laughed, leaving the room.

"Porno?" I asked eagerly.

"They playing," Asia said, quickly climbing on top of me.

We spent every moment of the rest of the tour together with the paparazzi catching every kiss and every hug.

I got a terse call from Shelby every time a photo was printed of me and Asia. I gave her the "It's entertainment" speech and a piece of jewelry, which always did the trick.

* * *

By the time I set out on my own tour, my album was already double platinum. As a result of the heavy demand, another thirty stops were added, and my price was up to thirty grand.

Donnie advised me that with the exposure from the tour, I should move another two million units—not to mention a couple hundred thousand in pocket money from after-parties.

Me, Bliz, and Desean hit every state like a tornado. I had six shows in New York, which allowed me to spend a couple days at home—no hotels, no room service, and just Ma Dukes.

"So what about Shelby?" my mother whined when I showed her the pictures of her grandson. "And why am I finding out a year later?"

"Ain't been no year. Dave ain't but, like, six or seven months," I corrected.

"That means you had over a year to tell me," she said, pinching my arm, "and what about Shelby? What she got to say about this handsome little fellow?"

"I mean, she…you know what I'm saying?" I stammered.

"You haven't told her, have you?" she said, pointing a finger. "She doesn't know!"

"No," I confessed meekly.

"Boy, are you crazy?" she said in disbelief. "This is not something you can keep secret. You have to tell her."

"So what you think of the album? You been watching my videos?" I said, changing the subject.

"I think you have a filthy mouth is what I think," she said, causing me to laugh at her disgusted expression. "Ain't nothing funny, crazy boy," she snapped. "They play that one nasty song 100 times a damn day. Everybody at the hospital saying, 'That's Nurse Angela's son'."

"You know you like that," I teased.

"I am proud of you, but…but what happened?" she asked seriously.

"A-yo, I had to give the people what they want," I said easily now that I had started believing it myself—and now that I was rich because of it.

"I used to love your little poems," she said, smiling fondly. "You had a poem for everything—and I mean everything! Oh, I do like the one they play on the radio now, the one with the girl.'

"'Delightful'? That's Asia, from Galaxy," I advised.

"Oh, but that video! That's just disgusting. Has Shelby seen that?" she asked.

"Dang, Ma! Who are you, her agent? Shelby is fine with it. It's art, entertainment," I said, frustrated.

"Okay, okay. Don't get upset. Don't want you to curse me out like one of your songs," she said sarcastically.

"You crazy, Ma," I said, kissing her cheek. "I'm 'bout to bounce. I'll be back before I leave the city."

"Wait, son," she said tentatively. "I need to speak with you about something."

The seriousness in her tone caused me to be concerned, so I sat back down next to her. "Are you okay, Ma?" I inquired.

"Me? Yeah, I'm fine, but...well, your dad...uh, your dad wants you to speak with him," she blurted.

It took a few seconds to process what she had said, so I asked her to repeat herself just to be sure I had heard her correctly.

"Your father. You need to call your father," she repeated under her breath.

"My father?" I asked, incredulous. "What? He must have seen a young nigga on TV, huh? Smell a little dough?"

"Baby, it's not like that. It's not his fault," she pleaded.

"Not like what? Whose fault is it? Mine?!" I yelled.

"No. It's mine," my mother admitted through her tears.

"I'm grown now. Too late for a Daddy now," I said, getting ready to leave.

"Please, baby, just—" was all she could get out before I stormed out of the apartment.

I saw my mother a couple of days later, before I left, and she forced his number on me. She said he was in Albuquerque, New Mexico. I had no intention of calling dude. *For what? He wasn't there to teach me to ride a bike. Shit, I still can't ride a bike.*

* * *

The tour took us to Jersey, down Philly way, and back up to CT. It was packed shows, followed by packed after-parties, followed by packed hotel rooms.

I was amazed at what chicks would do with me, for me, and to me just because I was famous. What was more amazing was that most of us let us tape them. They had to know that shit would eventually end up online.

That was why we made sure our faces never got caught on tape. When the sex tape of me and Asia got leaked, no one could say it was me. The media could only speculate, even though she called my name several times because no one saw my face. She, on the other hand, was clearly featured when she turned around to ride me backward. Asia refused to say who the male was in the tape—only that it was her man. The controversy got me twenty more tour stops, and she said she was going to get a solo deal out of it.

Of course Shelby called to complain, but in the end, she didn't have enough evidence, and I was acquitted of all charges.

Detroit, Gary, Cleveland, Cincinnati, and then Chi-town; the Midwest; the Deep South, and the West Coast; Washington State and—to my surprise—they were banging my shit in Oregon; down to Cali, Sacramento, San Diego, Vegas, and back over to the bay.

When we reached Albuquerque, we had a two-day rest before our show, and then we would be back on the road. I sat in the hotel room for hours, staring at the piece of paper, until Day intervened.

"A-yo, B, call him," he said, putting a hand on my shoulder.

"A'ight, yo," I relented, "but this nigga better have a bike."

CHAPTER 24

"Light residence," a cheerful voice sang with an accent I couldn't quite place.

I hesitated for a second, then hung up. For some reason, I caught an attitude and called right back. "Let me speak with David Light," I demanded.

"Sure. May I tell him who's calling?" the lovely voice responded, unfazed by my tone.

"Just put him on the phone!" I huffed.

"Sure...just one second," the woman said, putting the phone down.

A few moments later, my father was on the line. "David Light," he announced in a friendly, yet questioning tone.

"David Light, huh? Well, this is David Light too," I spat, full of contempt.

There was a silence on the line as he processed the words. "My...my son?" he muttered in disbelief. "David, as in my son?"

"That's what my mother claims," I said curtly.

"I've been waiting for you to call," he said anxiously.

"Yeah, I know what that's like," I shot back.

If he knew I was trying to bait him into an argument, I couldn't tell. He let all my sarcastic remarks pass without comment.

"I hear you're quite the celebrity," he said proudly. "They play your songs all day on the radio down here where I live. I live in Albuquerque. Ever been here?"

"You mean before now?" I quipped.

More silence to process, making me wonder if dude was a little slow. "You here now? In New Mexico?" he asked.

"Yeah. I got a show in the arena night after tomorrow," I replied.

"That's great! You gotta come see me!" he shouted.

I wanted to say no and tell him to go fuck himself and be done with it, but I didn't. I couldn't. The next thing I knew, I was giving a taxi driver his address.

I was dressed down in a plain One Ummah sweat suit and sneakers. I had no jewels on, but I had a couple stacks in my pocket in case the nigga was down on his luck. I had calmed down a little, until I got to his house at least. "Are you sure this is the right place?" I asked the cabbie as he came to a stop in an upscale subdivision.

"You said 487 Bell Harbor. This is the place," he said as I checked it against what was written on the paper in my hand.

"I guess so." I shrugged and passed a $100 bill forward.

"I don't have change for that," the driver said.

"Naw, keep it," I ordered, getting out of the car.

"Thanks, sir," he gushed. "Take my card. Call when you're ready, and the next trip's on me."

I stood in the driveway for several minutes, looking up at the large house. It was a typical southwestern stucco, three stories high with expansive landscaping. A new, shiny Jaguar sat in front of the two-car garage. "Oh, this nigga been balling while me and Ma Dukes in the fucking 'hood!" I said, psyching myself back up. I wasn't sure what to be mad about, exactly, but I had a pretty good attitude going by the time I rang the doorbell.

"Oh my God!" a beautiful, dark-skinned woman screamed when she pulled the door open. "You look just like your father." Her accent sounded almost British, not quite Caribbean. "Come, come," she said, pulling me into the house by my hand. "Your dad's back here." She led me to the den, where my dad was reclined in a plush leather chair.

"David?" he asked, rising gingerly from his seat.

I didn't know what to do or so, so I just stood there for a moment. "What's up, B?" I said as he made his way over to me.

"My son, my son," he said, engulfing me in his arms.

I didn't return his hug initially, but he held me tightly, rocking gently back and forth. I eventually joined the embrace as tears flowed freely from all of our eyes. Even the woman who had answered the door was crying.

"Come on in. Have a seat," he said, pointing to the sofa.

I finally took a good look at him and was amazed at how much he looked like me. I saw what the future me looked like, but I thought he looked older than the forty-five that he was supposed to be.

The conversation started slowly and built momentum as we went along. It was mainly small talk as I flipped through a photo album that featured mainly me. Some pictures contained him, some with my mom, but all of them had me in them. I glanced around the room and saw that it was full of more pictures of me.

The woman who had let me in peeked in and asked if we needed anything. I declined all offers over both of their insistence. She looked to be about my age but was far too dark to be his offspring. I caught a glimpse of her frame as she left and nodded approvingly. She filled out the light pink hospital scrubs quite well. Dad was obviously an ass man, like his son.

"A-yo, who dat? Your girl?" I finally asked.

"Who, Khadijah? No, no!" He chuckled. "She is my nurse."

"Nurse? What you got a nurse for?" I asked.

"Uh, let's talk about that later, okay?" he replied, making me more curious.

"A'ight. So where you been?" I asked, point blank.

"Where do I begin?" He signed.

"How 'bout the beginning?" I shot back.

He took a deep breath and began to tell his side of the story. "Your mom and I were both young when we met. She is a year younger than me, but she was the mature one, and when we found out she was pregnant, she grew up instantly. I didn't. I mean, I tried. Even bought her a little ring and asked her to marry me. I just…I couldn't keep it in my pants."

"I can relate." I laughed at my own dilemma with my own penis. Dude had a mind of its own.

"Well, she kept catching me. I'd say I was sorry and swear I wouldn't do it no more, then get caught again. When she found out I slept with her best friend, that was it. She vowed to never let me see you again, and she meant it. Your mom can be a very stubborn person."

"No! My mom?" I laughed, knowing full well just how stubborn she could be.

He pulled a box from the closet and dumped the contents on the sofa. I leafed through years of birthday cards and letters, all addressed to me, with "Return to Sender" written on them in my mother's handwriting.

"I sent cards every year on July 18, but they came right back. She wouldn't even take the money!"

"Okay, I know how Ma Dukes is, but why you ain't take her to court or something?" I asked wearily.

"Court?" he asked, incredulous. "Son, I was knee deep in the streets. Court was the last place I was trying to be. I got in some trouble, so I bounced out here to wait out the statute of limitations. I ended up in school, got a degree, and started my advertising company. I lived my life, but I never forgot about you."

"I see," I said, still flipping through the returned mail.

"Time for your meds," Khadijah said firmly. She handed my father a plastic pill cup filled with pills of assorted sizes and colors.

"Khadijah, let me formally introduce you to my son," he said proudly. The way he said "son" was the way I said it when referring to lil' Dave, and that made me proud as well.

I stood and extended my hand.

She lowered her gaze and giggled shyly as she took my hand. "Nice to meet you," she blurted before pulling her hand away and rushing from the room.

I got a kick out of her modesty, especially considering the type of women I met on tour.

"So, tell me about the music biz," my dad said.

"What's to tell? I'm the man right now," I said, not intending to brag.

He laughed my exact laugh. DNA is no joke, 'cause he moved the way I moved and vice versa. It was uncanny watching him.

After I filled him in on my career, he filled me in on his. He told me he'd worked for a major advertising company for years before striking out on his own. He was the creative force behind a good number of brands I was familiar with. "Remember the jingle for the Bomb-bey Energy Drink last year?" he asked gleefully.

"Yeah. The one with the corny rapper?" I laughed as the catchy ad came to mind.

"Hey! Watch ya'self!" He laughed. "Rapping is harder than it looks."

"Say word! That was you?" I said, cracking up. "I guess I got it naturally, huh?"

"Yeah. It was all going well until I got sick," he said morbidly.

"You look a'ight to me," I said, in hopes of cheering him up. I watched as sadness filled his eyes and the corners of his mouth turned down.

"It's pretty bad, son…terminal," he said. "Stage 4. There is no Stage 5."

"Cancer, B?" I said hotly. "And you just now telling me?"

"Told your mom months ago that I urgently needed to speak with you. I guess she finally decided to relay the message when I told her I was sick," he replied.

We kicked it for a while longer, until his meds put him to sleep.

I didn't feel right about just leaving while he was out, so I waited. I got hungry enough to look for the kitchen, in search of food.

"Hey there! Can I get you something?" Khadijah asked as I entered the kitchen.

"If you don't mind," I replied courteously. "I'm starved."

"No problem. I was just about to fix myself something, and food for one can feed two." She smiled the prettiest, whitest smile I'd probably ever seen. I watched her intently as she prepared the food, and I noticed again how pretty she was. She was too dark for my taste, but pretty nonetheless. Khadijah stood maybe five-two and was a good, solid 130. Her hair was done in thick braids that framed her smooth black face. "That's not polite," she said with a giggle when she caught me staring.

"My bad. So tell me about yourself," I said, trying to initiate some small talk.

"I may as well, since I already know all about you." She giggled. "I'm a year older than you. I'm from the Gambia."

"South America?" I asked ignorantly.

"No. East Africa," she corrected with another giggle. She rarely made eye contact as we talked, until the subject of my father came up. According to Khadijah, my dad was a cross between Martin Luther King and Muhammad Ali. She had been assigned as his healthcare nurse and worked through an agency until his health insurance ran out recently. "Those dirty kufar wanted to just leave him all alone!" she said, seething. "It's all about money with those people, so I quit. I stayed without pay. He is my dad too. We are family," she announced proudly.

"So how y'all getting by?" I wondered.

"I am taking real estate courses now, but I will quit school and find work. Your father doesn't know it, but he is running out of money," she whispered.

"You'll do no such thing," I said adamantly. I went in my pocket and retrieved the cash I had with me.

"No, we can't take your money. We will get by," Khadijah said confidently.

"I know *we* will," I said, including myself in the family. Suddenly, the weight of it all overwhelmed me. I had met my dad and found out I was going to lose him, all in the same day. I was supposed to be mad, to hate him, but I couldn't. He was a good dude, and his den was a shrine of my childhood. "I've been looking for him my whole life." I sobbed, and I couldn't remember the last time I'd cried.

"It's okay," Khadijah consoled, coming around the table and taking me into her arms.

I spent several minutes in her bosom, wracked with tears. I felt better after the good cry, albeit a little embarrassed. After I regained my composure, we picked our conversation back up.

"Your dad loves your music," she beamed. "Every time it comes on the radio, which is 100 times a day, he makes me turn it up."

"Oh yeah?" I asked. "How 'bout you? You like it?"

"Well…" she began, then paused, as if searching for the right words. "You have a very nasty mouth…filthy!" She chuckled.

I laughed with her, then explained how the record company had forced me to change my content. For the first time, I didn't try to justify it.

"You're okay, I guess. I'm more partial to John Mayer myself," she added.

When the sun peeked through the windows, we realized we had spent the entire night chatting. I ate breakfast with my dad when he awoke, and then I headed back to the hotel. After a couple of hours of sleep, I was back at his house.

I spent all my time in Albuquerque with my father and/or Khadijah. I only left to go destroy the arena, then again when it was time to move on.

My father said he would plug me in with some of his advertising connects and get me some endorsements. He even actually tried to give me some money to hold me over.

I made Khadijah pinky swear not to tell my dad about the money I gave her.

Since she wasn't familiar with a pinky swear, I told her she had to cut her finger off if she told.

I left with a vow to speak with them every day, and I did. No matter what city I was in, I made sure to call. I would talk to my dad until he fell asleep, then to Khadijah until the wee hours of the morning.

CHAPTER 25

W hen we finally returned to Atlanta, I had a check for over a million dollars waiting on me. It was a payment for the tour, and my first royalty check was about due as well.

Bliz got 200 grand for his contribution as the DJ, while day got 100. I found it hard to believe Desean was hot about getting less than Bliz. *Hot about $100,000 to travel around the country and fuck groupies? Fuck...man! Most niggas would die for that shot.*

All those zeros on that check made my Range Rover look suddenly old. With Shelby by my side and Desean in the backseat, I set off to replace my truck. "This looks like the place," I announced, pulling into the lot of an exotic car dealership. "This you," I said, tossing the keys and ownership of the Range to Desean.

"My nigga!" he said and pulled off to go spend some of his own money.

Suddenly, Shelby took off running, as if possessed. I laughed my ass off when she reached a convertible Porsche and tried to hug it. It wasn't so funny, though, when I did the same to a silver Aston Martin in the showroom.

"Eh...um...that vehicle is 185,000—dollars, that is," a snobby salesman said as he approached. His attitude pissed me off instantly.

We both looked each other down with our noses turned up.

He wore slacks, a tailored shirt, a bowtie, and a nice pair of wingtips, while I was sporting a baggy pair of One Ummah shorts, a wife-beater, and Tims.

"A-yo, what y'all getting for that Boxter out there?" I inquired.

"If you're referring to the Porsche, that...that *woman* is currently smudging, it's $94,000," he said. The way he emphasized the word "dollars" made me wonder if he thought I planned to pay with rubles or yen.

"A'ight. Give me both then," I said, producing my black card.

His demeanor changed instantly once he saw I was not some regular street nigga. I was a street nigga with cake, and that changed everything. "Can I get you anything else, Mr. Light?" he asked graciously, looking at my name on the card.

"Yeah. As a matter of fact, I'm feeling them wingtips," I said seriously.

The cars were given a quick wash and pulled up front as I completed the transaction. After the insurance cards were faxed over, we were on our way with $300,000 worth of automobiles and a shiny pair of shoes.

"Thank you, thank you. Please come back again," the barefoot salesman yelled as we left.

Shelby went straight to class, so I pulled into a Jaguar lot and copped Tanisha the same model my dad owned. I had them deliver it to the apartment, but I planned to be there for her to show her appreciation. I was hard just thinking about it.

When I got back to the condo, I saw that Day had already changed the rims on the Rover. I pulled in and headed upstairs.

Desean was fiddling with his camera when I walked in.

"What up, B?" I said, tossing my keys to him.

"Damn, son!" he exclaimed at the Aston Martin key ring. He put his camera down and reached in his pocket to show me his own surprise.

"What's this?" I asked as I caught the small velvet box. I was horrified when I opened it and saw the contents. "Please. Yo, please tell me this ain't what I think it is," I begged, staring at the large diamond solitaire.

"Ten stacks, B. You think she gonna like it?" he asked.

"She who?" I begged, hoping he was gonna say anything but.

"Veronica, nigga! I told you I'ma marry her," he snapped.

I sighed heavily and fell into a chair.

"What?" he demanded. "Fuck you huffin' and puffin' about?"

I sat there for a few moments, trying to figure out a way to put it delicately. In spite of my genius at lyrics, I couldn't really find the words this time. All that came out was, "Yo, don't marry that broad."

"Say what?" Day said, looking mortified. "I can't believe you just said that.

Yo, I love that girl."

"Why? 'Cause the pussy good? That's the only thing I've ever heard you say about her. 'She fine…The pussy good…Mean head game'. That's all good, but you don't get married for that," I reasoned.

"You jealous, B," Desean blurted. "That's all. You hate that this is something that ain't all about you."

"Whatever," I said, done with it. I wanted to tell him the truth, but I didn't see what good it would do.

"Look, B. Me and V getting married. You gon' hafta get used to it," he stated plainly. "Now, she on her way over here, and I got film class, so I would appreciate it if you kept it civil."

I sat on the sofa playing with one of the video cameras, recording myself doing a mock interview.

Veronica used her key and walked in a half-hour after Day left for class. "Hey, Lite," she said, looking around. "Where everybody at?"

I sucked my teeth in response and went back to filming myself.

Veronica went into Desean's room, only to return a few minutes later—naked. "I got something for you to record," she said, lying on the sofa.

I turned the camera on her and watched her masturbate through the viewfinder. By the time she climaxed, I was so turned on there was no turning back. I set the camera down and slid inside of her. My intention was to punish her for seducing me…again. I pounded her with everything I had. I was trying to hurt her, but she came again. The sight and sounds of her thrashing in ecstasy was too much for me and pushed me over the edge as well.

The second I came inside her, Shelby began ringing the intercom.

Me and Veronica scrambled to get up and get cleaned up. I put the camera down and used my shirt to wipe up the puddle we'd left on the leather sofa.

By the time Shelby walked in, I'd just finished washing my utensils in the sink, and I met her in the living room.

"Dave, why didn't you come help me?" she whined, her arms full of packages.

"My bad. I was busy playing in Desean's stuff," I said, holding up the camera.

CHAPTER 26

My album was at four million units sold and climbing The new video for "Wet Work" came out and pushed sales further. "Whose Pussy?" finally fell off the charts, but "Delightful" was holding strong.

With a three-million-dollar check for my publishing, it was time to fulfill a promise I'd made. I had forgiven my mom for keeping my dad away for my whole life, but I still wasn't really speaking to her. Every time it crossed my mind to call her, I called him instead. I figured since she stole his time, I would give him hers.

I had Desean shoot a video of the mini-mansion I purchased for her down in Henry County, just south of Atlanta. The house cost me almost $400,000, and the new Benz in the garage set me back another $80,000. It was all good though. My album money would be coming in any time. The way I figured it, that was another easy four or five million, so I had no problem blowing that little three million.

When my mom moved down, I took Tanisha and lil' Dave out as much as I could. Ma Dukes took an instant dislike to Tanisha—not for anything she did, so much as she was just pro-Shelby. She kept pretending not to remember her name. It was always "Hello, Tamika" or "Nice to see you again, Tonya." More often than not, she called her Shelby and followed it up with a fake apology.

While she may have been cold and spiteful to baby-mama, she doted over her grandson. Dave had his own room, with everything a kid could want. My mom began sucking up to Tanisha to get her to allow Dave to spend the weekends. Since Tanisha started clubbing again, it worked.

I always felt a sense of urgency whenever I saw my father's number flash on my phone. Even though we spoke daily, the six months he told me he had left had passed six months ago. I felt like I was on borrowed time.

Khadijah, through our daily conversations, had become my closest friend. Because she wanted nothing, expected nothing, and asked for nothing, I was able to share things with her that Shelby, Day, or Tanisha didn't even know.

"Hey, big head," I teased when my dad's number appeared on the caller ID. I knew it had to be Khadijah that time of night, because my dad always went to bed early with the help of his meds.

"It's time. You must come now," Khadijah cried.

I pushed the Aston Martin over 120mph as I flew to the airport. It took me three connections and $1,000 for the last-minute flight, but that didn't matter. I called my personal cab driver, Ali who scooped me from the airport and got me to my destination in a hurry.

Khadijah greeted me with a hug for the first time when I arrived. "The doctor is with him now," she said solemnly as we embraced. Even in light of the grim situation, I could not help but notice how good Khadijah felt against me—how soft she was and how clean she smelled. We stood there for several minutes, just holding each other, until the doctor came down the stairs to talk to us.

"Well, I gave him more morphine for pain, but I am afraid there is nothing else that can be done," he said compassionately. "If he expires, please call me, and I'll be right over. I'm so…sorry, folks."

I went up to the room where my dad was sleeping and sat down beside him. I held his hand and watched him as he slept fitfully. He seemed to be having a conversation with someone in his sleep. Sometimes he appeared to be answering questions, saying, "Allah, Muhammad, Islam…" I knew both he and Khadijah were Muslim, but I had never spoken in depth about religion, so I had no idea what he was talking about. Then, he kept telling someone that he couldn't leave yet because he was waiting on his son.

"I'm here, Dad," I whispered. "I'm here."

Khadijah came and went during the night, but we didn't speak. The three of us had grown so close from our conversations and visits. I had even brought lil' Dave out to meet them several times. Dave was in love with both of them.

I hadn't realized that I had dozed off until I heard Khadijah speaking the next morning. "Would you like some breakfast?" she asked sweetly.

"Huh? Um, yeah, if you don't mind," I answered groggily.

"Not you, big head." Khadijah laughed before turning back to my dad.

"Hey, Pop. You're up!" I said cheerfully.

"Hey, son. I've been waiting on you," he said alertly. He seemed so lucid that I thought maybe the doctor was wrong. My father seemed 100 percent healthy and alert. "I am hungry," he said, turning to Khadijah.

"Your favorite coming right up!" she sang and rushed off to prepare his food. She had been making cheese omelets and home fries every day in case it was his last.

"I won't have time to eat," he whispered in a confidential tone when she cleared the room. "He will be back to get me anytime now."

"Who?" I asked, puzzled. "The doctor?"

"Israfel," he said, still whispering. "He came last night, but I told him I wasn't going nowhere until my son got here."

"I'm here, Dad," I said, wondering if I should call the doctor, assuming that was who he meant.

"What will you worship after I'm gone?" he asked seriously.

"Um…I don't know," I answered honestly.

"Oh, my son, don't join anything in worship with Allah. Verily, joining others in worship with Allah is indeed a great sin," he said adamantly.

"Uh…okay. I won't," I said, still not sure what he was talking about.

"Remember son, chess not checkers," he said like he always did to end every conversation.

Just as Khadijah walked in with coffee, my dad took a deep breath.

"LA ILAHA ILLALLAH!" he said triumphantly before closing his eyes… for the last time.

Khadijah dropped the tray and ran screaming from the room.

The doctor arrived some thirty minutes after we called and signed the death certificate, eliminating the need for an autopsy.

I had no idea how a Muslim funeral would play out, but thankfully, all arrangements had been made. The process went so quickly that my father was in the ground by early evening the same day.

Back at the house, Khadijah was disconsolate.

I sat by the pool, reflecting on my father. I relived every conversation and laughed again at his jokes. I nodded affirmatively at his frequent advice, as if I could hear his voice.

"Success is its own reward. Money is only a byproduct of success," he often said.

My phone vibrated incessantly, causing me to chuck it into the pool. I felt a strange satisfaction watching it sink to the bottom.

I sat there for hours, laughing and crying until it was pitch black outside. When I went inside, I found Khadijah weeping in the den. I had no words to comfort her, so I took her in my arms and held her. I began kissing her tears away from her face.

She returned the gesture, and soon we had our tongues in each other's mouths.

It wasn't romantic in the typical sense as we kissed feverishly. It was about pain—about easing the pain. We frantically removed each other's clothes and dropped them to the floor.

Khadijah gasped loudly and drove her fingernails into my back as I pushed inside of her. She was so tight it hurt both of us. It was over seconds after it began, and we fell asleep in each other's arms.

In the morning, we were both embarrassed. We separated quickly and dressed without a word. I went to the bathroom and returned to find that Khadijah had left the house. Not knowing what to feel or think, I called Ali to take me back to the airport.

Back on the ground in Atlanta, I searched frantically for my phone. I chuckled and shook my head when I remembered it sinking into the pool.

I knew my people would be worried since I'd taken off without telling anyone, so I rustled up some change to use a payphone.

"Where were you at?" Shelby demanded when she answered her phone.

"New Mexico. My dad passed," I said solemnly.

"Oh no! I'm so sorry, baby," she said sincerely. "I have lab now, but can we talk later?"

I hung up without bothering to answer. I thought about calling Khadijah, but I just couldn't. Instead, I went to where my car was parked and headed home. Halfway there, I decided to go to Tanisha's instead. I had an overwhelming urge to see my son.

Both Tanisha and Dave rushed me at the door and competed for hug time. She cried at the news of my father's death and left us alone to cook for me.

Li'l Dave was talking up a storm, filling me in on everything I'd missed out on by not being around. I found out that Grandma had bought him new clothes, Pokémon socks, and that somebody named Uncle Sherm came by a lot.

When Dave got sleepy, I put him to bed and hit my weed stash. I rolled a blunt and grabbed a beer to unwind. I took a second to call Day from Tanisha's cell phone as I smoked.

"What's up, T? Where Lite?" Desean asked upon answering.

"This me, yo," I replied wearily from the events of the last forty-eight hours. I filled him in and graciously accepted his condolences.

As we spoke, Tanisha sat down beside me. She took my beer and used it to swallow a red pill before taking the blunt and pulling it.

"So what's been up?" I asked after giving my spiel. We hadn't really spoken much since he'd given V the ring.

"Well, all the footage is at the editor's. They got a rough edit for me to review before they finalize," he said. "I had them make us a little compilation of all the X-rated stuff on the side."

"That's what's up," I said halfheartedly. I listened to him go on and on about the DVD project, even though I wasn't the least bit interested. "A'ight, B, I'm out," I said when he paused to breathe.

"A'ight, yo," he said and hung up.

As soon as I put the phone down, Tanisha was all over me, purring like a kitten.

"What was that pill?" I asked turning to Tanisha.

"X!" she replied between kisses. "And I'm soooo horny!"

"You poppin' pills too now?" I asked, irritated. I didn't like the fact that the mother of my son was smoking and drinking more, but the pills straight pissed me off. I decided we needed to have a good talk, but not during lollipop time.

Tanisha sucked away all the tension and stress, and in the end, I decided our little talk could wait.

CHAPTER 27

The album jumped to five million, and Day knew it was time to drop the DVD. We met at the condo to review the final edit. It still had to go to the label for clearance. It seemed I didn't totally own me anymore and needed permission for everything—even things related to me.

"After this, the pornos," Desean said enthusiastically.

The DVD was well put together and very professional. It showed the whole process of me putting the album together and everyday life. It featured me onstage, backstage, and hanging out. It had all the videos I shot, as well as my final performance of the tour.

"A-yo, son, that shit is dope!" I said, giving Day a pound. I was genuinely impressed with the results.

"A'ight…and now, the pornos," he said, changing the disk.

I lit a blunt and settled in. The disk wasn't edited to the degree of the first one. They just strung together all the footage of the groupies that we'd compiled.

We cracked up at each other engaged in various sex acts on the road. Thankfully, neither of our faces could be seen, just in case the video fell into the wrong hands. For that purpose, we made each chick state her name and age before getting naked. That way, nobody could try to R. Kelly us later.

Near the end of the tape, Veronica popped up on the screen, masturbating on the very sofa we were sitting on.

"What the fuck is this?" Desean asked, confused.

"A-yo, B, I ain't trying to see your girl," I said, reaching for the remote. I knew what was coming next…or, should I say, cumming next.

"Hold up," Day said, snatching the remote before I could reach it.

"We don't need to see this," I implored, to no avail.

After Veronica exploded in ecstasy, I came into view and plunged inside of her. The tape revealed far more details than I remembered.

Desean looked horrified when V put her legs on my shoulders and gave it up completely. That was when he lost it. The first punch caught me square in the jaw and sent me onto my back. Desean commenced with whipping my ass. All I could do was try and cover myself from the onslaught. He was raining down blows with both hands.

"Oh, Lite! Beat this pussy! It's yours, baby!" Veronica yelled when she came, causing Desean to stop and look.

"I can't believe you!" he said calmly and retrieved the disk.

When he left the room, I took advantage of the reprieve and got the hell out of there.

* * *

"What the hell happened to you?" Tanisha asked, seeing my battered face.

I had a busted lip and nose and a large knot on my forehead. "Nothing. Some bullshit," I snapped, pulling away and falling on the sofa.

"Mm-hmm," she huffed and headed into the kitchen. "Here. Put this on that may not," she said, handing me an ice pack.

"On what?" I questioned.

"That bump on ya head. It may go away or it may not," she said sarcastically.

"So you think this shit is funny?" I barked.

"No, baby. Here," she said, pressing a pill into my mouth.

I took it with the beer she brought me and sat back.

"Get some rest. I gotta go get little Dave from my mama and drop him off at yours," Tanisha said, helping me out of my shirt. "Oh, hell naw!" she yelled at the sight of the claw marks Khadijah had left. "Who been scratching your back?"

"Uncle Sherm," I replied sarcastically, letting her know I knew about her extracurricular activities too. *I don't say nothing, so don't you.*

I fell asleep as soon as she walked out the door. When I woke up a couple hours later, I felt good…too good. My whole body felt like it had electric currents running through it. Even my "may not" was tingling. When Tanisha walked through the door, I was already on my feet. "A-yo, fuck you gave me, ma?" I demanded, rubbing my nipples.

"Dang, baby, you rolling!" She laughed, kicking off her shoes.

"Rolling? What you mean rolling? X-pill rolling?" I asked 100 miles a second.

"Yep, and you feel good, too, don't you?" she asked, pulling her sundress over her head.

I wanted to be pissed, but I felt too good. The sex was incredible—the best we'd ever had—and I began taking X on the regular after that.

* * *

Two days later, I finally ventured back to the condo. I checked the garage and entire block for Day's Range before I parked next to Shell's Porsche. I took my time going upstairs, afraid of what might be waiting for me.

"Okay, what happened?" Shell demanded as soon as I opened the front door.

"What happened with what?" I said, playing dumb. The fact that she was even there meant she didn't know. I had plenty of wiggle room.

"Desean was moving his stuff out when I got home, and…oh my God! Did y'all fight?" she said, reaching for what was left of my knot.

"Some bullshit," I replied, pushing her hand away.

"It's more than just some bullshit, David," she demanded.

"Why you ain't ask him then?" I snapped.

"I did!" she yelled back. "He said to ask you."

"You did then, and I said it's some bullshit. Nigga wanna bounce? Fuck him!" I yelled back. "Let's not forget I'm D-Lite. I made all this shit happen for all y'all, Desean included."

"You know what?" Shelby said earnestly. "You're changing. All this stuff is going to your head. I don't even know who you are anymore.

CHAPTER 28

By the time the album campaign wrapped up a year and a half after it began, I ended up moving five and a half million units stateside. Add that with two million more overseas, and four number one songs, six top tens, and features on five more top ten songs. In other words, I did the damn thing.

I just got another publishing check for six million, and my royalty check would be another seven. It was time to cop a house and a couple more cars. My plan was to get everything I wanted with my publishing and then follow Pops's advice and be frugal.

I finally built up the courage to call Khadijah, but the phone was disconnected. I heard from the probate lawyers some months back, but I never responded. The last time my dad had mentioned his Will, I told him to change the beneficiary from me to Khadijah. I felt she deserved the house for the way she'd taken care of him.

Even though I hadn't called, rarely a day went by that I didn't think about her. I felt a connection to her that grew by the day, even without us being in contact. In the end, my ego won out, and I decided, *I'm D-Lite! She should be calling me!*

When I reached the car lot, the same salesman who had initially chumped me off damn near broke his neck to greet me. "Mr. Light! A pleasure to see you again, sir," he gushed.

"'Sup, B?" I replied, looking over the lot. Then I spotted her, and I felt an erection slowly building as my eyes ran over the curves of a mineral gray Bentley Coupe. Next to her sat the newest Lamborghini, and my heart skipped a beat. "I'll take them," I said, getting teary-eyed.

"*Them*, sir?" the salesman asked anxiously.

"Yeah, both of them," I replied, reaching for my black card.

"Very good, sir," he said and bent down to remove his shoes.

After a good laugh, I completed the $750,000 purchase. I had spent damn near a mil', and it wasn't even noon!

My next stop was at a jewelry store, where I dropped $150,000 on trinkets for me and my girls.

The next day, Shell and I had an appointment with a realtor to pick a house. I was pissed but not surprised when Shelby backed out at the last minute. "I'm sure I'll love whatever you get," she said, detached.

When I got to the realtor's office, we both stared at each other in disbelief. She couldn't believe her prospective buyer of million-dollar homes was so young, and I couldn't believe she was so fine.

Ms. Lawrence had to be in her early forties, but she could have given a teenager a run for her money. She was as tall as me in the heels and had a heavy Southern belle demeanor that was just killing me. She must have had a team of people to get her into the tight skirt suit that barely held her all in. "You're Mr. Light?" she finally asked, breaking the awkward silence.

"Yes, ma'am," I said, politely extending my hand.

"Nice to meet you," she sang sweetly. "Let's go look at some houses, shall we?"

We walked out to the parking lot, where she remotely unlocked the doors of a 6 Series Beemer.

"If you don't mind," I said, hitting the remote that unlocked and started my Lambo, "I'd like to drive." I opened the door for Ms. Lawrence and checked out her frame as she slid into the car. Her legs opened enough to give me a good view of the sky-blue panties concealing her goods.

"Careful! You're too young for that," she teased, catching me looking at her crotch.

I got in and put the car in gear as the massive V12 growled.

"Wet Work" just so happened to be playing on the radio, and Ms. Lawrence reached over to turn it off. "Ugh! I hate that stuff," she said with a grimace.

"Yeah, I ain't crazy about it either," I said, putting the address of the first stop into the navigator.

"So tell me, Mr. Light, what do you do?" she said, initializing small talk.

"Me? I'm a rapper." I laughed.

"I'm sorry!" She blushed. "I...I um—"

"It's cool, ma. Like I said, I ain't crazy about it myself," I said, checking out her thick thighs.

I was shocked to see what a million bucks could get me in the city. The first couple of houses were large older homes in the Grant Park section. They were nicely done but had zero land, and the 'hood was right around the corner. For a mil', I needed to be a little further from the ghetto.

We slid over to the Midtown area, where I refused to even get out of the car. The tiny bungalows were smaller than the tree house my mom built for Dave in her backyard.

"I do have something I bet you would love," Ms. Lawrence said seductively.

"I bet you do," I said eagerly.

"Un-uh. Trust me, child, what you're thinking about, you can't handle," she said so seriously that I believed her. "I mean a house that just came on the market, but it's a little more than you say you're ready to spend."

"How much more?" I asked, caught in her brown eyes.

"It's listed at 4.5, but I'm sure I can work something out," she said, licking her lips.

"Where to?" I demanded.

We made our way to 285 and exited on Peachtree Industrial Parkway and followed it out to Duluth. The navigation led us to a gated golf community with beautiful homes.

"This is more like it!" I said, marveling at the three-story homes with large lots.

"There it is," Ms. Lawrence announced triumphantly.

I pulled the car into the driveway and took off running toward the house. I was at the front steps when I remembered Ms. Lawrence. "My bad," I said apologetically and opened the door.

She reached for my hand and gave me a long, deliberate view of her crotch.

I got so hard so quick that I felt lightheaded.

"Are you okay?" She chuckled at my dilemma. "Told you...you are not ready for that."

I was sold on the house as soon as she swung the door open. The marble foyer glistened from the huge chandelier at the top of the dual staircase. "I'll take it," I said breathlessly.

"You sure you don't want to see the rest of it?" She laughed.

The rest of it was spectacular—10,000 feet of opulence. There was a huge dining room off the foyer with enough room for one of those long-ass tables like in the movies, except this was real life, and I was really in a house with three fireplaces on the first floor alone. The kitchen was marble and granite, with a large center island boasting a restaurant-worthy grill. There were also two sub-zero fridges and all the latest appliances.

The second level contained four large bedrooms. Ms. Lawrence only laughed when I kept asking which one was the master. I didn't get the joke until the third floor.

The entire third level of the house was the master bedroom—or, better yet, suite. It had a sitting room as big as the apartment I'd grown up in.

There were not just his and her sinks the house had connected, yet private his and her bathrooms. They met in the middle at a huge Jacuzzi tub and glass-enclosed shower stall.

I still had yet to see the whole house, but when I walked out onto the master suite deck, I had seen enough. Ms. Lawrence joined me and felt the need to point out the pool, Jacuzzi, and other amenities I could clearly see.

My father's advice about biting off more than I could chew rushed to my mind. "Don't finance anything. Buy only what you can afford to pay for right now," he always lamented. "The sun don't shine forever, son." *It's shining now.*

The realtor must have been a mind reader, because the second I decided it was too much house for too much money, she hugged me from behind. "What do I have to do to get you to buy this house, Mr. Light?" she said, pressing her body against mine.

"I'm not sure I can…well, I, uh…" I stuttered, my blood running from one head to the other.

"Come on," she demanded, leading me back into the master bedroom. She stripped me roughly, then laid me on my back. I tried to protest, but she hushed me. After putting a condom on me, she mounted me and rode off. The woman totally ignored me; it was between her and my dick. When I tried to speak again, she cupped a hand over my mouth and shut me up. She rode me hard and fast. When she began whining that she was about to cum, I had to focus so I could join her.

The next thing I knew, I was signing papers. I agreed to use the two million I'd planned to spend, then pay it off in a year or two with my show money.

"Four million!" Shelby exclaimed. "What possessed you to spend four million dollars on a house?"

Since I couldn't explain, I just gave her the tour, and her objections lessened with each room. "I can pay it off next month with my royalty check or just use show money," I explained. I planned to use Ms. Lawrence's method of persuasion as soon as the tour reached the bedroom. It had worked on me, and I was sure it would work on Shelby.

CHAPTER 29

" **A**-yo, what the fuck is this?" I screamed at the sight of my so-called royalty check. "I sold five mil'! Where's the rest of my money?"

"Relax, Lite, my boy," Donnie said, pissing me off further. "Let's look at your books and see what's going on." He handed me a copy of my books and went over them line by line. "Okay, according to your contract, you are to be paid at a rate of $1 per unit," he began.

"Damn straight," I cut in, "so 5.5 million units equals 5.5 million dollars!"

"Exactly," Donnie proclaimed, as if I'd won a prize. "That's the starting figure. Now, let's tally up the deductions. Uncle Sam took $2.2 million off the top for your personal income tax. Management's 20 percent comes out to $1.1 million. You had a $100,000 advance, another million dollars for production, videos, company credit cards, Range Rover, condo, tour support…"

The staggering list of deductions made me feel lucky for the one-million-dollar check I was holding. It could have been worse if Day wasn't there to make sure I kept my publishing money.

"Here, Lite. Call these people," he said, handing me a business card for an accounting firm. "They will not only manage your funds, but they'll aggressively invest and grow them for you. You still have a million more from your overseas sales, and if you need cash, I can always book a tour," he said.

"Book the tour!" I demanded and stormed out of his office. I refused to let him see me cry.

I took his advice and called the accounting firm. I liked the part about them flipping my dough, but I balked at their suggestion of turning over the two million I had in my accounts. I did give them Power of Attorney for everything that came in, including my overseas money and all the money from the tour that we were about to embark on. As for my after-party money, I planned to fuck that up as usual.

Me and Bliz loaded up on kush, X-pills, and Viagra for the tour. We needed someone to take Day's spot as assistant and cameraman. Bliz suggested a dude named Boon from Decatur. At six-three, 200 and change, he could have been our security too.

The tour crisscrossed the country haphazardly, and wherever I went, I rocked a sold-out show. Every city was the same thing: show, after-party, sex.

I thought about Day often, wishing he was there. I wished things were like they used to be. I wished my ego hadn't gotten too big to call and ask his forgiveness, but it had.

I called Tanisha and lil' Dave, as was my habit whenever I got to another city. I was in my hotel room in Oklahoma City, doing my routine, when Bliz stuck his head in the door.

"A-yo, come to our room when you get off the phone," he said excitedly.

I nodded my agreement as Tanisha's phone went to voicemail. I hung up without leaving a message, then dialed Ma Dukes. After speaking with her, I chopped it up with my son.

My next call was to Shelby, who didn't pick up but texted me right away. I traded a few texts with her before heading to Bliz and Boon's room. "What do we have here?" I said, walking into the suite.

"Need you ask?" Bliz laughed, pointing to the three naked girls performing for Boon and his camera.

The young women were all thick, healthy, young country girls doing whatever Boon directed. Only problem was they were all too dark for me.

"I'm out," I announced after a few minutes, to everyone's dismay.

"A-yo, what the fuck, son?" Bliz asked, following me out into the hallway. "We got three freaks ready to do whatever, but they asking for you."

"Son, you know I don't fuck with that dark meat." I laughed.

"Make an exception, nigga. Just close your eyes and pull your dick out," he pleaded. "Son, you be buggin' with this light skin/dark skin shit. You can't tell me you ain't never had no black chick."

My mind flashed to Khadijah. Man, I missed her. No one knew about her, not even Day. She was personal, and I didn't want to share her with anyone. "No, no black girls, B," I lied on my way back to my room.

I dialed the old number for my dad's house for the 100th time and got the same result: nothing. It didn't matter, though, because our next stop was in Albuquerque, and I intended to find her.

As soon as I stepped off the plane in New Mexico, I took off in a cab to my dad's house. Using the spare key, I searched the empty house in vain. I couldn't understand why she wouldn't be there. My dad had left the house to her, as far as I knew. *Where would she go? And why?*

I did an interview for the local radio station to drum up some hype for the show, but I used the time trying to locate Khadijah. I invited her to the show and the after-party and even gave the name of the hotel where we were staying.

The radio DJ, along with Bliz and Boon, watched me curiously as I sweated Khadijah. About fifty girls called in claiming to be her or saying they'd be willing to be her, but none of them actually were.

After the after-party, Bliz and Boon brought a load of groupies back to the hotel, but I wasn't in the mood.

Shelby's phone went to voicemail, so I listened to her voice and hung up. I realized we hadn't actually spoken in weeks.

Tanisha answered from a club, but the music was so loud that we couldn't hear each other. I hung up, frustrated, and lit a blunt to smoke myself to sleep.

We pulled out of New Mexico the next day to head for Texas, then Missouri, then back up to Kansas. Our last stop in the U.S. was New York, so we could fly out of JFK.

I was excited about the overseas leg of the tour. Donnie ended up booking more shows due to the demand: five shows in London, then Ireland, then the rest of Europe.

Boon lost his mind going to Amsterdam; the idea of legalized prostitution and weed was too much for him. "So let me get this straight…I can order a blunt and a blowjob?" he asked skeptically. "Some bud and some butt? Kush and bush?" After our show, me and Bliz had to drag his big ass back on the plane.

Germany, France, Italy, and Japan were next. We hit places I had never even heard of, but they'd heard of me. It was crazy going to places where they didn't even speak English, but they knew the words to my songs.

"Congrats. The tour caused a surge in sales," Donnie said enthusiastically. "This is the perfect setup for the next album."

"What's up with that DVD thing?" I asked, curious about how Desean's project went. I had signed away all rights to it from the beginning, so I had no financial stake in it. I just wanted to make sure he was all right.

"That's doing great—over half a million in sales," he said. He ended the call by saying he would see me the following week, meaning the tour was over. We'd been gone for months, and it was finally time to head home.

I tried Shelby again to let her know I would be home soon. I was prepared to leave a message, so when she actually picked up, it caught me off guard.

Shell was yelling so loudly that I couldn't make out what she was saying.

"Whoa! Slow down, ma! I miss you, too, but I can't understand anything you're saying." I laughed.

"I said," she began slowly, "you are a worthless, lowdown piece of shit! You got a kid?"

"What the hell are you talking about?" I asked, genuinely confused.

"A baby, motherfucker!" she screamed. "A K-I-D!"

"You talking about that Spanish chick back home? Joe Frasier's mother." I laughed. "That ain't my kid."

"I ain't talking 'bout New York. Who the fuck you think you are, ODB with kids everywhere?" she said, still yelling.

"ODB? You crazy!" I laughed, trying to lighten the mood.

"You got paternity suits, and you think shit is funny? This shit funny to you, nigga?" she demanded.

"Hold up…paternity?" I asked, now getting heated myself. "How the fuck Tanisha gonna do some foul shit like that? I take care of our son. I give her plenty money, bought her a Jag'. The bitch stays in my condo. Fuck she suing me for?"

The line went silent for so long I thought the call had dropped.

"Hello?" I checked before hanging up to redial.

"You're Tanisha's baby's father?" she asked, incredulous.

"Ain't that who you talking about?" I said, puzzled.

"No, faggot! Some bitch in New fucking Mexico filed paternity papers on your trifling ass! They just served them," she spat viciously.

"New Mexico?" I repeated. "I ain't hit nothing out there."

"Oh yeah? What you say, um…fuck 'em then fuck 'em?" She laughed humorlessly. "Says Khadijah Amin. That ring a bell?"

"Khadijah? You talked to Khadijah?" I asked excitedly. "Did she leave a number."

"You know what? Fuck you, nigga," she said, exasperated, and hung up.

I started to call back, but I knew she wouldn't answer. My best bet was to go to the nearest jewelry store for a bribe. I dialed my dad's old number instead. It was still disconnected.

An hour later, Tanisha called me yelling too. "Why Shelby just come over here and punch me in my eye?"

I wasn't surprised that Shelby's Porsche wasn't in the driveway, 'cause she was hardly home anyway. I marched inside, carrying trinkets from all over the world, including a five-carat champagne-colored diamond ring from Belgium.

The first thing I noticed when I walked into the foyer was a note taped to the mirror, rolled up inside of her engagement ring. I discarded the note and went to see if Shelby still lived there.

I breathed a sigh of relief when I walked into the bedroom and saw her overflowing jewelry box was still on the dresser. I took that as a good sign, because no woman would leave behind a half a million dollars' worth of jewels.

My hopes were dashed, though, when I went into her closet and saw the bare walls and floor. Not one shoe, sock, or stitch of clothing remained. All of her personal effects were removed from the bathroom as well.

I dialed her number again, as I had been doing since we'd touched down in America, then hung up when I heard her phone ringing behind me in the bedroom. Curiosity propelled me back down the steps to read the note. It was as if I heard Shelby's voice as I read the short letter: "Fuck this ring, the house, the money, and the jewelry. But most of all, fuck your punk ass."

CHAPTER 30

"Lite, my boy!" Donnie said cheerfully as I walked into his office for some emergency meeting.

"I ain't your boy. Now get to the point," I demanded, not bothering to hide my contempt. "My wifey left me, and I got to go to court next week for some paternity shit."

"Well, this is one of those good news/bad news scenarios," Donnie said delicately.

"Not necessarily bad news," Amy chirped. "I think we can work it to your advantage."

"Will somebody please get to the point?" I snapped. "What's with all the parables?"

"Okay, well…um, the good news is that the tour went well. We generated a ton of new sales, not to mention the million or two you made," he began.

"Isn't that great?" Amy cheered.

"We have a slew of endorsement deals out of the blue. Bomb-bey Energy and One Ummah both want you bad," Donnie added.

I smiled, knowing my dad's influence had landed me the deals. He had put major money in my pocket from the hereafter. "And the bad news?" I asked, relaxed from the good news.

"Not bad…let's not say bad," Amy said cautiously.

"Okay, well, um…it's your old friend Ace. He just signed with Murder Kill Murder Records, and uh…well, there's a song," Donnie said, beating around the bush.

"So?" I asked bluntly. "Fuck that got to do with me?"

"Well, it's a dis' song," Amy blurted, "and it really sucks."

"He's just trying to get some exposure at your expense," Donnie said. "Just ignore it. He'll go away."

"Yeah, don't feed into it," Amy pleaded.

"A-yo, let me hear it…NOW!" I demanded.

They looked at each other, then Donnie picked up his stereo remote and pressed play.

I sat up to get a good listen as an interpolation of B.I.G.'s "Who Shot Ya?" boomed through the speakers.

"WHO SHOT YA? I DID. WHAT YA GON' DO?
WHO SHOT YA? BITCH NIGGA PROBABLY GON' SUE

LET ME TELL Y'ALL 'BOUT A FAKE GANGSTA NAMED LITE
HE LOVE TO BATTLE CUZ HE TOO SCARED TO FIGHT
INDUSTRY WHORE, NOTHING MORE THAN A FUCKIN' FLUNKY
STUDIO THUG FRONTIN' LIKE HE WAS SERVING JUNKIES
LIKE CHUCK D SAID, *DON'T BELIEVE THE HYPE*
THIS NIGGA LITE AIN'T NEVER SOLD A ROCK IN HIS LIFE
YOU AIN'T FOOLING ME SON. I KNOW WHO YOU ARE
LAST TIME I SAW YOU, I LEFT YOU WITH A SCAR
IT'S LITE'S OUT NOW THAT ACE IS IN THE PLACE
YOU AIN'T SHIT NIGGA, I'LL TELL YOU TO YOUR FACE
WACK ASS NIGGA, SPITTING THEM WACK-ASS RAPS
YOU GO LIKE A HO WHEN THE GUNS START TO CLAP
I KNOW THIS FOR A FACT, SEEN IT WITH MY OWN EYES
NOW YOU ON THE TV FRONTIN' AND SELLING LIES
I'M THE REAL GANGSTA LITE, NOT YOU
YOU SCREAMED LIKE A BITCH WHEN I SHOT YOU

WHO SHOT YA? I SHOT YA. WHAT YA GON' DO.
WHO SHOT YA? BITCH NIGGA PROBABLY GON' SUE."

I sat there with my mouth open in stunned silence as Ace blasted me for another two verses. When the song ended, Donnie and Amy waited anxiously for my reaction.

It started as a small chuckle, then grew. Soon, tears were rolling down my face from my laughter.

"That's the spirit! Laugh it off." Donnie laughed.

"This guy is fresh out of jail, looking for a meal ticket, that's all," Amy added.

"He sure ate my food," I said between laughs. "Really, I'm laughing at you two."

"Us? What did we do?" Amy laughed.

"Y'all out ya damn minds if you think I'm gonna let that shit pass," I said adamantly. "I'm a battle rapper. I eat rappers. This is what I do," I said as I walked out, "and I'ma do it. I'ma do me now."

Donnie and Amy called after me, but I wasn't trying to hear what they were talking about.

I simply yelled back down the hall, "I'ma do me now!"

* * *

Ace's song came out and blew up quickly. Every time one of my songs played, his was almost sure to follow. He was eating off my plate, getting a whole lot of experience and exposure at my expense.

The final straw came when I heard my son running around the condo talking about "Who shot ya?"

"A-yo, where the fuck he get that from?" I barked at Tanisha.

"They be playing it all the time," she whined.

"Well, turn it off!" I yelled, frustrated and embarrassed.

"I'm 'bout to take him to your mom's house 'cause I'm going to the club with Meka and them," Tanisha said.

"Shit, what else is new? He stay over there 'cause your ass stay in clubs," I spat back.

"Well, if you would let us move in with you, then you won't have to worry about me in no clubs," she appealed.

"Have a good time at the club," I said, shutting that move-in shit down for the 100th time. Ever since Shelby had left, Tanisha had been trying to slide her ass in there. I really wasn't feeling her lately. All the smoking, drinking, and pill-popping was starting to show. She used to take pride in her long brown hair, but now it was either a ponytail or stuffed under some weave. If I didn't know any better, I would have sworn she was sniffing coke too.

Lil' Dave was getting big, and the nigga cursed like a sailor. He all, "Nigga this, nigga that." I had no idea where that lil' nigga was getting that shit from.

Bliz damn near lived at the house with me. We turned the mansion into our own private club. Every night, we invited strippers or groupies or both. My life had literally become sex, drugs, and hip-hop.

* * *

I ended up taking Dave with me when I flew into Albuquerque for my court date. I called ahead and had all the utilities turned on at the house since I had decided to spend a week alone there with my son. Donnie tried to book me a show for a quick twenty-five grand, but I declined.

My mind was swimming as we rode to the courthouse. I couldn't understand why Khadijah would put a baby on me. I had lost Shelby behind that shit, and we really didn't even have sex. "It's impossible," I thought aloud.

"Nothing is impossible, Daddy," Dave interjected.

I doubt if he even understood what he said, but I drilled it in his head regularly. "That's right, my nigga," I said proudly.

The information board listing docket numbers put me on the fifth floor. Dave took off running straight for Khadijah when we stopped on the elevator.

I wanted to be mad at her, but she was beautiful, and I missed her. She was talking to a short, older white woman until Dave jumped in her arms.

She must have asked about me, because he pointed back to the elevators, where I was still standing. All the anger left when she smiled at me.

"Hey, you," I said as I walked up.

"Hey, yourself," she said, hugging me. "You mad at me?"

"Very," I replied, holding her tightly. "I missed you too."

"Whose baby?" Dave demanded, breaking up our reunion.

"I'm sorry, dear," Khadijah cooed as she picked up the infant. "Meet your father."

Before I could say a word, Khadijah handed the little girl to me. As I inspected her face, she pulled off one of her socks.

"Look…she has your father's toes," Khadijah said proudly.

"No, she has *her* father's toes," I corrected, looking at my daughter.

"I tried to call you, but your phone was off," she whined.

"Long story." I laughed, thinking again about my phone, sinking to the bottom of the pool. "What's her name?"

"Zakiyyah Na'eema," Khadijah said softly.

"That's pretty. What does it mean?" I asked.

"Pure delight." She laughed. "Named after you."

"Is this the plaintiff, the child's father," the white lady said, interrupting the reunion.

"Who is you?" I asked, irritated by both the interruption and being referred to as "the plaintiff."

"I'm Ms. Chin from Social Services," she said, handing me a card that I didn't want.

"I'm cool," I replied, refusing the card.

"Well, as you know, we are here to establish paternity and support," she said.

Khadijah looked embarrassed, so I came to her rescue. "A-yo, they a'ight," I announced. "I got them."

Khadijah had to withdraw the petition, and I signed the birth certificate. I ended up owing the state a few grand for aid they had paid. I wrote a check and left with my family.

We shared an awkward silence on the ride back, until I asked the million-dollar question: "How did we get here? What happened?" I wondered aloud.

"Well, um, when Dad passed, we…I mean, I…I'm not sure. Lord knows I didn't intend to lose my virginity like that," she said, pausing. "I have no idea. We were in so much pain."

"That did ease the pain," I suggested."

"Heck no! That stuff hurt!" Khadijah laughed.

"Next time will be better, I promise," I offered.

"Next time I do that, I will be married," she said adamantly.

"By tonight?" I said, sizing her up.

"You are so silly. I missed you." She laughed.

"So how you end up on Social Services? Why didn't you just stay in the house?" I asked.

"Well, first, when I missed my period, I just would not believe that I was pregnant. I mean, it was only ten seconds, so—"

"Hey! It wasn't no ten seconds," I said in my own defense.

"Anyway…" Khadijah laughed before continuing. "I was six months along before I accepted it. Then the probate people said they didn't have anyone listed as a tenant, so they had me evicted. I ended up in a small apartment, on welfare. I was content to raise her alone, but I remembered how your dad hated missing out on your life. I couldn't do that to her…or to you."

"Why didn't you call the label? They could have reached me," I said, feeling guilty. I remembered the lawyer leaving messages and sending letters about my dad's estate, but I had just ignored them. I had put her on the street, with my baby!

"I called the label and told them I needed to speak with you, but they told me to go to your fan page," she said, disgusted, "like I was some groupie." Khadijah began crying softly as she spoke.

My mind was made up. "You never have to worry about anything ever again. I'll never leave you guys," I promised.

I kept my promise the whole time I was there. For the whole week in New Mexico, I stayed with Khadijah and my children. I took the time to bond with Dave and my new daughter.

Khadijah went to school during the day, leaving me to change diapers and fix bottles—something I'd never done with Dave, and I loved it.

She cleaned out her small apartment and moved back into Dad's house. I never made a move on her and was totally content just to have her company.

I e-mailed pictures of Zakiyyah to my mom, who was delighted to have a granddaughter. She and Khadijah spoke and became fast friends.

We were all in a somber mood when it was time for lil' Dave and me to return to Atlanta. After I put the kids in bed, Khadijah and I settled into the den to watch TV.

While channel-surfing, we ran across the new video for Ace's dis' song, "Who Shot Ya?" It featured pictures of me, as well as a lookalike who made me look like a straight herb.

"What the heck was that?" Khadijah asked hotly.

"Some hater tryina eat off me," I said, trying to contain my anger. "My label said to ignore him, so I'm gonna let it pass."

"Let it pass?" she exclaimed. "Oh no. You must get him."

CHAPTER 31

I was only back in Atlanta long enough to pack and head back out to L.A. for the Music Awards. I was up for four of them: Song of the Year for "Delightful"; Best Collaboration for "Robbing Spree"; New Artist; and Album of the Year.

I tried to get Khadijah to go out to the show with me, but she declined. Tanisha begged to go, but her increasing drug use was turning me off. The sober week I'd spent in New Mexico had given me a new outlook on things, and I pondered that while smoking a blunt.

Bliz and Boon both ended up flying out west with me. Asia and I were scheduled to perform "Delightful" live. After the sexless week I'd spent with Khadijah, I couldn't wait to see her.

Walking down the red carpet was like déjà vu, jolting me back to that dream I'd dreamt and daydreamt since I was ten, only now it was real. My favorite rappers were really saying "What's up?" to me, really suggesting we get together and do something. It was real and surreal at the same time.

I was in the middle of an interview with one of the video channels when some commotion up the street drew everyone's attention. There was some sort of protest going on, complete with picket signs and chants. As the protesters grew closer and their signs came into view, it was clear what they were protesting: me!

It was that clown Ace and a group of people holding signs that read "Lite's Out!" as they chanted the same. "Lite's out! Ace in the place!"

The stunned reporter could only stick her microphone on my face for comment.

I wanted to speak my mind, but Donnie and Amy had made me promise not to say anything. "I think he wants some attention." I chuckled. "Now, if you'll excuse me, I have a couple of awards to pick up." I was up against some stiff competition, so I regretted the cocky statement the second it left my lips. It was too late to take it back, though, so I slumped in my chair and sulked. I cast Bliz and Boon a puzzled look when they stood up and began clapping at me. "I won?" I asked, shocked. "I fucking won?"

Since I hadn't been paying attention, I didn't know the award was for Best New Artist. The thought of winning was so far removed from me that I had nothing prepared. I accepted the trophy graciously and freestyled an acceptance speech. "First and foremost, I want to thank God," I said, drawing applause. "Next, to my fans, who understand what I'm trying to do." When the next round of applause died down, I held the award up to heaven and remembered my dad. "To Pop Dukes, thanks for all the advice. I'm still trying to figure out some of what you said and apply it. You was right…chess, not checkers!" I went on and thanked my mom, Khadijah, the label, and everyone I could think of, until the music began signaling that my time was up.

When I got back to my seat, my Blackberry began vibrating nonstop: congratulations from Khadijah, Donnie, Amy, and Guy, as well as a few people I forgot to mention.

I was apologizing to Tanisha when another text came in, telling me I was needed backstage. It was time for Asia and I to perform.

"Hey, boo," Asia said, giving me a tight hug. "I missed you."

"Missed you too," I said, admiring her clothless outfit. My mind flashed to Khadijah, sitting at home with our daughter, watching me perform with the half-naked girl.

When we hit the stage, I kept that in mind and kept my distance—avoided her like the plague, more like it. Every time she tried to shimmy up close, I did a little two-step away from her. It came across as playful, given the reports of us dating, and no one was the wiser. After the show, she slid me her room keycard for the after-the-after-party party.

I didn't expect to win any more after Song of the Year went to B-Bop and Album of the Year went to Erv-G, but me, Sig, and Red Clay won for "Robbing Spree" as well.

After they thanked their people, I got another minute for shout-outs of my own. "This one is for the Bronx, the ATL, and my bitch Ace!" I said, laughing off the stage.

* * *

Not only did those two statues look good on my mantle, but it was also good for business. Donnie was about to book ten guest appearances at $68,000 a pop. That would keep me ringing until the next album dropped.

I was supposed to start on the next album but decided I needed a vacation. I planned to take Dave back out to Albuquerque and hang out for a month or two.

Even though Dave was at my mom's house, I still swung by the condo to check on Tanisha. Knowing nothing sexual was popping off with Khadijah, I wanted a little lollipop action before I bounced. But lollipop time had lost its magic. In fact, I was semi-disgusted watching Tanisha bob her weave to please me. She kept sniffling and rubbing her nose. When a line of snot escaped a nostril, I was done.

"What's wrong? It's not good?" she asked, feeling me go limp in her mouth.

"Yeah, you cool, ma. I gotta bounce," I said, getting myself together.

"Okay," she said sadly, then perked back up. "Can I have some money?"

I really couldn't believe she had the audacity to ask me for more money. She was living rent free, pushing a Jag', and getting five stacks a month already to take care of a kid who was never even there. Still, I reached in my pocket and peeled off a couple of layers.

"Thank you!" she sang when I handed her the cash, and she leaned up to kiss me.

"Don't mention it," I said, giving her my cheek.

* * *

Khadijah picked us up in the Jag' and had a big reunion with Dave, trading kisses. "Hey, you," she said, smiling at me.

"Hey. What, no kisses for me?" I said, feeling a tad bit jealous.

"When you step your game up, you can have all the kisses you want," she replied.

"Yeah, Daddy. Step your game up," lil' Dave demanded.

Zakiyyah squealed with delight when she saw me and reached for me to pick her up.

"At least somebody loves me," I said, scooping my daughter from her stroller.

She gave me all of her attention until Dave came and stole her too.

Sometimes I caught Khadijah giving me love-struck stares, but it went no further than that. We stayed up late, talking into the night, just like we did before my father passed. Our relationship did not involve sex, but it was stronger and purer than what I shared with Shelby or Tanisha. Sometimes she caught me giving her love-struck stares as well.

The time I spent with my kids was priceless—bedtime stories, playing in the park, every single second.

We had been there two weeks already when I decided to call Tanisha and let her know her son was out of town.

"Hello?" Tanisha slurred into the phone.

"Tanisha?" I had to ask, unsure if it was her.

"It's me, Lite," she said groggily. "You just missed your son. I just put him in bed. He was asking about you."

As she spoke, I went upstairs to the kids' room just to make sure I wasn't tripping. "Oh, okay then," I said, watching my son sleep 1,000 miles away from her.

"Who dat?" a male voice said before Tanisha could cover the receiver.

"It's just my baby-daddy," I heard her reply in a hush.

* * *

The month flew by so quickly that it was over before I knew it. I was having a cup of coffee, watching Khadijah do some cleaning before taking Dave and me to the airport. She was so graceful that the room lit up everywhere she stepped.

That was when I realized I was in love. I had already loved her, but now I was in love and told her so. "You know, I am so in love with you," I blurted out uncontrollably.

"Where did that come from?" Khadijah laughed.

"The bottom of my heart," I said sincerely. "I have been in love with you for some time—even before my dad died, before we...well, before Zakiyyah."

"Well, you should love me." She chuckled. "All you gotta do is step your game up. I know this doesn't compare to the glitz and glitter of your life, but we're family. Step your game up!"

"I don't know what that means," I finally admitted. All month, that was all I'd been hearing, "Step your game up."

"You don't want to understand then. The signs are everywhere," she said sadly.

We rode to the airport in silence, everyone consumed by their own thoughts. Khadijah looked sad, I was confused, and little Dave was just pissed. I practically had to drag his stubborn little ass to the plane. Little dude had his lip poked out and refused to speak to me. "I know, my dude. I hate to leave too," I consoled.

"So step your game up then!" he said, pointing at a billboard, an ad for a local jewelry store whose tagline was exactly that. It featured a man slipping a ring on a smiling woman's finger.

No wonder I had been hearing it all month! The ads were everywhere, including on radio and TV.

"A-yo, come back and get me," I demanded when Khadijah answered the phone.

"What? What's wrong? Where's Dave?" she demanded.

"Everything is cool. Chill," I said. "We just gotta go to the courthouse."

"Courthouse? For what?" she asked, confused.

"So I can step my game up," I replied proudly. "We need to get married. I finally saw the signs."

"Are you...sure?" she asked skeptically. "How did you finally figure it out?"

"A little angel showed me," I said, looking at my son.

"Tell the angel he left his truck in the car." Khadijah laughed.

After a quick civil ceremony, I was back at the airport. Our honeymoon was a kiss and a strawberry Bomb-bey from out of the machine. I hated to leave, but the Black Tree Awards were being taped in Atlanta the next day.

I would have blown it off if I wasn't up for five of them. I was in the running for Song of the Year for "Delightful"; Best New Artist; Best Rap Album; again for Collaboration on "Robbing Spree"; and the "Wet Work" video.

The promoters intended to create some excitement by booking both me and Ace to perform. He had a new single entitled "Lite's Out," and it was beginning to make some noise. Ace was fully intending to build a career off me.

Initially, I was supposed to perform "Delightful" with Asia, but for reasons unknown, she pulled out at the last minute. I decided to do another song, but then Bliz showed me the latest copy of *Beat Street.* On the cover were Ace and Asia, hugging up under the caption, "Lite's Out."

"What the fuck?" I said, quickly turning to the article.

In it, Asia said that our relationship was a publicity stunt cooked up by the label. She also said I was a studio gangster and that Ace was her real man. She ended the interview by letting everyone know she had a solo album coming out on Murder Kill Murder Records.

"Talk about a publicity stunt!" I laughed, in spite of how hot I was. "Oh, I'm gonna let this nigga have it."

"The bitch too," Bliz said animatedly. "Get that bitch too."

Boon had brought a bunch of wild-ass Decatur niggas just in case anything popped off.

The night was going along great. I had won for Best New Artist and again for the "Wet Work" video. I was onstage giving my shout-outs to all the usual suspects, and as fate would have it, the second I mentioned my wife, I had direct eye contact with Shelby.

She and Desean were seated a couple rows in, and I made up my mind to see them after the show. It was time to man up and apologize. I gave one last shout-out to my fifth grade teacher, Mrs. Hunter, and left the stage.

The crowd whooped it up pretty good when Ace took the stage and did his bullshit dis' song, "Lite's Out." They only got into it to instigate the whole affair. Dude couldn't see me with the fucking Hubble telescope, and they knew it. They wanted beef, and they were gonna get it.

I laughed as Ace spent his whole time onstage looking for me in the audience. What he didn't know was that me and half of Glenwood Avenue were stage left.

He finished the corny song and made a few more slanderous remarks before exiting stage right. The crowd applauded him as he walked off, but they lost their collective minds when I walked on.

"Y'all liked that?" I asked the bloodthirsty crowd.

Ace and company tried to come back onstage as the audience jeered, but they were held back by the rent-a-cops.

Bliz dropped the instrumental to Tupac's "Hit 'em up," and I came out swinging.

"I DON'T CALL THE COPS. I CALL NIGGAS WITH GLOCKS...

TO COME THROUGH WITH THE BURNERS AND SCORCH THE BLOCK...

PULL OUT THEM STREET SWEEPERS AND CLEAN YA CLOCK...

AND I DON'T GIVE A FUCK ABOUT WHO GOT SHOT...

KEEP TALKING RECKLESS, AND YOU'RE GONNA FEEL THE PAIN...

I'LL LEAVE YOUR ASS HEADLESS LIKE ICHABOD CRANE...

I KEEP GUNS IN MY ATTIC IN CASE NIGGAS WANT STATIC...

SEMIS AND AUTOMATICS TO LET YOU FUCK NIGGAS HAVE IT...

YOU BUDGET-FUCK LITTLE BROKE-ASS NIGGA...

LITE'S LARGER THAN LIFE, DOING SALES LIKE JIGGA...

SHOOTING AT ME IS YOUR ONLY CLAIM TO FAME...

NOW YOU TRYNA COME UP BY USING MY NAME...

NIGGA, YOUR ARMS TOO SHORT TO BOX WITH GOD...

YOU DEALT ME IN, PLAYER, SO I'MA PULL YOUR CARD...

WE CAN BATTLE OR FIGHT ANYPLACE THAT YOU WANT TO...

DON'T TRY TO HIDE, 'CAUSE I WILL COME AND HUNT YOU."

The crowd lost it, and so did Ace. This time, he and his goons pushed past security, who were all too busy watching the show to notice. Right there on national TV, we engaged in an all-out brawl.

The melee lasted a few minutes, until Atlanta PD took control of the situation, and with fifty people fighting, guess who got arrested. Me!

Once I posted bail, I went home, lit a blunt, and called my wife.

Khadijah had no doubt seen the fiasco and had been blowing my phones up ever since. "Hey, handsome," she said sweetly when she picked up. "Are you okay?"

"I'm cool. Sorry about that," I said sincerely.

"Oh, man, that was so cool!" Khadijah laughed.

We joked about the situation for a few more minutes, until I begged off the phone. Khadijah ended the call by telling me she had a surprise for me.

G STREET CHRONICLES
~A NEW URBAN DYNASTY~

WWW.GSTREETCHRONICLES.COM

I slept late into the next morning, until I heard activity downstairs. I assumed it was Bliz, but then I smelled food cooking and knew full well that Bliz, the takeout king, wasn't cooking nothing.

When I went down to investigate, I found Khadijah cooking and Zakiyyah in a walker.

"Hey, baby! What are you doing here?" I exclaimed. "And what are you wearing?"

"Visiting my husband…and this?" she said, pointing to her headscarf. "It's a hijab. It's what all good Muslim women wear. My beauty is only for my husband's eyes."

"Sounds good" I said, scooping my daughter out of her walker. "So, um, when does your husband get to see some of that booty…eh…beauty?"

"Soon, Mr. Man, very soon," Khadijah said shyly. "The kids need another companion, so you have work to do."

After eating, I gave Khadijah and Zakiyyah a tour of the house.

She made wisecracks the whole way. "Easy come, easy go," she quipped at the million dollars' worth of cars in the garage. "A fool and his money soon part," she remarked at the half-million in jewels lying on my dresser.

Zakiyyah's eyes grew huge at the sight of all the shiny trinkets, so I put her on my bed and poured the jewels all around her.

"So, how much money do you waste…um, I mean spend?" she asked, astonished.

"I have no idea." I laughed, even though it wasn't funny. I had been so high for so long that I had no clue.

"The sun don't shine forever." She signed.

We both grew silent at the reminder of my father; he used to say that all the time.

"Well, I got, like, two mil' in checking," I said proudly.

"In a checking account?" she asked, shaking her head. "You have a family. You must make wiser choices."

"I know. That's why I got, like, five or six million with my accountants," I replied.

"Is it five or six?" she said, still shaking her head. "There is a difference, you know. How is it being invested?" She continued shaking her head when I told her I didn't know.

"A'ight, I'll tell you what, Ms. Pricewaterhouse," I said sharply out of embarrassment, "I'll give you some money and see what you can do." I spitefully wrote out a personal check for one million dollars, figuring that when she went out and blew it like any woman would, she couldn't complain anymore about my spending habits. *I'll probably sell twice as many records next time,* I reasoned. *The sun may not shine forever, but it's sure as hell shining now.*

* * *

My mother and Khadijah had spoken so much over the phone over the last few months that they were like old friends by the time they finally met in person. After my mom fussed over her granddaughter, I took Zakiyyah out back on Dave's swing set.

I was so amazed by my daughter—the way she looked at me and hung on my every word. I regretted that I wasn't able to share moments like that with lil' Dave when he was that young. My only solace came from the fact that we were straight for life. My kids would never live in the 'hood. Their futures were secure.

My thoughts were interrupted by a commotion inside the house. I went to see what the fuss was about and found Tanisha raising hell. She was dropping Dave off and flipped out when she ran into Khadijah. "Un-uh! Don't you be calling her no mommy!" she yelled. "I'm you goddamn mama!"

"A-yo, be easy," I demanded, walking in.

"Hell to the naw! I ain't leaving my baby with no bitch," she screamed.

"Now calm down, Tanisha," my mom said nicely, but I heard the danger in her voice. For all the education, sororities, and country clubs, Ma Dukes was still that chick from Webster projects!

Khadijah only made matters worse by laughing. "So I must be the bitch?" she asked with a chuckle. "You sure can pick 'em!"

"We out!" Tanisha fumed, dragging my son out of the house, kicking and screaming, so I followed her out.

My mother was getting upset. "You wanna kick her ass?" she asked Khadijah as I left.

"A-yo, what the fuck was that all about?" I demanded, taking her by the arm.

Up close, I could see her eyes were red, and I could smell liquor on her breath. "You out here DUI with my kid?" I said, getting in her face.

"I ain't drunk, you motherfucker!" she yelled, letting go of Dave.

He took advantage of the situation and ran back into the house.

Tanisha exploded into tears and jumped into her car. I had barely cleared the tires when she sped off. I did feel bad for her, having to find out I was married like that.

* * *

The only time I left Khadijah and the kids was when I went to see Guy at the studio. Feeling benevolent, I dropped lil' Dave off with Tanisha for the day.

My label wasn't supporting me in my feud with Ace, and they didn't have to. It was personal. The song was going straight to the radio and on Bliz's next mix tape. It was time to let Ace have it, him and that nasty bitch Asia.

As usual, me and Guy smoked a few blunts as we worked, and as usual, we got into one of our monumental debates—only this time, he started it.

"You're becoming quite the studio gangsta, aren't you?" he said as we listened to a playback of my unusually violent song.

"Studio gangsta? Who the fuck you calling a studio gangsta?" I demanded.

"You, Lite." He laughed. "Come on. I know a studio gangsta when I see one."

"You need to check ya'self. You white people the ones fucking up the game,"

I spat.

"What?" he asked, incredulous. "How on Earth do you figure that?"

"Y'all the ones pushing all the sex and violence in *our* music, and then you go home to the suburbs. I'm from the 'hood, and I see the results of that shit," I said hotly.

"First, I seriously doubt you're from the 'hood." He chuckled. "I remember when you first came, you were all 'Yes, please, and thank you'. Now you got Glocks? And as for white people promoting sex and violence, puh-lease! Black people do more to destroy themselves than anything in creation. You don't see cows killing other cows just 'cause they from a different pasture or a different color or just 'cause it's fucking Friday night!"

"Man, I aint—"

"Hold up. I'm not done," Guy said, cutting me off. "Bob Johnson, Debra Lee, Katherine Hughes, um…Christina Norman—all billionaires from promoting sex and violence, and they are black. Do you think I would write a rap about casual, carefree sex if my people accounted for half of all the HIV infections? Or about selling drugs when they know they got a drug addict in the family? Hell no!"

"Well, I ain't got no crack-heads in my family," I lied. My mind flashed to my Uncle Speedo. Dude was worth about a mil' till that pipe got him. In the end, he died broke and alone in a hospice from CRA, crack-related AIDS. "Fuck you, nigga!" I yelled and stormed out. The surest way to win an argument with a white person is to call them a nigga. They don't know what to say to that. There's no comeback. Halfway down the hallway, a thought came to me, so I went back. "Same time tomorrow?" I asked, as if the argument never happened.

"You betcha!" Guy replied cheerfully.

Like I said, we argued all the time, but it was all love.

* * *

Something was troubling my soul as I drove home. Guy's words had hit home, but it was more than that. When I pulled up to the condo and saw police cars and an ambulance, my heart sank.

My fears were confirmed as paramedics rushed lil' Dave out on a stretcher. Tanisha was right behind them, crying hysterically.

"What happened?" I asked, grabbing her by both shoulders.

"I-I don't...I don't know! He just...he just passed out," she said. She jumped in the Lambo beside me, and we chased the ambulance to Children's Hospital.

"We're gonna have to run a full battery of tests to determine what's wrong," the doctor informed us. "To save valuable time," he said, pausing to look us both in the eye, "did he have access to any drugs or medication?"

Tanisha began blinking rapidly, signaling the fact that she was about to lie. "No, nothing," she said so unconvincingly that even the doctor frowned.

"It would make our job easier and save your son valuable time," he stressed to Tanisha.

"I said I don't know," she said curtly, causing the doctor to storm off.

"A-yo, what he took?" I asked seriously as soon as the doctor was out of earshot.

"X," she whispered softly. "He got into my pills."

"I can't believe you!" I spat before taking off in search of the doctor to tell him the truth.

"I figured that might be the case," the doctor sympathized. "It happens daily in this city. At least we know how to treat him now."

As the doctor went to treat my son for MDMA ingestion, I went to find Tanisha so I could put my foot in her ass. I ran back to the waiting room, but she was gone. I called Khadijah to let her know what was going on, and she was there in a flash.

Khadijah was absolutely livid about the whole situation. She griped nonstop as I bounced Zakiyyah on my knee. "She needs a good African ass-whooping," she fumed. "That's it. Dave comes back to Albuquerque with me. When you want to see your family, that's where we'll be."

She was still muttering threats when two police officers accompanied a woman to the nurses' station. After a brief dialog, the nurse pointed at us, sending the trio in our direction.

"Excuse me, Mr. Light? I'm Lisa Jones from Child Protective Services," the woman said sternly while extending her card.

"I'm cool. I got my own Child Protective Service," I said, nodding toward Khadijah.

"You're Mrs. Light?" Ms. Jones asked Khadijah.

The two officers looked like they were ready to pounce if she answered in the affirmative.

"Actually, I am Mrs. Light, but unfortunately, I am not the biological mother," she replied.

I gave a brief explanation of the day's events, as well as the address to the condo.

Ms. Jones nodded to the police, who set off to speak with Tanisha. "There will be a custody hearing in a week or two. The child will be in foster care until then," she said casually.

I was set to blow, but Khadijah placed a hand on my knee to stop me before speaking up herself. "Ms., um, Jones, are you carrying a gun?" she asked politely.

"Why no," she replied, puzzled by the odd question.

"The reason I ask is because the only way you're taking that boy is over my dead body," Khadijah said stoically.

Ms. Jones obviously took her at her word and schedule an emergency hearing for the next day, since Dave would be staying in the hospital overnight for observation.

The judge was swayed by Ms. Jones's recommendation and awarded us full custody. Khadijah and the kids promptly flew out to New Mexico the very same day.

If not for a promise I had made, I would have joined them, but I had agreed to help Boon out at his new club.

I dropped by Bliz's studio to give him a copy of the scathing dis' song.

His girl Tosha was there, rubbing her pregnant belly as she sat on the sofa. "Hey, Lite," Tosha said sweetly as I entered the control room.

"Hey, yourself. Oh, don't get up," I teased.

"Ha-ha, very funny." She chuckled at the remark. "I can't wait to get this thing out of me. Supposed to done came already."

"Don't be calling my baby no thing," Bliz said, finally looking up from the computer. "What up, B? How's little man?"

"Dave straight, yo. He out west with wifey," I replied.

"Wifey?" Tosha chuckled. "I can't believe you got married."

"And to a dark-skinned woman," Bliz exclaimed.

"You know what they say...the darker the berry—" Tosha began.

"The sweeter the juice!" me and Bliz finished.

"Sorry to hear about y'all son. Ol' girl been going out bad—smoking e'rry day, poppin' pills, snorting, and fucking with some ol' lowlife niggas." Tosha frowned.

"I kinda feel like it's my fault," I admitted. "I coulda did more, been there for her."

"Shittin' me!" Tosha exclaimed. "If anything, you slowed her down for a minute. Ol' girl need to grow up."

"Yeah, that's what her moms said," I agreed. "That's why nobody gonna bail her out. She need time to think. Our son almost died."

"You ready for tonight?" Bliz asked as I stood to leave.

"No. I'm ready to go home to my family," I replied, "but a promise is a promise."

My homeboy from Brooklyn, Andrew Mayes, was now the program director at the radio station, so I took the song straight to him.

"This shit banging, fam'!" he said after a playback in his office. "'Bout time you got at that nigga, B. Can't believe son tried you like that."

"That's what's up," I said, giving him a pound and hug before I left.

He said he was gonna run it every hour on the hour, and he kept his word. I heard it twice on my forty-minute ride home. By 8 that night, it was the most requested song. The fans loved it!

My label, on the other hand, was pissed. They threatened to send a cease and desist letter first thing in the morning. With all the uproar, at least there would be a big showing for the new club.

Boon opened his new club dead in the 'hood on Candler Road in Decatur. He took over the lease on a failed club and renamed it—what else?—The Boon Boon Room.

As I navigated through the parking lot, all I saw were young thugs and thugettes—gold teeth and dreads for the males and as little as possible for the females.

The hoochies flirted shamelessly as the Bentley floated through.

"Boy, y'all lucky I'm married," I thought aloud as a couple of chicks caught my eye.

I couldn't ascertain why, but I had a sense of foreboding as I made my way around the rear of the club. Something just didn't sit right with me. *I'ma just wreck this shit and get out of here.*

I actually entertained the thought of going straight to the airport after the show and catching the first thing smoking to my family. I mused about copping a private jet off the next album. *I did eight times platinum the first time, and this time I'ma do ten!*

Even the mood backstage was unusually subdued. Normally, me, Bliz, and Boon would be drinking champagne and smoking blunts while some groupie played with herself for the camera. Instead, we were contemplating the future.

"A-yo, I only been married for a minute, but I highly recommend it," I advised sincerely.

"I feel you, B. I'ma wife Tosh up as soon as she drop that load," Bliz added.

"She ain't had that kid yet?" Boon exclaimed. "Girl been pregnant for a year."

"Seems like." Bliz laughed. "S'posed to had it last week. They got me on a short leash now."

"Y'all niggas tripping," Boon boomed. "Don't let me find out y'all niggas getting soft on me."

We shared a good laugh and headed for the stage. We had to wait for security to break up a few fights before we could begin, and again I fought the urge to just leave. I couldn't let my man down.

Initially, I had no energy or enthusiasm, but the crunk crowd got me motivated. I kicked whatever song they yelled out. Of course, my dudes wanted that 'hood shit like "Robbing Spree" and "Wet Work," while the girls screamed for "Whose Pussy?"

I wrapped up and was trying to leave, but they demanded my dis' song about Ace and Asia. Donnie had already warned me not to perform the song, but I did it anyway.

After the show, Boon walked me and Bliz out back to our cars. As soon as we got outside good, we were confronted.

"What's up now, nigga?" Ace said, running up on me.

As soon as he came into reach, I threw a haymaker and knocked him down. With him out the way, I ran to help Bliz with the two guys he was trading punches with.

Boon was just knocking niggas out left and right—out their shoes, shirts, and consciousness. When he finished with his, he came over and scattered the rest.

"Gun!" Bliz yelled and tackled me as shots rang out.

Boon went down from a shot in his calf, but Bliz had me covered with his body. We lay there for a few seconds after we heard cars pulling off.

"A-yo, you can get up now," I told Bliz, but he didn't respond.

I pushed him up enough to look into his lifeless eyes. He took a shot to the back of the head when he tackled me. Bliz was gone!

His phone began ringing as he lay there, and then again as he was loaded into a body bag. The painful irony was that it was Tosha calling to announce the birth of his son.

CHAPTER 33

A week after Bliz's death, his funeral was held in one of Atlanta's mega-churches. Thousands of relatives, friends, and fans came to pay their respects to another one of rap's fallen soldiers. The industry's biggest stars, some of whom got their break as a result of one of his mix tapes, were in attendance.

At their request, I sat with Bliz's mother, Tosha, and the son he would never meet in this life. We tried to console each other, but none we were all inconsolable.

"It's not your fault," Bliz's mother said, pulling my head onto her shoulder. "My son loved you. He died proving that."

"Wasn't nothing you could have done," Tosha added, patting my hand.

Me? I wasn't so sure. *I should have listened to my management and not responded. Maybe if I didn't perform that song that night...* "From Allah we come and to Allah we must return," I said, echoing the words Khadijah had said at my father's passing.

Those closest to Bliz didn't hold me responsible, but they were the only ones who didn't. I was openly scorned by almost everyone else. I got dirty looks, eye rolls, and no one would talk to me. They played some of Bliz's music from over the years but exclude everything featuring me. That was despite the fact that "Wet Work" was the biggest song of his career. His production of that song made him a millionaire and set his family straight for life.

Not only was I prevented from performing at the memorial concert, but I wasn't even invited. After his casket was covered, I went straight to the airport and went home.

Khadijah saw that I wasn't in the best of spirits and gave me plenty of space to brood.

I turned on the TV in hopes of preventing the tragic scene from replaying in my head, but it was still being run. One of the music channels—the one that would never get another D-Lite video—put a new spin on the affair. They showed footage of me leaving the police station the night of the shooting and suggested that I was a snitch. Never mind the fact that it was one of Ace's own people who gave him up.

One of the cats Boon knocked out was still sleeping when the police arrived. They thought he was dead, too, until they heard him snoring. When he came to, he told police all about Ace's plan to kill me. He laid out the ambush, told them what Ace was driving, and even told them where he was headed. Ace was taken into custody and could be convicted on the strength of his own people. Nevertheless, I was the snitch.

I thought I was disgusted at the foul twist they put on it, but wifey was .38 hot! "Ugh!" Khadijah groaned, alerting me to her presence. "Now he's the hero and you're the bad guy?"

Over the next month, Donnie and Amy called, texted, and e-mailed me incessantly. I had flat out refused to work—no shows, no interviews—and I was long overdue on starting the new album.

Khadijah ran around doing her little real estate thing, and lil' Dave was in pre-k, leaving me alone with my daughter. Zakiyyah's favorite game was "Bling Bling," where she dressed up in all my jewelry. Watching her play with hundreds of thousands of dollars worth of trinkets put things in their proper perspective. I never rocked my jewels again. Even when she flushed a $25,000 ring down the toilet, she was far more upset about it than I was. "Aw, shit," she said as the yellow diamond cluster swirled away into oblivion.

"Shit is right," I agreed.

Khadijah was taking her little investing seriously. She was always trying to tell me about this property or that deal, but I hardly listened. She didn't have to report to me. I was just glad she was happy and doing her thing. If she liked it, I loved it. Besides, I had, like, seven million with my accountant.

When I could steal a little time alone, I went down to my dad's office to play around on the recording equipment. I listened to the jingles and taglines he made and tried to make my own. Advertising is a lot harder than making a song.

I was a rapper, and trying to market to diverse demographics was altogether different.

My wife had been sick a couple of mornings, so it was no surprise to either of us when we found out she was pregnant.

"We need a minivan," she said with her lip poked out, positive pregnancy test in hand.

After a long embrace, I vowed she would not have to spend the pregnancy alone. "I couldn't be here the last time, but I promise I will be here for this one," I swore.

"Don't you gotta go back to Atlanta and make some more of your dirty songs?" Khadijah asked, trying not to laugh but failing.

"I'm taking a vacation," I announced. "Let's go somewhere."

"Where?" Khadijah asked excitedly.

"Anywhere you want. Just name it," I replied.

"Kids, go pack! We're going to Africa!" she yelled upstairs.

As spontaneously as the trip came about, it still took weeks of preparation before we could leave. We had to get passports for the kids and begin anti-malaria protocol.

Choosing the lesser of the two evils, I called Amy instead of Donnie to break the news.

"Please, please, please do the album first," she begged.

"Can't do, ma. Made a promise," I advised.

"Okay. If not the album, then at least a single please. I'll do that thing you like," she pleaded.

"There's nothing you can do." I chuckled, amused by the proposition.

"Okay, Lite, if you insist." She sighed. "Hey, maybe I can play it up as a Dave Chappelle type of deal. We can send a camera crew and—"

"Amy," I cut in, "I'll see you when I get back."

I couldn't remember the last time I shopped in a mall, but that was where my wife insisted we go buy clothes for the trip. After picking up clothes for the kids, Khadijah dragged me into one of those cheap jewelry outlets.

"A-yo, I'll call my jeweler. He'll make whatever you want," I protested.

"Listen, mister, I never got a ring, and I want one now," she fussed.

She and Dave looked at rings while Zakiyyah and I checked out watches.

"Oh how precious!" the saleslady gushed at my daughter. "And look at your pretty jewels. Oh my God! Those are real diamonds!"

"Bling bling," Zakiyyah said, happily offering her a $100,000 chain.

"Will you please stop clowning around and come on?" Khadijah beckoned.

We left the stunned saleslady and joined her across the store.

"These are nice," I lied, looking at the plain wedding bands. "What is it? Platinum? White gold?"

"Actually, they are sterling," the salesman said dryly. After the fuss Zakiyyah had made with her jewels, the salesman was anticipating a large sale and commission.

"Babe, you know Muslim men can't wear gold," Khadijah chided through clenched teeth.

"And, babe, you know I'm not Muslim," I replied through clenched teeth of my own.

"Not yet. Pay the man," she demanded.

I shrugged my shoulders and handed the guy a twenty for both rings and turned to leave.

"Don't forget your change," the salesman said sarcastically.

* * *

We arrived in Banjul, the capital city of the Gambia, from a connecting flight out of London. Africa was everything I thought it would be and at the same time, nothing I expected.

The hotel was a decent four-star place with excellent service. Since Khadijah spoke both the local dialects of Wolof and Mandinka, we got special treatment. After a few days of touristy stuff, we ventured out to the countryside to see her family.

That was when I saw that the Gambia was, in fact, a third-world country. The people were poor but not downtrodden. It was quite the opposite, in fact. They were happy. No one had much of anything, yet they were willing to share what little they did have. "Food for one can feed two" was their mantra.

Khadijah's mother spoke no English but insisted on talking to me nonstop. Sometimes Khadijah translated, but other times she just laughed. Even when Khadijah wasn't around, her mother spoke to me. I would just smile and nod, having no idea what I was agreeing to.

The first time we sat down for dinner, her mother set a pot of rice on the table. I waited for the rest of the dishes, but none came.

"Dig in, dear. That's all," Khadijah instructed.

The next day, I bought my mother-in-law a cow. After slaughtering it, she quickly distributed the meat to all her family and friends until nothing remained.

The next day, I did the same, and so did she. "I'ma buy a whole herd and see how she does with that," I joked to Khadijah.

"The exact same thing." She laughed. "I send her money all the time, and she would rather give it away than spend it on herself."

Her mother seemed to understand what we were saying and said something in reply.

"What?" I asked, curious as to the seriousness of the statement she made.

"She said she will get it back when she meets her Lord. All her charity will be waiting," Khadijah explained.

I found out that the Gambia was a Muslim country, which explained why everyone was so hospitable. They greeted us with peace and asked about our health, our family, friends, business, and even pets. A greeting could take ten minutes or more, and complete strangers told me they loved me.

Our time in the peaceful country passed so quickly I almost hated to leave. Khadijah was in a hurry to get back to her little investments and didn't want to have the baby anywhere but in America.

I hid the $20,000 I had left over in one of her mother's cooking pots, and it was time to go home.

CHAPTER 34

I had so many e-mails, voicemails, and texts that it would have been impossible to reply to them all, so I just ignored them. IRS this, mortgage company that—nothing important.

It wasn't until after the birth of our son Asad that I finally called the label. The plan was to enjoy a few more weeks welcoming the newest addition to our family.

The kids flipped over having a new sibling. Dave gave him his favorite toy truck, and Zakiyyah gave him an iced-out Rolex.

Donnie was all stoic and businesslike when he came on the line. "Mr. Light, you are in breach of your contract," he said in a threatening tone. He was trying to be hard, but I heard his voice quiver. He wanted to cry. As my manager, he was eating off my plate, so my long hiatus had put a dent in his purse.

"Man, don't get ya panties in a bunch," I teased. "D-Lite is back, ready to work." I said out of my mouth what wasn't in my heart. I didn't even know who D-Lite was anymore. I knew who I was but not what they made me. That D-Lite didn't exist anymore; he died with Bliz.

Khadijah refused to go to Atlanta while I did my album. Get this: She claimed she couldn't leave *her* business. I made over twenty million, but she couldn't leave her business.

We agreed that I would commute back and forth from Atlanta to Albuquerque—Mondays through Thursdays in the studio and Fridays through Sundays at home. My wife was non-negotiable on Fridays, insisting that I attend the Mosque with her.

The first night back in my Atlanta house was so awkward that I couldn't sleep a wink. The memories of Shelby and Bliz were in every room. The empty condo wasn't much of an option with the reality of how I had disrespected my best friend waiting there for me. In the end, I decided to get a room.

If there was one consolation to being home, it was my garage. The sight of my exotic whips brought a smile to my face. I walked around fondling their curves, trying to decide who would be my companion. When I narrowed it down to two, I flipped a coin. "Heads, Bentley…tails, Porsche truck," I said, watching the tumbling quarter. "Heads! Excellent choice."

I checked into a suite downtown and got some rest before heading to the studio.

Guy greeted me warmly before we got into one of our many heated debates. We argued over nothing until Boon came through to hang out for a while. Then, we all listened to tracks from A-list producers, looking for a vehicle for my first single. I heard plenty of bangers, but there was nothing that just moved me.

"Say, Lite, you heard this yet?" Boon asked, passing his MP3 player.

"You know Donnie want only A-listers," Gary warned.

"My nigga, Bliz is on top of the A-list," I said hotly.

"Let's give a listen then," Guy said, giving in without a fight.

He plugged the small player into the system, and the track immediately made all heads nod. It had a sample of TLC's "Creep" and Tosha singing the hook.

"Hurry up. Gimme a pen," I demanded as the lyrics filled my head.

Guy loaded the song from the MP3 straight into Pro-Tools as Boon lit a blunt.

I wrote while the blunt made its way around to me, and I took it out of habit. As soon as it touched my lips, it dawned on me how long it had been since I'd smoked. I enjoyed my sobriety and passed it off without a pull. There was no sense going backwards now.

I was back in my zone once I hit the booth. I only had one verse written down, so I freestyled the rest. The words were coming to me like one of those karaoke machines that displays the lyrics on a screen.

Guy and Boon flipped over the final product, but I was ambivalent. The song was sound and probably hit material, but it wasn't me. For the first time since selling out, I felt like a sellout.

"You got one there, shawty," Boon said enthusiastically.

"I agree," Guy cosigned. "Donnie may wanna change the track though."

"I couldn't care less what he does," I said. "After I deliver this album, I'm done. I quit."

"Quit?!" Boon exclaimed.

"Quit, B. I'm just not feeling it no more." I sighed.

* * *

My wife and kids practically threw me a party when I got home. Khadijah claimed they existed when I was gone but lived when I was home, and I felt the same way.

"So, did you get any work done?" Khadijah asked with forced enthusiasm.

"Yeah. Actually, I did," I replied. "Got a song done. I'll let you hear it when the kids go to sleep."

"Uh-oh. That bad?" Khadijah laughed.

Once the kids were fed, bathed, read to, and tucked in, we met back in the den.

"OKAY, LET'S HAVE IT, MR. NASTY MOUTH." SHE LAUGHED.

"IT'S NOT THAT BAD," I SAID, PRESSING PLAY ON THE REMOTE.

"SO FAR, SO GOOD," KHADIJAH SAID ABOUT THE TRACK AND LYRICS.

THEN MY VERSE SAID,

"WHAT'S UP, MA? WHATCHA TRYINA GET INTO?...

CAN I COME THROUGH AND CUT YOU UP WITH MY GINSU?...

I GOT A SAMURAI SWORD THAT AS HARD AS A BOARD...

YOU KNOW ME, MR. LOW-KEY, SLIPPING IN THE BACK DOOR...

AS SOON AS YOU'RE ALONE, JUST PICK UP THE PHONE...

AND WE CAN MOAN AND GROAN UNTIL YA MAN COMES HOME...

NO FLOWERS OR CANDY, THAT'S NOT WHAT YOU EXPECT...

YOU CALL ME LIKE FEDEX, ON TIME WITH GOOD SEX...

I'M YOUR SUBSTITUTE CUTTER. I COME WHEN YOU CALL...

THERE'S SIXTY-NINE POSITIONS, AND WE'VE BEEN THROUGH 'EM ALL...

D-LITE'S THAT—"

Click.

Khadijah turned off the song and put on a frown. "You are so nasty." She grimaced.

"What? I ain't even say nothing." I laughed, grateful she didn't hear the next verse about threesomes.

"I just don't get it," Khadijah said, confused. "I mean, you talk about stuff you don't really do. Why must it always be about sex and violence?"

"First off," I began defensively, "Superman can't really fly. It's entertainment. Next, sex and violence is the reality of the streets."

"Which street? Certainly not Bell Harbor." She laughed. "You just read *Cat in the Hat* to your kids. That's who you are."

The next day, I stole my wife's John Mayer CD and took it downstairs. I made a loop of his song, "Waiting on the World to Change," then beefed up the drums. I played it over and over until a script played in my head.

"I CAREFULLY CONTEMPLATED THE CONTENT OF THE QUR'AN…

COMPARING IT IN CONJUNCTION TO WHAT'S CURRENTLY GOING ON…

THEY SAY MUSLIMS BEEN TERRORIZING THE WORLD FOR AGES…

BUT LOOK IN THEIR BOOK. THAT'S NOT ON NONE OF THE PAGES…

IT PAINTS PICTURES IN PARAGRAPHS, AS PRETTY AS PARADISE…

WHILE FALSE PROPHETS FOR PROFIT PREACH FOR A PRICE…

CREATING CONFIDENT CHARACTERS CONSISTENT WITH CHRIST…

SINCERE SOUL-SEARCHING SUGGEST I SACRIFICE…

IN THE NAME OF GOD OR IN THE NAME OF SATAN…

THE KEY IS TO FEAR ALLAH AND THEN BE PATIENT…

HATERS GONNA HATE. LET 'EM KEEP ON HATIN'…

THE WORLD IS GONNA CHANGE, SO I'MA KEEP WAITIN'.

"BRAVO! NOW THAT'S WHAT'S UP!" KHADIJAH CHEERED BEHIND ME.

"YOU LIKE THAT?" I ASKED, FEELING VULNERABLE.

"NO. I LOVE IT." SHE SMILED. "THAT'S MORE BEFITTING OF A MUSLIM MAN."

"But I'm not…oh, forget it," I said, exasperated. Khadijah made statements like that all the time. She didn't push religion on me other than that. I really did read her Qur'an, but we would have to wait and see what happened.

"It's different," Donnie said, waving his hand. "That was a monster song, so the recognition will help. The crossover appeal…yeah, I think we have something."

I tried not to laugh at him talking himself into something.

"Who did you say produced it?" Donnie asked, catching me off guard.

"Um, DJ Ramel," I said, snatching a name out of thin air. "Yeah, he did

Signature's whole album."

"Sig! He did good numbers. And he cleared the samples?" Donnie asked.

"Of course," I lied, not knowing how to do all of that anyway. It couldn't be that big a deal, as many sample songs as I heard every day.

"Let's run with it," he exclaimed, snapping his fingers. The gesture reminded me of Damon Wayans on *In Living Color*, "two snaps in a circle," and it cracked me up.

"What's so funny?" Donnie chuckled, wanting in on the joke.

"I'm just happy, that's all," I said, still laughing.

I swung by the condo to see what was up with Tanisha, but there was still no trace of her. I called her mother, who said she was fine, but she offered no further information. She did scold me real good about not bringing lil' Dave to see her.

My last stop before heading to the hotel was home. I was still a fly guy, so changing cars was a must. While I was there, I skimmed through the growing pile of mail. I processed it into two groups: junk and more junk. "IRS, urgent, junk," I said, tossing it in the pile. "Mortgage company, more junk."

An austere knock on the front door disturbed my recycling.

"A-yo, who the fuck banging on my shit like five-o?" I demanded.

"Uh, sir, it's the DeKalb County Sherriff's Office," came the reply. "Are you Mr. Light?"

"Yes, sir. How may I be of assistance?" I asked, totally switching gears.

Instead of a reply, he handed me a subpoena. Ace was set to go on trial, and I was listed as a witness for the state.

Somehow, the media caught wind of the subpoena and ran wild with the story. Every music channel and rap rag picked up on it and added their own spin. "Snitch or Tattletale?" read the cover of one publication—the same magazine I'd helped sell millions of copies by gracing their cover. Now, they openly scorned me.

"Just ignore it. Do not testify," Donnie begged. "The most they can do is give you thirty days. This way, you rep' stays intact."

"Thirty days? Man, you do it!" I replied sharply. The three or four a week without my family was already hard enough. Thirty days was out of the question.

The district attorney briefed me on what I should or could say. Actually, he tried to tell me what to say. The thought caused me to chuckle as the bailiff attempted to swear me in. I found the irony of swearing to tell a lie amusing.

DA: "State your name and occupation for the record."

Me: "David Light, entertainer…I guess."

DA: "Tell the jury in your own words what happened the night Marion Creekmore was fatally wounded."

Me: "Who? Oh, Bliz. Well, I did a show at the Boon Boon Room and got into a fight with Ace out back."

DA: "Did the defendant shoot at you?"

Me: "I don't know. I didn't see."

DA: "Didn't you tell me you saw him with a gun? Saw him shooting?"

Me: "No. That was what you told me."

DA: "Well, did the defendant shoot you in New York City several years ago?"

Me: "Some coward shot me from the back. I didn't see who it was."

DA: "That'll be all. Step down!"

The DA was hot. Before I could actually step down, Ace's attorney grilled me as well. He reiterated the fact that I didn't actually see the shooting or Ace with a gun. If anything, my testimony helped his defense.

I was pretty hot too. The whole "no snitching" shit was some bullshit. Son tried to kill me and killed my best friend, but I was somehow the bad guy. It didn't make no sense.

Whatever advantage I gave the defense was ruined when Ace's co-defendant took the stand. He was given immunity from prosecution and made the most of it. He gave them all the necessary elements to prove malice murder.

After Ace's "friend" testified, the state rested. The defense called a parade of "witnesses," who shamelessly perjured themselves. Have them tell it, Ace was at church preaching a sermon at the time of the shooting.

It was to no avail. The jury deliberated for a whole ten minutes before finding Ace guilty on all counts. The judge sentenced him to life plus five years in the state prison.

* * *

Donnie called me after news of the verdict and threw an all-out tantrum. "You're dead! You fucking killed yourself," he whined. "No one wants to work with you! They've canceled all your guest spots. The promoters won't book you either."

"A-yo, fuck them!" I shot. "Matter fact, fuck them, fuck you, fuck—"

Click.

He hung up on me before I had a chance to fuck the world.

That night, I went into the studio and took my frustration out in the booth. In my anger, I took the whole world to task. I spoke about Darfur, Palestine, and the AIDS crisis. I rapped about the corrupt criminal justice system and all the crooked politicians.

I spared no one—not even the very profession that made me rich. I snitched on all the bullshit and dirty tricks of the music biz, from the radio stations with their pay for play and the thieving managers and scandalous promoters.

Then I turned the spotlight on myself. I took aim at me and my peers and how we were glorifying the very 'hoods we ran from as soon as we got our coins up; how we were perpetuating the same bullshit that had destroyed our communities and our own families.

Guy lined up the tracks, and I knocked them down. I had so much pent up inside that I didn't even need to write that shit down. For the first time in a long time, I spat it right from my heart. I kept it real…for real.

The seven songs I did that night, along with the six I'd already completed, fulfilled my obligation. My two-album contract was satisfied, and I could finally go home—right after I submitted the product to the label.

"What the fuck is this?" Donnie exploded as he finished screening the album. "Who do you think you are, Common or Talib Kweli or somebody? No one wants to hear this positive shit. Sex and violence, Lite, that's what they want. Sex and violence, like we told you!"

I had to hide my face in my hands to stop myself from laughing. Son was fuming!

"No one gets shot, stabbed, fucked or nothing!" he screamed. "Sex and violence! That's rap music."

"Look, man," I said, taking to my feet. "This is the album. I'm done. I'm going home, you can shoot, stab and then fuck yourself."

CHAPTER 35

The first single off the album was "Substitute Cutter." Even without the video that I refused to shoot, it took off like a rocket. We sold 300,000 units the first week on the strength of the single alone.

My decimated fan base still propelled me to a number one album and platinum in a month. Then they dropped the single "Waiting" containing the unauthorized sample. It was added to all the urban, pop, and alternative stations in the country.

Then it bit us in the ass. A cease and desist letter pulled the song from the air, and I was summoned back to Atlanta. Mr. Jennings called me from his private number and flew me on his private jet for what he called "a meeting of extreme importance."

"We have been sued by the copyright holders of the sample used in your latest single entitled 'Waiting'," Mr. Jennings began.

The meeting was attended by several of the label's attorneys, who scribbled furiously every time Mr. Jennings spoke, breathed, or blinked.

"Now, the producer of the song is listed as a DJ Ramel, and he had the duty and responsibility of clearing the sample," he advised in general. Then he spoke directly to me. "We are unable to even confirm the existence of this person. Who is he?" he asked. "And where can we find him?"

"Right here. He's me," I confessed, looking down at my feet. "I produced it myself."

"In that case, we are in direct violation," the head of the label's legal team advised. "With the cease and desist order in place, we are forced to pull all units from stores, effective immediately."

"What are we looking at to make this thing go away?" Mr. Jennings asked.

"Well, of course they will get any publishing monies generated thus far, and the suite is demanding ten million. I believe I can negotiate half of that," the lawyer explained.

"So what, we gotta take the song off and put it back out?" I asked naïvely. "If you want, I can do another song. That's not a problem." I felt horrible for costing the company so much money. Mr. J. had showed me nothing but love, and I was determined to make it up to him.

"Lite," Mr. Jennings said, finally looking at me again, "we're not going to re-release the album."

"So what exactly does that mean? What y'all want me to do?" I said, almost pleading.

"It means you're free to go, Lite," he answered before getting up and leaving the room.

I stood to leave after Mr. J., but the attorney stopped me. "Of course we will send you a statement once all receipts are tallied.," he said.

"Of course," I agreed, not having a clue what he meant.

When I passed the receptionist, she lowered her head, letting me know I was persona non grata. I paused to look at all the platinum plaques on the wall, including mine. I was stuck for a second until Mr. J.'s statement echoed in my head: "You are free to go."

* * *

"What the fuck?!" I exclaimed as I pulled up to my mansion. The place was buzzing with activity that I didn't order. There were several moving trucks, flatbed trailers, and a couple of sheriff's cars.

I pulled my Bentley to a sudden stop at the flatbed and blocked my Aston Martin from being loaded.

A deputy saw the maneuver and was by my side before I could get out the car all the way.

"Fuck is going on?" I demanded. "This is *my* car, *my* house."

"You'll have to speak with the agent in charge," the deputy advised, almost apologetically.

"Agent in charge? FBI?" I asked, puzzled.

"No…IRS," a small, mouse like man announced proudly, producing his badge.

"Okay, so what the fuck you doing here?" I asked, approaching the little man.

He looked like he wanted to run, but a glance at the sheriff's deputy gave him the courage to stand his ground. "I'm Carl Fletcher, with the Internal Revenue Service," he said confidently. "We are seizing the home, cars, and furnishings for failure to pay taxes."

"Taxes? Fuck outta here!" I laughed. "My accountant handles all that."

"Evidently not," he replied flippantly. "You are some three million in arrears. We have a court order, and a warrant may be issued."

"Let me get to the bottom of this," I pleaded. I flipped my phone open, but the label had already disconnected my line. I guess they weren't planning on spending another dime on me. "Hold on! I'ma run downtown and find out who wrong," I said, reaching for my car door.

"Excuse me, Mr. Light," the agent said, checking his pad, "but that Bentley GT is on the list of assets. It's now the property of the United States."

* * *

I snatched my change from the cabbie and stormed into the office of my accounting firm.

The secretary gasped, started by my sudden entrance.

"Where's Stein?" I demanded, but I didn't wait for an answer. I barged down the hall to his office as she called behind me, trying to stop me. I pushed into his empty office and stared in bewilderment. Everything was still intact except for any trace of Stein. Gone were the family pictures, nameplate, and putting green. The plants, the plaques, and everything were absent, including the man himself. I plopped down in his overstuffed leather chair and dropped my face into my hands in despair. I was on the verge of tears until another man walked in.

"Excuse me, sir," he began unsurely. "I'm Gilbert Vasser, president of the firm. If I can get you to accompany me to my office, I'll try to explain."

"All I want to know is where my money is," I demanded. "Cut me a check. I got, like, seven or eight mil' with you guys."

"Um, it is not quite as simple as cutting a check," Mr. Vasser explained. "Mr. Stein had been embezzling from his clients, as well as from the company. It seems he lost a ton of money on bad investments, and then there was the gambling, extramarital affairs, and personal extravagances. He looted us all, sir."

"A-yo, B, how much of my dough is left?" I asked, rubbing my now-throbbing temples.

"I'm sorry, Mr. Light, but all your funds have been depleted," he said solemnly.

"I'll kill him!" I swore bitterly. "I'll fucking cut his hands off and then kill him."

"Well, I'm afraid that's not a viable option," Mr. Vasser said, as if he'd contemplated it himself.

"Why the fuck not?" I demanded. "I ain't going out bad! I'll be damned if that nigga lives it up on my dime."

"No, that won't happen, I assure you," he said, fighting a smile from forming in the corners of his mouth. "He was found dead a couple of days ago. Stein committed…uh, he killed himself."

"So I'm just out?" I asked, stunned.

"Please be patient with us, Mr. Light. A full investigation is underway. As soon as the full scope of the situation is ascertained, you will be offered a settlement," he advised.

"A settlement? How the fuck you gonna give me a settlement on my own money? I want every penny of mine's!" I yelled, storming out of the office the same way I'd stormed in.

CHAPTER 36

T he $300,000 left in my personal account had been frozen, along with the black card and the other credit cards I carried. My lawyer said it could take years to recover the funds.

We had a little under $100,000 left in the account Khadijah maintained for the household. Besides that, we were broke, and I had to explain that to my wife.

I moped around for days, trying to figure out how to tell her I'd pulled an MC Hammer. If I hadn't transferred the house to her, we would have been homeless as well.

Khadijah had been running around excited about something and trying to talk, but I'd been ducking her. Finally, she caught me in the den, and I couldn't run. "Okay, Mr. Man, let's have it," she demanded. My wife had her *"Don't play with me"* face on, so I had to come clean.

"We're broke. I blooped," I blurted. "That eighty-seven stacks in the household account is all that's left." I went on and detailed the lawsuit and my album getting pulled. I told her about the fiasco with the accountant and losing all my assets. "And to top it all off..." I sighed. "I'ma end up owing my label."

When I finished my spiel, Khadijah simply sucked her teeth.

"Is that all I get?" I asked, incredulous. "We're broke, and that's all you got to say?"

"You should listen to your wife sometimes. I—" she began, but I jumped in and cut her off before she had a chance to say *"I told you so."*

"Whoa, ma! Let's not forget about the mil' I gave you." I chuckled. "How much of that's left?"

"Put your shoes on," she demanded and stood. "Let's go. I have something to show you since you don't listen."

As we loaded the kids into the minivan, I was again reminded of the reckless spending that had gotten me into that mess. Khadijah had told me to get a simple minivan to fit the kids and their stuff, $24,000, no problem, but by the time I got TVs and DVD players and rims and all the bells and whistles, I'd spent twice that.

Khadijah was still wearing her *"Don't play with me"* face, so we rode in silence. It wasn't like I was scared of her or nothing; I'm just saying. Since she knew where we were going, she did the driving.

Khadijah pulled to a stop at the entrance of a nearly completed subdivision. She sat there for a few seconds, waiting on me to say something. "Well?" she inquired when I kept quiet.

"I'm sorry. I, um…I don't get it," I confessed, almost timidly.

"The sign, baby. Read the sign," she said in the tone usually reserved for one of the kids.

"Uh, Lighthouse Cove," I read.

"Okay. And…" she coaxed, as if the sign was supposed to explain why we were there.

"Still nothing," I admitted.

"Lighthouse Cove, and we are the lights and the…?" she asked, leading me on.

"You wanna buy a house?" I asked, dumbfounded.

"Baby, these are *our* houses—all of them! I built them," she said shaking her head.

"I'm sorry. I still don't get it," I said, still clueless.

"I have been trying to tell you for almost a year, but you never listen," she said sharply.

"Well, you got my attention now," I said eagerly.

"You wrote me a check for a million dollars. I bought a few housed, fixed 'em up, and resold them. I doubled my money in a year. I got a loan for these sixty acres, then worked a deal with the builders," she explained slowly so I could keep up. "Fifty houses in the low $500,000s!"

"That's…twenty-five mil'?" I asked after doing the mental math.

"Gross, yes, but $200,000 off each unit goes to the builders, and $400,000 to the bank for the land," she explained.

"That's still, like, $10 million!" I yelled. "Baby, we got ten million!"

"Well, not *we*, actually—*me*. My company does." She chuckled. "But if you need a job or something…"

"Yeah, I need a job." I laughed.

"What can you do?" Khadijah teased.

I pointed at our kids for a reply.

"You're hired!" she yelled.

CHAPTER 37

As much as I tried, I could not get my mother to move out west with us. Even the offer of a new house couldn't budge her from her adopted city. She spent two Christmases in a row with us in New Mexico, so the next one was on us.

After a warm reunion with my mother in Atlanta, I pretty much got ignored. Khadijah and my mom were best friends, and I was left in the cold.

Finally, I decided to take my mom's car and cruise around the city. Atlanta grew so fast that if you blinked, something new would pop up by the time you opened your eyes.

The mailman pulled up as I was pulling to, so I got the mail and tossed it on the passenger seat. My eyes caught a familiar name, and I picked up the envelope. "Mr. and Mrs. Salaam," I read aloud. Ma had told me he stayed in touch, but I never let her tell me more than that. That chapter of my life was closed. *Or is it?* I thought as I entered Desean's address into the navigation system. I thought about calling ahead but decided against it. It was time to man up, and I needed to do that in person.

Not bad, I thought as the car directed me into an upscale subdivision in Cobb County. "Son doin' a'ight for himself."

I took note of the new Range Rover and BMW sitting in the driveway as I made my way up the walk.

There was a little boy pushing a truck around the porch when I got to it. "I know you," he said, looking up at me with Desean's eyes. "You're Uncle Lite!"

"That's me," I said proudly. "Where's your daddy?"

"I'll get my mommy," he said, abandoning his truck and yelling for his mother. "Mommy!"

I turned and looked around the neighborhood as I waited. I silently prayed that the boy's mommy wouldn't be Veronica. *Nothing could be worse than that.*

"Yes, honey?" a familiar voice rang behind me.

It took me a second to process the voice, but the result didn't make any sense. *Can't be,* I thought. But when I turned around, it was. There was Shelby, standing in the front door.

"Oh my God!" she exclaimed at the sight of me. She lifted her hands to her open mouth, revealing that she was at least six months pregnant. "Go...go get your father," she said with a gasp, setting her son in motion.

We stood there staring at each other until the door opened again.

"What's Dave talking about Uncle...Lite?" he questioned, until he saw me. He froze and joined the staring contest that Shelby and I were engaged in.

Their son didn't know what to think. He alternated between looking at his parents, then at me, then back at his parents.

I conceded and turned to go back to the car.

As I pulled on the door handle, Day came down the steps. "A-yo, Lite!" he called out as he neared.

I let go of the handle and met him halfway up the walk. We stood there for a few moments, then embraced. We held each other tightly, crying and laughing at the same time.

Shelby came over and joined the group hug. We broke off, and I nodded approvingly at my friends. No words were spoken; none were needed.

I turned on my heels, got into the car, and drove off without a backward glance.

CHAPTER 38

Tanisha was sitting in the living room with lil' Dave hugging her neck when I got back to my mom's. Her appearance had changed so much that I might have passed her on the street and not noticed her. Braids replaced the once-exotic hairstyles, and a pair of stylish frames took the place of colorful contacts. She had picked up a little weight, but she looked good—healthy.

She, Khadijah, and my mom were chatting it up like old friends, and the sight of the trio made my heart smile.

"Hey, ladies," I said cheerfully upon entering the room.

"Lite!" Tanisha exclaimed, springing to her feet. She looked toward Khadijah, who gave a slight nod before moving.

"Hey, girl," I said, giving her a warm hug.

"Hey, ya'self." She laughed. "Can we talk?"

I looked toward Khadijah. Then we excused ourselves to the kitchen and had a long-overdue talk.

"What can I say? Sorry don't cut it," Tanisha began, with tears welling up in her eyes.

"Sorry is plenty," I said, feeling a little misty-eyed myself. "I could have and should have done better by you."

"No. If anything, you and Dave were more than I deserved." She sobbed.

"Can I ask where you been?" I said, as my curiosity got the best of me.

"Jail." She sniffled, trying not to lose her composure. "I started messing around with this drug dealer. I used to let him use my car, but I ain't know he kept dope in it. I got pulled over one day 'cause of that warrant when lil' Dave...

well, you know."

"It's okay, lil' mama," I comforted with a hug.

"So I was going to jail anyway, but when they impounded my car and found drugs and a gun, it was a whole other story," she explained.

"So dude let you fall for his work?" I asked in disbelief. "Where they do that at?"

"I called his punk ass and told him what was up, and I ain't heard from him since." She laughed bitterly. "I ended with five years behind his shit."

"A-yo, you was eating coochie in there?" I asked seriously.

"No, boy!" She laughed. "Let me finish. I did get myself together in there. I got my cosmetology license, got saved, and got sober. Then, somehow, my mama got money for me to open my own salon when I got home."

I guess she expected me to come clean about giving her the money, but I didn't. I had already heard much of the story from Tosha.

"Well, thank you." Tanisha smiled. "For…well, for everything. Lil' Dave looks so happy. Thank you."

"My pleasure," I said.

CHAPTER 39

With all the women in the house, I decided to hit Boon up and see what he was up to.

"D-fuckin'-Lite!" he exclaimed at the sound of my voice.

"Daniel Boon! What's the biz?" I inquired.

"It's all good, man. I stepped my game all the way up. Dumped that dump in Decatur and got me a new spot downtown, B's Playhouse," he announced proudly. It had to be the hottest club in Atlanta. The radio ran spots for it every couple of seconds, it seemed.

"That's what's up! I gotta come check it out one day," I said, not really meaning it. If I never set foot in a club again in life, it would have been cool with me.

"One day? Nigga, you need to come down tonight. We got a packed house," he exclaimed.

"Wifey ain't letting me hit no club, son," I said, happy to have a good excuse.

"Huh? Put her on the phone," Boon demanded. "I'm 'bout to free you for the night."

"A'ight." I laughed and called for my wife. I know there is no way she gonna go for me going out. "It's Boon," I told Khadijah as I passed the phone.

"Hello, Mr. Boon," Khadijah sang cordially. Her end of the conversation consisted of a series of "Mm-hmm…okay…I see…" followed by a surprising "We'll be there then."

"Be where?" I asked when she passed the phone back.

Khadijah just smirked and walked off.

"Shit backfired!" Boon laughed when I got back on the line.

"A-yo, what the fuck did you say?" I asked, shocked by his achievement.

"The truth, shawty. You ain't did your swan song," he said stoically. "Go out like you came in, shawty—mic in hand!"

* * *

"You're gonna start a fashion trend," I joked to my wife when she stepped out of the car. She was dressed in her usual headscarf and over garment that was worn by pious Muslim women.

"For the better." She laughed. "At least someone will have some clothes on."

"You sure you up for this?" I asked, knowing she had never stepped foot inside a nightclub before. She had also never seen how women responded to me when I was onstage.

"Sure!" she cheered. "Have fun. Like Mr. Boon said, you must have a swan song."

The DJ cut the music as Boon walked out onstage.

"Ladies and gentlemen, I have a very special gest here tonight—a good friend of mine," he announced proudly. "Give it up for D-Lite!"

About half the club clapped just because Boon told them to. The other half seemed unsure of what to do until Red Clay and other celebrities in the packed VIP section took to their feet.

For once, I couldn't think of nothing fly to say, so I went straight into my act. Whatever song the DJ threw on, I spat. I started to balk when "Whose Pussy?" came on, but wife gave me the nod from side stage.

After performing every song from both albums, including the forbidden "Waitin'," I tried to leave the stage, but the crowd wasn't hearing it. They were too busy demanding a freestyle. As the chant grew louder, I had no choice.

"THIS RIGHT HERE IS GONNA BE MY SWAN SONG...

SOMETHING TANGIBLE YOU CAN FEEL AND PUT YOUR HANDS ON...

AT FIRST I DIDN'T UNDERSTAND WHAT SON SAID...

BUT NAS WAS RIGHT. HIP-HOP IS DEAD...

'CAUSE WE SPIT RHYMES ABOUT THE WORST DEEDS UNDER THE SUN...

RAPPER'S D~LITE

Most times, we lying about stuff we ain't never done...

jockeying for position, everyone flossing and frontin'...

fussing and fighting, black men dying over nothing...

Don't look at me odd. I'm just stating the facts...

that rap is the worst thing to happen to blacks...

since the introduction of crack...

Word to Ma Dukes, you know it's the truth...

Just look at how badly we've corrupted our youth...

Got 'em thinking it's cool to smoke, drink, and pop pills...

like our communities ain't already plagued with enough ills...

Sad to see all these beautiful black faces...

knowing 10 percent of the population makes half of all the AIDS cases...

We created an environment where almost anything goes...

cultivating a whole generation of pimps, hustlers, and hoes...

Material riches, hitting switches, that's the name of the game...

but dude who works hard at his job is considered a lame...

I gotta make a confession to y'all tonight...

D-Lite ain't never bust a gun in his life...

My whole career was just one big front...

'cause the folks at the label say that's what y'all want...

Now it's time for me to grab them and shake' em...

Peace be unto you all, as-salaamu alaykum. That's a rap!"

G STREET CHRONICLES
~A NEW URBAN DYNASTY~

WWW.GSTREETCHRONICLES.COM

I don't hear from Desean and Shelby, but according to Ma, they are doing well. They had another son and are working on another. Day has been doing well for himself, shooting documentaries, and Shelby has a bustling OB-GYN office.

Veronica became a video vixen and wrote a tell-all book about the entertainers she's bedded over the years. Thankfully, she left me out.

Donnie and Raynard moved to New York and got married. Auntie Ray sent me some pictures of him and his bride…or, uh, groom. Well, y'all know what I'm sayin'.

Amy moved up the ranks at Third Eye Records. She is still doing whatever it takes to please her artists, I'm sure.

Tanisha is doing well. She married some guy she met at her mother's church and is now expecting again. She and lil' Dave speak almost daily and they see each other often.

Khadijah has done the damn thing with her company! She built a couple more subdivisions and even a strip mall. Her current project is a mosque and a housing complex in her native home, the Gambia.

After sitting around the house for a while, I decided to reopen my dad's advertising company. I'm doing jingles and marketing campaigns for some of America's biggest companies. I went from a spokesman to agency of record to One Ummah clothing and Bomb-bey Energy Drinks. I think my Pops would be proud of that.

Ace is serving his life sentence in a close security, Level 5 prison. Of course, he's still tryna rap. He recently won Best Rapper on the Yard, taking home thirty packs of ramen noodles and a bag of coffee. That fool claims a reversible error was committed during his trial and is all wrapped up in appeals now. He swears to get revenge on the whole industry, me included. In fact, the title of his next album is supposed to be *Rapper's Revenge*. Sounds more like a book sequel if you ask me.

Be sure to check out other titles
by
Sa'id Salaam

Trap House

Chronicles of a Junky
Short Story Series

Dope Boy
Short Story Series

When the streets threaten to rip a family empire apart, will La Familia give into the streets' wishes or will they stand together and continue to rule.

Tree and Von are best friends who have been raised as brothers. When unequal power becomes an issue in the family, some members begin to do things on their own—definitely leading to disaster.

With Blood shed on the street and La Familia divided, shocking secrets will be revealed that will guarantee someone from La Familia will not be coming home.

G STREET CHRONICLES
~ PRESENTS ~

MONEY IS THE ROOT OF ALL EVIL

BOOSTERS

A NOVEL

SABRINA A. EUBANKS
AUTHOR OF *CHASING BLISS & FAME AND LOWLO* SHORT STORY SERIES

Quinn Whitaker is too smart for his own good. He and his close friends, Lonzo and Fitzi, have made a steady income out of shoplifting and petty thievery with Quinn masterminding their every move. The stakes change when they're presented with the opportunity to rob a drug dealer and increase their cash flow… but that move also changes the game. It whets Quinn's appetite to move on to the next big thing, and awakens his diabolical genius to master the craft and conquer the art of "the heist."

Lonzo and Fitzi come along for the ride of stealing big with Quinn as orchestrator, but when a simple job and blind luck leave them with more money than they ever dreamed of, the foundation of their friendship is eroded by greed, ego, distrust and murder. Quinn pushes past his aversion to taking lives and sets his sights on grabbing the brass ring – a job so big, so out of their league, it's unimaginable – but Quinn knows it can be done.

They say the love of money is the root of all evil. Will their friendship survive their quest to have it all, or will greed, envy, secrets and lust destroy them all?

We'd like to thank you for supporting G Street Chronicles and invite you to join our social networks. Please be sure to post a review when you're finished reading.

Facebook
G Street Chronicles
&
G Street Chronicles "A New Urban Dynasty" Readers' Group

Twitter